Her bottom lip quivered, and Rinehart wanted to kiss away her pain.

Because she was in pain. He could feel it biting at his gut. "I'm not the enemy, Laura."

"You work for the enemy," she countered with gentle force.

"So do you."

"You keep saying that," she pointed out, a hint of frustration in her voice. Somehow they were leaning close, the distance closing.

"Because it's true."

"Why should I believe you don't want what he does?"

His voice held confidence. "You know I don't."

She opened her mouth, shut it. A charge darted through the air. "Then what? What *do you* want, Rinehart?" Her voice came out husky, laden with the sexual tension flowering between them.

There was only one answer to her question, only one way to respond. "You," he whispered hoarsely.

Books by Lisa Renee Jones

Silhouette Nocturne

*The Beast Within #28
*Beast of Desire #36
*Beast of Darkness #43
*Captive of the Beast #63

*The Knights of White

LISA RENEE JONES

is an author of paranormal and contemporary romance. Having previously lived in Austin, Texas, Lisa has recently moved to New York. Before becoming a writer, Lisa worked as a corporate executive, often taking the red-eye flight out of town and flying home just in time to make a Little League ball game. Her award-winning company, LRJ Staffing Services, had offices in Texas and Nashville. Lisa was recognized by *Entrepreneur Magazine* in 1998 for running one of the top-ten growing businesses owned by women.

Now Lisa has the joy of filling her days with the stories playing in her head, turning them into novels she hopes you enjoy!

You can visit her at www.lisareneejones.com.

CAPTIVE OF THE BEAST

LISA RENEE JONES

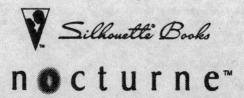

Silhouette Books

n⚫cturne™

To all those who supported me while I wrote this book and
somehow managed to move across the country at the same time.
Special thanks to Jean for her wonderful ideas and input. To Janice,
the perfectionist who makes me better. To my family, whom I love
and adore. And last, but not least, to my readers for allowing me the
joy of writing. I hope I can return that joy with a wonderful story.

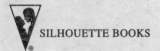

SILHOUETTE BOOKS

ISBN-13: 978-0-373-61810-1
ISBN-10:   0-373-61810-7

Recycling programs
for this product may
not exist in your area.

CAPTIVE OF THE BEAST

www.silhouettenocturne.com

Printed in U.S.A.

Dear Reader,

I am excited to bring you Rinehart's story—he is a Knight of White some of you will remember from past stories. Rinehart is a real hero of heroes: a military man who has lived a life devoted to protecting others; a loner who has felt the pain of loss and doesn't intend to experience it again. But love has a funny way of finding you when you least expect it. He's about to meet his match in Laura Johnson. And look out, sparks are about to fly.

The heroine in this story, Laura Johnson, is quite the loner herself, but with good reason. She isn't like everyone around her. Not only can she read people's emotions, she can move things with her mind; both are abilities that force her into a life shrouded with secrecy and danger. When demons set their sights on using her for their own gain, she must learn to embrace her abilities, and to trust Rinehart if she is to survive.

Captive of the Beast is a story about overcoming our insecurities, a story of personal discovery, of learning to see beyond insecurities to embrace life and become stronger in the process. You can learn more about THE KNIGHTS OF WHITE at Theknightsofwhite.com. Happy reading!

Lisa Renee Jones

The Knights of White

Sentenced to an eternity on earth for killing his brother Abel, Cain became angry and sought the favor of the underworld. By doing so, it is said that he was granted magical powers and given leave from the physical plane. But his gifts came with a price. Cain must oversee the Darkland Beasts, evil beings who walk the earth. Hungry for power, he builds his army of beasts by stealing male souls.

Over time, the scale of good and evil began to tilt. The archangel Raphael, the healer of the earth, was given the duty of balancing the scale again. To do this, he assigned Salvador, his most trusted companion, the duty of saving those souls worthy of serving good against evil. These unique individuals, victims of the Darkland Beasts, are given back their souls and enlisted in an elite army—the Knights of White.

But in each of these knights still lurks a beast of darkness. Each knight must face their beast and defeat it. Each knight must prove himself worthy of the soul returned to him, and capable of facing the underworld without defeat.

These knights must also prove themselves worthy of a mate born of all that is pure and good. If they do so, then, and only then, will these knights become all that they can be—magical warriors against evil, gifted with love that will guide them through darkness to light.

Prologue

Moonlight glinted off the sword Rinehart masterfully swept through the neck of the Demon foot soldier, a Darkland Beast. A second later, the beastly body lit up in flames and dissolved into ash.

Around him, his fellow Knights, Des, Max and Rock—brothers not by blood but by oath and by choice—challenged their opponents, as well. A quick inspection told him his battles were complete; he was not needed. Disappointed, Rinehart sheathed his saber.

Normally, a night spent fighting by his brothers' side fed his primal urges and calmed the darkness within. But not tonight. Not any night as of late. No matter how many Beasts he slew, he could not defeat the one inside himself.

Rinehart, Knight of White, was slipping into darkness and he knew it. Fortunately, no one around him did.

He started walking toward the van, eyeing the horizon, hoping for more battles, for more fuel to fight the war raging inside him. But there were no more Beasts this night. No more distractions from the turmoil that ate at his tainted soul. For now, he had to settle for his usual game of charades, of pretending he was fine, that he was made of steel.

Born into a military family, he'd learned from walking age how a soldier held himself in check, how to school his features into that steel mask. Like any lifetime soldier, he didn't have a name. Just an initial. In his case, the initial *W* had represented his birth name of William. But he was simply Rinehart now—would be forevermore. His immortality, the result of being converted to a Knight, had allowed him ninety-five years to practice this hard exterior, his shell of unaffected solidarity among the Knights.

The Knights were once all human; they were converted to Demons by the Beasts before being saved by Salvador, their creator. But the taint of evil still played inside them all, still clung to the souls that Salvador had returned to each of them, and without their mates, the pure ones who would counter the taint of the Beast, they would eventually be destroyed by it. Some survived longer than others without a mate. No one knew why that was. Rinehart could hear the clock ticking in his head. He was certain he would be one of those men going down sooner rather than later, and he hated that weakness inside himself.

But it was there, burning him up, claiming him.

He had to find a way to control it before it was too late.

* * *

An hour after leaving the battlefield behind, the Knights' van pulled to a halt in front of Jaguar Ranch, the central operations facility for the Knights of White. To the rest of the world, it was simply one of the largest ranches in the world at fifteen thousand acres. Sitting just outside Brownsville, Texas, the ranch often spawned rumors of Demon hunters living within its confines. Usually these stories surfaced when the myths of Matamoras monsters were raging hot, and rightfully so. Those stories were true, of course, and the monsters were, in fact, Demons.

Rinehart shoved open the back door of the van and jumped to the graveled driveway in front of the main house. His fellow Knights, Des and Rock, followed behind him. Max, who had been driving, rounded the front of the van just as his mate, Sarah, ran down the front stairs to greet him. Next came Jessica, who rushed toward Des, her mate. Rinehart ground his teeth and shoved his cowboy hat low over his eyes. He was happy as hell for brothers finding their mates. It simply ground home a hard core truth that didn't sit well right about now. He wasn't likely to find a mate before Hell found him.

Marisol, their healer, stepped out onto the porch, as she always did upon their return. With one touch, she could heal their wounds. Fortunately, tonight no one needed her. Well, almost no one. Rock had it bad for Marisol. And judging from the puppy-dog eyes he was casting in her direction, he was feeling the attraction now. The way the kid responded to Marisol, Rinehart wondered if she were his mate. A damnable situation, considering healers weren't allowed physical pleasures. They were another breed, one the Knights knew little about. But they knew the rule: no touching. That meant no peace for Rock. Not now. Not ever. If Marisol were his mate, something had to change or Rock would be destined for darkness.

On that note, Rinehart decided he and the kid needed some extra exertion. "Don't know about you," Rinehart said, stepping to his side, "but I could go for some more hunting. This time, for some female company. What say we head to town?"

Rock cut his gaze from Marisol, his lips tight, his expression strained. "Hell, yeah, man. I'm down for that. Let's roll."

There had been a time not so long ago when he would have acted like other women were taboo. But Marisol had been shutting him out lately, and he'd stopped fighting his needs.

Their leader, Jag, pushed open the screen door and joined Marisol on the porch. Tall and broad, his dark hair touching his shoulders, Jag charged the air with the force of his presence. With each passing day since Jag had found his mate, he seemed to grow more powerful, more gifted with magic. Though each Knight who mated had found he wielded new powers, Jag, being leader, wielded far more than any of them had imagined possible.

Max had started toward the house, and Rinehart called after him. "Max, man," he shouted. "Toss me the keys." The keys flew through the air, and Rinehart captured them in his palm, preparing to depart.

"Not so fast, Rinehart," Jag called out, sauntering toward him.

Rinehart rested his weight on his back leg and waited for Jag's approach. For some reason, a warning flared in his gut and adrenaline rushed through his body, his heart thrumming wickedly against his breastbone. He kept his expression nonchalant as Jag stopped in front of him. "What's cookin', boss?"

"A woman in need," Jag commented, crossing his arms in front of his chest, his assessing gaze settling on Rinehart's face. "A woman with gifts the Beasts plan to exploit. She and a small group of humans she considers family are being held captive on an island off the Gulf of Mexico. Your assignment is to extract her and her people, and bring them here where we can protect them." His voice lifted with a hint of urgency. "You up to the challenge?"

Rinehart almost laughed at that. When was he not up to the challenge? A slow grin touched his lips, his blood heating with the thrill of danger. "I'm her man."

"You better be," Jag said. "Because you're to extract her from the hands of the Beasts at all costs." He repeated the words with emphasis. "*All* costs. I'll deal with any fallout." He scrubbed his jaw, obviously bothered by the order he'd just given. The sound of Jag's mate, Karen, calling his name floated across the air. "There's a detailed file waiting for you in your room." Jag turned with the words, ending the conversation with the finality of his departure as he headed toward the house.

Rinehart stood there, watching their leader walk

away. If he'd read the story between the lines correctly—and he was pretty damn sure he had—Jag had just ordered him to bring back this woman, dead or alive, to potentially break one of those golden rules: Thou shall not kill a human.

Rinehart felt another rush of adrenaline chase blood through his veins, felt a chill race up his spine despite the hundred-degree-plus humidity. Who the hell was this woman? Or rather, who was she going to be if he didn't save her? He drew a breath and started walking, an urgency to see that file setting his heels on fire. Whoever, or whatever, this woman may be now or in the future, she had become his responsibility. A responsibility he would not fail—one way or the other.

Chapter 1

Dr. Laura Johnson had a secret. She was different, able to manipulate objects with her mind, able to read people's emotions, and sense danger and tragedy before they became reality.

Her parents had always thought that hiding her abilities was for the best. They'd warned her that there were people who would be greedy and power hungry, people who would be enticed to misuse the power behind her secret. And now, fifteen years later, both her parents having passed on, she still remembered their words, understood them, lived the truth they held.

Hiding those abilities had become second nature. In fact, her research exposed her to others like herself, people with similar gifts, and still she remained silent. She knew it was the right choice. Pretending to be no different than everyone else around her was as much a part of each day as brushing her teeth and having morning coffee with her favorite vanilla creamer. Sometimes she even convinced herself it was true, that she was like everyone else.

Staring out the window of the government lab off the Texas coast where she'd been working the past two years, she watched the ocean crash against the rocks of the secluded island facility. It was eight in the morning, and she'd been up well before sunrise, unable to sleep. Every nerve ending in her body was raw, frazzled, and she didn't know why. Her instincts screamed with warnings, with a promise of danger. With the promise of her secret exposed.

She struggled with why she was feeling such a thing. She had felt unease for a while now, ever since Captain Walch had taken over the island's operations six months before. The man wasn't a good person. Not even close. He'd use her patients for the wrong things with a snap of the fingers; in fact, several times now he'd hinted at the power that duplicating their skills could wield. But Walch wasn't the cause of this uneasiness. Her instincts tingled with a warning like nothing she'd ever experienced before. The word *malice* leapt into her mind as if part of some warning system that her instincts had set off. And considering her instincts were uniquely accurate, she trusted them.

Behind her, the lab door opened and closed, and Laura turned to find her favorite patient, a firestarter named Kresley, walking toward her. With red hair several shades lighter than Laura's dark auburn coloring, Kresley drew fast attention whenever she walked into a room. Her striking blue eyes and waiflike figure reminded Laura of a sea nymph from a fairy tale.

Kresley was the only patient Laura had brought with her to the island. Now a woman of twenty, the young girl had become close to Laura's heart. After Kresley's parents had turned away from her, treating her as if she were a freak, Laura had taken her into her home.

"What in the world are you doing up so early?" Laura asked, knowing how fitfully Kresley slept most nights.

Kresley smiled. "I had a bad dream last night."

In her present state of unease, Laura wouldn't have thought she could laugh, but she did. "Most people don't smile over a bad dream, you know, but since the alarms in your room didn't go off, I assume that can mean only one thing."

"Yep," Kresley said, nodding. "I had a nightmare and didn't start a fire. I'm controlling my power even in my sleep."

"Wonderful!" Laura said. She moved forward and hugged Kresley, pleased she'd called her firestarting ability a power rather than a curse, as she often did. Maybe it was hypocritical, considering how she felt about her own abilities, but Laura had grown up with something that had given her the confidence these kids didn't have— parents who loved her, parents who made sure she knew she mattered and, although she had to be secretive about her powers, she was special to them.

While working for the University of Texas, Laura had discovered the genetic marker that created certain people's gifts, or powers. Once that discovery had been published, she'd been invited to the island to help a group of people with problems similar to Kresley's—they couldn't control their powers. And now, two years later, Laura had finally found the missing piece of the puzzle and created a retrovirus correction. Thankfully, it appeared to be working.

Laura had inherited four other patients when she'd come to the island, all kept locked away like animals. They were prisoners because they lacked control over their gifts. She suspected they would all love a little trip off the island.

She was starting to tell Kresley this wish when the door opened, and Captain Walch appeared in the entryway. Tall, with a muscular build and dark hair, Walch wore stiffly pressed, army-green dress pants and a white button-down shirt sturdy enough to display medals. His dark hair was cut short, his cheekbones were high and sharp, his nose long and pointed. As usual, his face was emotionless, even militant. Except for his eyes—they raked over Laura with a lusty inspection.

His gaze narrowed on Kresley and then refocused on Laura. "We need to talk," he said.

Obviously he wasn't keen on small talk on Kresley's behalf. Not that he ever was. "Alone," he added.

Laura turned to Kresley. "I'll meet you in the coffee shop in a few minutes."

Kresley hesitated, protectiveness flashing in her blue eyes. The two of them were close, and Kresley knew how much Laura hated being alone with Walch. "It's

okay," Laura assured her. "I'll only be a few minutes."
Kresley nodded and headed for the door, never glancing
at Walch again.

Laura crossed her arms in front of her body, wishing
for her lab coat—anything to cover her black dress. Not
that the simple shell of a dress was anything but conservative, but Walch had a way of making her feel
naked.

The door shut behind Kresley before either of them
spoke. "You seem edgy, Laura," Walch commented.
"Something on your mind?"

Laura felt more than edgy—she felt defensive for no
good reason. "Actually, yes," she said, forcing herself to
seize the opportunity. She knew Walch: he'd make
whatever point he had come there to make and then dart
away. She needed to be aggressive. "I think it's time to
test the patients' control. A trip off the island would
allow me to see how they respond to real-world stimu-
lations."

His response came fast—too fast, in fact. "You're
feeling good about your progress, then?"

Why did this feel like a trick question? "It's moving
along well," she agreed cautiously, "but they still need
regular injections to maintain the corrections I've
made."

"There won't be a trip right now. Not anytime soon,
for that matter. I have a team of researchers joining you
later this week. They've shown me enough documen-
tation to convince me they can clone your patients' gifts
in others. As I've mentioned on several occasions, the
military finds this concept intriguing. More than intri-

guing—it's an absolute necessity. This *will* happen. We *expect* it to happen."

She drew in a surprised breath. Visitors? A research team? No wonder she was on edge. "I didn't sign up for this. That's not what I'm here for."

He seemed unaffected by her response, in fact, was prepared for it. "If you want to continue receiving the funding and resources to complete your work, you'll make this happen."

"Is that a threat?" she demanded.

"Call it what you want, but we both know this is the next logical step in your work. We need to do this before someone else does. Our men must be the most deadly, the most well equipped."

"By creating weapons of war," she said. "I won't do it. I came to help these people, not to fight wars. That's your job, not mine."

"You came here because you wanted our money and resources. You have all the resources you could dream of here and a chance to be a part of changing the world. Fix *them* while you help *us*. Think about what the next step in your research can mean to the future. It's not about creating war—it's about eliminating it." His expression turned intense, emotion actually evident for once—emotion laced with hunger and greed. "When one opponent is the strongest, the others don't fight. They don't dare. You will be creating peace."

She stared at him, swallowing hard. He was different from before. Darker. Evil seemed to cling to him, a second skin. She could feel it, primal, potent.

She had to get off this island. She would come back for her patients, but if she didn't leave they might all be stuck here. Despite her fears, her voice was low but firm. "I've overstayed my welcome here. I want to go home." He took a step toward her. Instinctively, she backed up. Already close to the window, her heels hit the baseboard. Her hands went to her sides, pressing against the ceiling-to-floor glass panels behind her.

"You have a job to do, and I suggest you accept that," he said. He stood so close to her that the toes of his shoes were almost touching her sandals. "You will welcome your new research team with open arms, and you will eagerly aid their efforts." He paused, his eyes lowering to her lips, lingering there before lifting. "And you will do so because it's in the best interests of both you and your patients."

"What does that mean?" she asked, fear fluttering in her stomach. It was fear for her patients, and fear because there was more going on here than she understood and she wished she knew what.

"It means that you are being monitored, Laura. You always have been. Anything you do that might interfere with our goals will be penalized. If you value the safety of your patients, then I'd stay on task." He leaned in, his body far too near, his mouth brushing her earlobe. "And remember...I'll be close." He eased back and looked into her eyes. "And I'll be watching."

For the first time since she was a teen, Laura fought the rise of her powers, fought the desire to use them against this man. No...*Beast*. The word came to her clearly. He was a power-hungry Beast. Her adrenaline raged, her nerve endings stood on end. With effort she reined in the rush of energy, drew in a discreet, calming breath.

"Fine," she said. "I'll do it. I'll help clone the marker."

He smiled, evil. "That's my girl." His finger ran down her cheek, and she shivered with repulsion. A second later, he stepped away from her, and Laura felt as if a heavy weight had been lifted from her shoulders. "Your new research team will be here Friday morning," he said. "I trust you'll be ready for them."

She glared at him, not agreeing, not daring to disagree. She couldn't say or do anything until she knew what her next step would be. But as he exited the room, giving her one more lust-filled look over his shoulder, she knew one thing for certain. She had no intention of doing what he demanded. Somehow, some way, she was going to get off this island, and she was taking her patients with her. Their own powers were resources they themselves could put to use for escape if it came down to it. But she'd need to stockpile their medication first and plan carefully.

Then, they were out of here. One way or another, they were getting off this island.

Chapter 2

Rinehart stepped onto the sandy beach of his island destination, after a long night on a boat spent, in part, blindfolded. Behind him several military police officers followed, one of them informing him their ride would be there shortly.

Only these soldiers weren't men. Not anymore. They were Beasts in human disguises. Beasts that reeked of evil. The hardest part of the trip had been not killing them. No. That wasn't true. The hardest part was thinking about his past, about the time he'd spent in the military and then the FBI. About the night he'd led his men on a mission deep into Mexico, his mind distracted by personal matters, by a woman, to be exact—a matter that should have been left at home. His team had fallen that night, ambushed by Beasts. He'd failed his men and his country. Why Salvador had saved him, converted him to a Knight of White, he didn't know. Still didn't. But when he'd finally pulled himself out of the self-hatred that day had created, he'd vowed to both himself and Salvador he would never fail the Knights.

Max, Rock, Des and their newest Knight, Lucan, joined him on the beachfront, reminding him of that vow. He had a damn good team who had worked miracles to get them here today. "My skin is crawling from being so near those bastards," Des murmured under his breath, touching the arrowhead necklace he wore around his neck as a reminder of his Native American mother. Something he did often in troubled times.

"I hear ya, man," Rinehart said. "We can't get this job done fast enough to suit me."

Rock came up on the other side of Rinehart. Like the rest of them, he wore khakis and a collar shirt. Gone was his standard attire of jeans, T-shirt and cowboy hat. But the more conservative clothing did nothing to contain his impetuous youth. "Remind me why I can't take their heads right now," he said.

Rinehart shook his head; that statement spoke worlds about why Rinehart kept Rock attached to his hip. If anyone were going to beat Rock's ass, it would be him. "You gotta learn some patience, kid," Max said, joining them, egging on Rock with the kid reference. They all knew he hated it.

Max had learned that lesson and plenty more in his time, Rinehart thought. It had been Max who had designed their background stories for this mission, complete with any document known to man supporting their identities—and he'd done it with the ease of a pro.

And who would have believed that Lucan, an old friend of Max's, with his propensity for leather and hot women, could pull that long blond hair back, put on a pair of glasses, and transform into a lab-coated scientific geek?

Once they'd thrown out the bait, spreading the word in high-profile circles that they were looking for financial backing, Walch had started circling like the vulture he was. Lucan had reeled him in. Of course, their offer to be the guinea pigs for the cloning project gave Walch the extra incentive. It also ensured that Walch didn't try to convert them to Beasts and discover they weren't human.

"Here comes your ride," one of the soldiers said, nodding toward an approaching Jeep.

Rinehart's gaze lifted and locked on the incoming vehicle, his attention riveted to the petite woman on the passenger's side. Her long auburn hair blowing around her pale, bare shoulders drew his gaze. He knew Laura Johnson from her picture and had studied her life, her work and her habits prior to her time on the island—just as he had studied every one of his extraction targets. But the single photo in that file of her in a lab coat, hair pulled back in a prim little knot, had done her no justice. Laura Johnson was a looker with a capital *L*. And she was a smart one, too. And not just because of her degrees, or the work she did, but because, evidently, she despised Walch, the man sitting in the Jeep with her; he could see that from her expression, her tense posture.

The Jeep pulled to a stop and Walch exited the vehicle, making a quick path to meet Rinehart, hand extended. "Welcome, Mr. Rinehart." He glanced at the other Knights and nodded. "Welcome to you all. I trust your trip was satisfactory?"

Rinehart ground his teeth and glanced at Walch's hand; he had no interest in touching him. His hands went to his hips; his weight shifted onto his back foot. "If being blindfolded is a luxury, then it was a bucket of joy."

Walch's lips thinned; a frown formed between his thin brows as he withdrew his hand. "There are necessary evils to security, Mr. Rinehart. I'm sure a man of your background and stature can understand such a thing."

Rinehart understood all right. He understood he wanted this over and done with. "My men are tired and hungry and won't all fit into that Jeep you have there."

"Transportation will arrive for your group momentarily. I thought you and I could have a private chat on the way to your quarters." He glanced at the Jeep. "I interrupted our lead researcher's morning run so you could meet her." He motioned Rinehart forward. "Shall we?"

In the distance, Rinehart noted a convoy of approaching vehicles and eyed Des in an effort to gauge his thoughts on the situation. And not because Des was the unofficial second-in-command of the Knights. On this mission Rinehart was number one, and Des would respect that. But since his recent mating, Des had acquired a special talent that seemed to be growing with each passing day. He often had visions of the future, flashes that warned of trouble. A damn nifty little trick when they were hunting Demons.

Des inclined his head at Rinehart. "We're good, man."

Rinehart glanced at Walch, and they turned to depart.

The minute Rinehart's eyes gravitated to the Jeep, they connected with Laura's; the jolt that followed packed the heat of a fireball. He'd caught her staring at him and, with the discovery, found the definite presence of instant, shared attraction.

He sauntered toward her. A smile touched his lips as he noted the sweetness in her reaction and the guilt that flashed across her lovely, heart-shaped face. Much to his surprise, despite the light tinge of red flooding her cheeks, she didn't cower under his returned attention. She held his gaze, studying him with interest, as if sizing him up.

When he arrived beside the vehicle, he reached over the passenger's-side door and offered his hand. "Nice to meet you, Dr. Johnson. I'm William Rinehart, but you can call me Rinehart." He lowered his voice slightly. "All my friends do."

Surprise flashed in her eyes as she tentatively extended her hand to him. "I prefer Laura." The instant their hands touched, her lashes fluttered, hiding her reaction to the connection.

Rinehart didn't know what she felt in that moment, and hell, he wasn't sure he knew what *he* felt except...hot. Burning up, in fact. Ironically her palm was cool and soft against his, a direct contrast to the scorching sensation flooding his body. His groin tightened, his heart raced. His blood coursed with molten heat. This was not a normal reaction to a woman. Not by a long shot. He tightened his fingers around hers, somehow afraid if he didn't, she might escape as he struggled to identify what was happening to him. If only she would look at him, so he could see into her eyes.

The sound of Walch opening his door drew Rinehart back to the present, and he forced himself to release Laura's hand. Walch settled behind the steering wheel and patted the spot next to him. "Make room for Mr. Rinehart."

One look at Laura's expression and Rinehart knew she didn't want to sit next to Walch. "Maybe I should wait for the next car," he suggested, wanting to save her the discomfort, even as he hated missing the opportunity to be near her, to figure out his reaction to her.

"Nonsense," Walch said. "You two need to get busy on this project. Laura doesn't mind being a little cramped." He glanced at Laura, who stared straight ahead. "Do you, Laura?"

Laura eased across the seat toward Walch, casting Rinehart a silent thank-you for his efforts. Walch's gaze dropped, devoured Laura's bare legs, which she left on Rinehart's side of the gearshift, thank God. Unfamiliar possessiveness rushed over Rinehart, urging him to protect Laura. He barely contained a desire to yank Walch out of the Jeep and pound him.

He jerked open the passenger's-side door and slid in beside Laura. One thing for sure—Laura wasn't going anywhere alone with that man. Ever. Not now that he was around.

Possessiveness roared through his body. Saving Laura had suddenly become personal, and this mission just a little more complicated. He didn't know what this woman was doing to him, but she was doing it in a big way. Laura Johnson and her patients were leaving this place with him, and he didn't care who had to roll over to make it happen. And if Walch knew what was good for him, he'd better keep his beady little eyes to himself.

Rinehart was going to enjoy taking that bastard's head.

By the time the Jeep pulled up to the main research facility—a half-circle-shaped, black-glass building— Laura knew she was in trouble. The drive back to the main research facility, which also housed Laura's apartment, had been filled with chatter about each of Laura's patients. On the surface the conversation seemed typical enough, considering the circumstances. But nothing was typical about Laura's reaction to Rinehart.

She was on fire, hot all over, aware of him as a man in an unnatural way. Aware of herself as a woman in a way that was downright frightening. Perhaps because she'd managed so effectively to push that part of herself into a place of dormancy—until now. Until this man drew the fire beneath the surface to a reality without even trying. She wanted to hate Rinehart, a man who was here to force her research to proceed in a direction she didn't want to go. Yet…she found herself drawn to him.

Rinehart slid out of the Jeep and held the door open for her. At the same moment, Walch excused himself to take a cell phone call a few steps out of hearing range. Laura scooted out of the vehicle and found herself staring up at Rinehart, when she'd promised herself she wouldn't make eye contact.

He was tall, standing a good foot above her five-four height, his body honed, a fighting machine. Military, present or past—she didn't know which, but he was definitely military. Confirming her theory, she observed that his light brown hair was trimmed neatly, his square jaw clean-shaven. But the dead giveaway was the lethal quality that clung to him, much as it had to her father and his Special Forces buddies. That "ready to go to battle" air they wore like a second skin. Which meant he'd push his agenda as dogmatically as her father always had—he wouldn't stop until he gotten what he'd come for. Damn this attraction she felt toward him. It was being wasted on a man to whom she was going to give a proverbial butt kicking.

He pushed the door shut, but didn't step away from Laura, didn't give her any space. He stood within whispering range, the wind drawing on his spicy male scent and insinuating it into her nostrils. Tempting her, teasing her, reminding her that this man had some control over her, control that she didn't want to allow.

"You don't like Walch much, do you?" he asked softly.

"Not one bit," she replied, unafraid of the truth, but not willing to announce it on a loudspeaker, either. Walch knew how she felt about him, but he had an ego that if wounded publicly would put him on the attack.

Rinehart studied her a moment, and then laughed, a soft timbre that danced along her nerve endings and made her ache in intimate places. Appalled, embarrassed, she crossed her arms in front of her chest. What was wrong with her?

"I like honesty," Rinehart said. "We should get along well."

"Don't be so sure of that," she warned, not wanting to get along with this man, not wanting to be this attracted to him. Besides, his reason for being on this island made him her enemy.

He narrowed his blue eyes on her. Deep blue with little speckles of green. "Not sure about me liking your honesty?" he asked. "Or not sure if we'll get along?"

"Either," she said. "We don't share the same agenda, which means we don't share the same values. Frankly, we're destined to clash."

"I don't know about agendas, though I'd love to compare notes. But I have to say," he added, "*clashing* isn't the word I'd choose to describe our interaction so far." His voice softened; his eyes darkened. "More like—"

"I'm ready," Walch said, drawing their attention before Rinehart could finish his sentence.

Laura took a step backward, distancing herself from Rinehart, wishing she knew what he'd been about to say, while realizing it shouldn't matter. "I need to take a shower before I do anything, and I have patients scheduled to meet me in the lab in an hour."

"Perfect," Walch said. "I want Rinehart and his team working with you every step of the way. That starts here and now. Today."

Laura ground her teeth. "I'm not sure that's the best way to make this work. My patients—"

"It'll work," Walch said. "Make it work."

She clamped down on her rising temper, feeling Rinehart's eyes on her face, feeling him watching her.

Her gaze went to his, avoiding Walch's. "I'll see you in an hour," she said, her voice low and curt.

Without waiting for a reply, she departed, walking toward the residential housing entrance at the side of the building. She heard Rinehart call her name and ignored him, heard Walch make some nasty comment, and ignored that, too. Getting all worked up wasn't going to help her or her patients. The clock was ticking, and she had to get off this island. Rinehart was a complication that she could do without, but she would handle him, just as she would Walch.

Rinehart watched as Laura departed and Walch stepped to his side. "Take a long, hard look, Mr. Rinehart. Because she's your new pet project. She has secrets and I want them exposed. And after watching you two together, I believe you're the man to get them for me."

Slowly, Rinehart turned his head toward Walch, irritated despite the fact that this turn of events worked in his favor. He needed to get close to Laura, and it seemed Walch was going to give him a free ticket to get there. "What kind of secrets?"

"I think she has abilities just as her patients do. In fact, I think she is more powerful than all the rest of them together."

Walch had Rinehart's attention now, but he carefully schooled his features to barely contained boredom. "What are you basing this assessment on?" he asked.

Walch leaned against the Jeep, crossing his arms in front of his body, his expression gloating. As if he had done something no one else could. "Laura apparently doesn't give me enough credit for my analytical skills. I didn't take her reports at face value. I checked them out. To create a retrovirus that corrected the defective marker in patients who can't control their abilities, she would have required a perfect specimen without the same flaws."

"And her reports didn't indicate such a requirement?"

"Not even a slight indication," Walch said. "But the facts are the facts. She had to have a perfect specimen to make that virus, and I believe that specimen came from Laura herself."

Rinehart believed Walch was right, which was all the more reason to act otherwise. "Why hide something like this when she is already involved with this type of research?" He shook his head. "It doesn't make sense. Maybe the specimen is from a patient."

"It's not," Walch said. "She inherited these patients from us. All except for the firestarter, who clearly had no control until she began injections of the retrovirus. As to why she's hiding her abilities, I don't know and, frankly, I don't care. I just want her secret exposed."

"It could be a past patient," Rinehart countered. "One she didn't bring to the island."

"No," Walch said. "It's Laura. I know it is. And tell me why either of us would screw with cloning patients who need injections when we can clone Laura's genetic code and make perfect soldiers?"

Jag's warning came back to him: Laura was dangerous in the hands of the Beasts. "She doesn't want any part of this," Rinehart commented. "You won't get her help willingly."

Walch cast him an impatient look. "Based on how she looked at you, if anyone can make her willing, it's you. I'll give you a few days to seduce her into cooperation."

Rinehart needed to show resistance, but not too much. This seduction plan would get him close to Laura. But he also didn't want to agree too easily. "I didn't come here to play some bedroom game, Captain. I came here to make my research a reality."

"You came here for my money and resources. If you want them, you'll do as I say."

Rinehart raised his eyebrows. "Don't you mean the government's money and resources?"

"I *am* the government, Mr. Rinehart, and don't you forget it." There was no mistaking the threat lacing his words. "I'm also a resourceful man, accustomed to getting what I want. My superiors like that about me." He pushed off the Jeep. "Let me show you just how resourceful." He started walking, as though expecting Rinehart to fall into step.

Balling his hands by his sides, Rinehart grimaced. This was the first time he'd ever had to tolerate a Beast rather than simply killing it. And damn if it wasn't testing his restraint to the limits.

Chapter 3

A few minutes later, Rinehart and Walch stood inside a small apartment that seemed as much laboratory as it did living quarters. What his living arrangements had to do with Walch's resourcefulness, he had no idea. Shiny white tile covered the floors, and when combined with the bright white walls, the effect was damn near blinding. The closest things to color in the room were the cream-colored leather couch and the marble coffee table.

"This will be your temporary home. Very temporary, I hope. I want this project nailed down rapidly. Your men are one floor up."

Rinehart would be done in a few days, all right, but not in the way Walch meant. He'd be ending this project and delivering Walch and his men to hell, minus their plan for super-soldier Beasts.

Playing his role, Rinehart was quick to counter Walch's statement with caution. "I feel compelled to remind you that our work has been limited to animals thus far. We've never tried to reproduce our results with humans."

"I don't want words of caution, Mr. Rinehart. I want results. I want every soldier on this island to become an unstoppable weapon in the next generation of warfare, human weapons that can't be stopped."

Rinehart digested that statement with concern. There were two thousand people on this island. Not only could they not be allowed to become human experiments in this weapon's creation, they couldn't be left as prey for the Beasts.

Walch continued, "As I mentioned, I'm a resourceful man, and I plan to arm you with every tool possible to ensure success." He picked up a remote from the coffee table. "When I saw how well your first meeting was progressing with Laura, I took the liberty of calling my programmer. He's given you access to a special feature on your television that I've found quite helpful in the past. I'm sure you will, as well." His lips twitched, a hint of an evil smile playing on them. He hit the power button. The screen filled with the image of a bathroom, with a woman behind a shower curtain humming a soft tune, her voice dancing along his nerve endings with a familiar, warming sensation. Recognition came first, followed by rage. Pure, white-hot rage. *Laura.* Rinehart's temples pulsed, his blood thickened. This son of a bitch was taping Laura.

With extreme effort, he sucked in a breath and strug-

gled for control. Never before had he felt such a desire
to hurt someone as he did toward Walch right then.
Never before had his dark side felt this close to the
surface. He could feel himself about to snap, the primitive emotions normally reserved for battle taking hold
of him. His feelings of possessiveness toward Laura
were unnatural; his reactions to her, too intense. *Mate.*
That word took him back for a minute, made him pause.
Was Laura his mate? Could it be? If his protectiveness
toward her was any indication, the answer was yes.

He drew a discreet, deep breath, reasoning with
himself, reminding himself of his duty to his men, his
commitment to bring innocents to safety.

Now Rinehart ground his teeth as he funneled
rational thoughts through his mind and forced out the
primitive ones, measuring his actions. The Knights were
outnumbered on this island, and his rash actions could
get them killed.

His gaze settled on Walch, and Rinehart realized
with relief that the man—no, the *Beast*—had not
noticed his anger. Walch was too busy staring at the television screen, waiting for Laura to exit that shower.
With his gaze still riveted on Laura's image, Walch
spoke, making it obvious he was aware of Rinehart's attention on him. "If she uses her powers, or attempts to
escape, we will know." He glanced at Rinehart, his eyes
glinting with lust. "Makes for interesting television, I
might add." Then his tone changed. "Bed her and get
her confidence. I want her powers exposed, and her
cooperation in hand. If you can't get through to her and
fast, I'll force her submission."

"How exactly will you do that?" Rinehart asked, tension coiling in his gut.

He snorted. "Easy. She treats those damn patients like her children. If I threaten them, she'll do whatever we want. Of course, I've gotten to know her well enough to know, in that scenario, she'd be plotting against us at every turn. I'd prefer that you get through to her. In a perfect world, you'll get her close, milk her for what she's worth and make her disposable. There might even be a bonus in it for you."

Rinehart could guess what that meant for Laura. He doubted seriously that the Beasts would kill her as they did other human women. They'd convert her into a Beast and turn her into a weapon. *Over my dead body,* he vowed silently.

"I'll take care of Laura," he said, his voice low and clipped, hating this role he had to play. "You just get ready to write me that bonus check."

"That's what I want to hear," Walch said, his eyes lighting with victory a second before he studied Laura's image again. His lips twisted in an evil smile, as he appeared to reluctantly turn his attention back to Rinehart. "I'll give you some privacy to study Laura's habits more intimately." He set the remote on the table. "Enjoy your stay, Mr. Rinehart."

The door shut and Rinehart charged toward it focused on one thing—his total outrage. He wanted to get his hands on Walch and make him pay for what he was doing to Laura. As his hand gripped the doorknob, he reined himself in. With extreme willpower he forced himself to pause, to think through his actions. The

Knights were outnumbered here. No matter how much he wanted to kill Walch for what he was doing to Laura, he couldn't. Not yet.

He forced himself to walk to the couch, to sit down and attempt to both understand and reel in his emotions. Suddenly, his eyes were on the television, fixed on Laura as she stepped out of the shower, gloriously naked and dripping water. A low growl escaped his throat as his groin tightened without his consent. He grabbed the remote and turned it off, even as a word played in his head. *Mine.* Damn it! Guilt overtook him for what he'd just seen. For wanting to leave that image of Laura playing, wanting to see her naked.

But not like this. Not like some freaking Peeping Tom.

He pushed to his feet again, scrubbing his jaw, wired with rage all over again. Thinking about Walch watching Laura in her most private moments ate him alive. It couldn't continue. Wouldn't continue. He froze in stride. Those cameras were coming out of Laura's room, and they were coming out today. While Laura was in the lab, he and Max would make it happen. Walch couldn't do a damn thing about it, either. If he tried, Rinehart would threaten to tell Laura about the cameras, which would be the kiss of death to her cooperation. Clearly, Walch believed Laura's cooperation held value, and he believed Rinehart was the way to get it.

Rinehart couldn't wait for the confrontation that would come when Walch found out he'd lost his surveillance of Laura. *Bring it on,* he thought. *Bring. It. On.*

He was in charge of what happened here. It was time Walch started to learn that.

Despite the tiny victory this plan would achieve for Rinehart, another troubling thought came to mind. Laura had become the focus of the Beasts' plan to enhance their soldiers and defeat the Knights. Laura. A woman—logic said—who could be his mate. Why else would she incite such intense emotions in him when no other could? Yet Laura, the woman who might well be the mate who could save his soul from the darkness, had perhaps become the biggest threat the Knights had ever faced.

If she were as powerful as Walch thought her to be, then Laura's gifts, duplicated in the Beasts, could shift the power from good to evil. Laura might well hold more than his future in her hands. She could hold the future of the Knights, and even humankind, in her hands.

Still furious over Walch's little peep show at Laura's expense, Rinehart found his way to the lab entrance at the same moment that a stairwell door opened a few feet away. Des appeared in the doorway, followed by Max, Rock and Lucan. Rinehart didn't ask why they had bypassed the elevators. He knew. They were exploring, getting to know the undisclosed details of their location, preparing for whatever might come their way and expecting the worst.

"I assume you got the same deluxe welcoming package I got in my room?" Rinehart asked, as they communed in a circle in the hallway. "Cameras, mikes, electronic accessories?"

"Oh, yeah," Max confirmed. "We're wired tight."

Rinehart ground his teeth. "Walch gets off on

watching *everyone* here, male and female. And by watching, I mean *every* intimate moment."

Des cursed in Spanish. "That piece of—"

"Garbage," Rinehart finished for him, with Lucan chiming in at the same time.

"There's no reason to watch her bathroom besides simple, perverted exploitation," Rinehart added. "I'm taking out the cameras."

"And when Walch finds out?" Max asked.

Rinehart's eyes lifted to the ceiling, to an air vent that was perfect for a hidden camera. He hoped like hell there was one; he hoped Walch was listening right now. "Walch can kiss my tight, white ass." His gaze riveted back to Max's. "I plan to spend a lot of time in that room, and I'm not doing it with an audience. I'm here to make scientific history, not provide X-rated entertainment."

Max's eyes narrowed, an inquiry shining in the steely depths. He wanted to say more, to ask questions; he couldn't with an audience. Instead, he smiled. "Can't blame you for that. I've got a nifty little signal disrupter you can plant once you're inside."

"Company arriving," Des warned.

Rinehart turned to see Laura approaching, and his heart raced with the sight of her. God, she was beautiful. Classically so. The silky mass of her auburn hair was primly pulled back in a knot at her neck, enhancing the high cut of her aristocratic cheekbones and the fairness of her ivory-perfect skin. She wore a simple black dress and black heels that came off as sleek and stylish; the long legs he'd admired only an hour before were sexy and bare.

She was the epitome of simple elegance. A woman meant to be on the arm of a man of status. Not some soldier who knew nothing but survival. Which meant he had to be wrong—she couldn't be his mate. But this knowledge did nothing to tame the desire raging inside him, the desire burning for reward. He watched her walk, becoming aroused at the sultry sway of her hips. She stopped in front of them, her arms crossing beneath her full breasts, tension dancing off her like an electric charge.

His gaze lifted to her red, painted lips. He wanted to taste her.

"Hello, Laura." Her eyes met his for a flicker of a moment before her lashes lowered. But in that moment, he'd seen the same heat of awareness he felt for her reflected in her own gaze. And he'd seen her conflict over those feelings. She thought he was the enemy, yet she still wanted him.

He burned to look into those eyes again. "I'd like you to meet my men," he said, forcing her to give him her attention again as he indicated each man as he spoke. "Max, Rock, Lucan and Des. Lucan has invested a lot of time in this project. I think you will find his research of interest."

"I have no interest in turning humans into weapons," she countered, "and I won't take all of you into my lab. You'll scare my patients. If I had my way, I wouldn't take any of you."

Rinehart ignored the cutting remark. "Understandable," he conceded. "Max and Rock handle security. Myself, Des and Lucan will be involved with the actual laboratory studies."

Her brows dipped, confusion registering in her expression. "You brought security personnel to a military facility?"

Rinehart pinned her in a steady gaze. "I trust my men." The inference being that he trusted no one else, especially not Walch. He hoped they could bond on that issue.

She studied him a moment. "I don't," she said finally.

Okay, so much for bonding. Though he didn't like her response, her directness didn't surprise him, not after his earlier encounter with her. "We'll earn your trust," he vowed.

Her reply was instant, her words as sharp as a saber sword. "Don't waste the effort. It won't work." She turned away, shutting down a rebuttal. The lab door opened and quickly shut behind her.

Rinehart let out a heavy sigh. Jag hadn't exaggerated when he said this assignment would be a challenge, and judging from the looks on the other Knights' faces, they agreed. Laura was that and so much more. But he'd earn her trust, or he'd die trying.

A low whistle slipped from Des's lips. "This is going to get interesting. I can't wait to see how you're going to manage that time in her room you mentioned. Right now, I don't think she'd give you time in hell."

Rinehart shot Des an irritated look. "I'll manage," he promised. "You can count on it."

Two hours later, Rinehart and his men sat around a lab table and watched as Carol, Laura's twenty-five-year-old patient, finished moving a chair with her mind, the last of a thirty-minute demonstration of her powers. Before her had been the twenty-year-old twins, Jacob and Jared, who were superhero strong, able to bend steel with their minds.

The chair slid from one side of the room to the other. Completing her task, Carol laced her fingers together in front of her, her long raven hair lying in silky waves around her shoulders. She was a lovely, young girl, but her skin was unnaturally pale, with dark circles distinct beneath her pale eyes.

"Shall I continue?" she asked, her attention fixed on Rinehart rather than on Laura, the depths of her stare radiating an empty quality, a quality that spoke of a Beast's influence. Rinehart was certain that Carol had not been converted yet; she was simply being controlled. One bite from a Beast, and a soul could linger between life and death indefinitely.

"I think we've seen enough," Laura said, answering the question with a hint of a sharp tone.

Carol's attention slowly slid to Laura, boring into her almost angrily before she said, "Very well." She turned on her heels and slowly walked toward the door.

Rinehart noted Laura's frown, the worry shimmering deep in her eyes. Laura sensed something was wrong with Carol, perhaps could see it in her changing behavior. In the way a weakened soul allowed the influence of evil to slide into its core.

Laura seemed to shake herself, tearing her attention away from Carol's departure and back to the table. With the firestarter having yet to show up, only one patient remained ready to show off his talents. A tall, lanky, sixteen-year-old kid named Blake stood up and smiled. "My turn." Laura laughed softly, the sound trickling over Rinehart's nerve endings like a soft lover's caress. Damn. Her impact on him was downright unnerving in its ability to overwhelm and control him.

"What are you laughing for?" Blake asked, but his grin said he knew why.

"I never thought I'd see the day when you would be eager to show off your gift rather than deny it exists." Laura winked at Blake. "We've come a long way, baby."

"Bring it on," Des challenged. "Show us what you got."

Then, despite having read Jag's reports about Blake, Rinehart sat in startled disbelief as Blake disappeared, faded away into invisibility, and then several seconds later reappeared in the same spot. He didn't orb as only a few select Knights and Beasts could do. He simply made himself invisible. The other patients' gifts had been amazing. But this—this was unbelievably dangerous. In the hands of the Beasts, downright deadly.

"Unfreaking believable," Des murmured beside him, rubbing his eyes as if they were tricking him.

A quick look at Lucan said he was thinking the same thing as Rinehart. This kid was danger with a capital *D*.

Blake grinned again, baring bright, white teeth. "Pretty cool, huh?" he asked, a childlike quality coming through that made him appear more twelve than sixteen. But then, he'd lived a sheltered life.

"Yes," Laura said. "It's cool." She glanced at the clock. "Don't you have to study for that algebra exam tomorrow?"

Blake's slender shoulders slumped. "I hate algebra."

"All the more reason to study," she reminded him, and cut her gaze from his, her eyes colliding with Rinehart's. And just like that, emotions rushed over Rinehart. The worry Laura felt about this reached across the room and tore a hole in his gut. That emotion, *her emotion,* somehow became his, and it did so with such a definitive presence, the impact damn near shook him to the core. Was he losing his mind? Rinehart narrowed his gaze on hers, searching. Did she have an ability that was creating this weird link to her emotions. Emotions that formed words in his mind—her words, her thoughts. *Blake deserves a good life. He deserves to get away from this place. I have to get him out of here.*

Someone spoke, breaking the spell, pulling him back to reality. Blake. Blake had agreed to study for his test. Explained something about a tutor to Lucan. Laura jerked her attention away from Rinehart and smiled weakly at Blake as he said his farewells.

"He's a good kid," Laura said, watching him leave.

Good kid or not, the more Rinehart considered Blake's ability, the more concerned he became. "Blake's clothes disappeared when he did. How is that possible?"

She hesitated before answering. "He cloaks himself and anything he is touching at the time."

The room fell silent with that bombshell, and somehow, Rinehart managed to keep his "oh, shit" to himself. Blake was a deadly weapon and Laura knew it. So did Walch. A Beast that inherited this ability could kill without ever being seen. That couldn't happen, and he had no doubt Des and Lucan were in full agreement.

"Like I said," Laura added when no one spoke.

"Blake's a good kid. So are the twins. They'd never hurt a flea."

Rinehart noticed she didn't mention Carol, who she clearly believed had taken a dark turn. What about Kresley? he wondered. Was there a reason she wasn't here? And what about Walch's claim that Laura herself was the source of the serum? Did she have an ability, as Walch claimed? Did she represent a threat that reached beyond scientific knowledge?

"Their abilities could be deadly in the wrong hands," Laura added, almost as if she responded to his silent questions. "Duplicating them and handing them out like candy could be catastrophic." She pushed to her feet. "I guess deadly is what you're counting on, seeing as how you're out to use your great cloning discovery to create human weapons rather than cure diseases." She opened her mouth to say more and quickly sealed her lips. Then, "I need to grab some supplies in the back office. If Kresley arrives, I suggest you send her back to me. She sets fires when she gets uncomfortable, and I can assure you, this group will make her uncomfortable. I know it does me." She turned and walked away, with her verbal slap delivered, anger charging the air in her wake.

Des leaned back and ran his hands down his legs. "I'd say that went about as well as paying a topless dancer with dog treats."

Rinehart sighed. "I'll go talk to her," he said, pushing to his feet.

Des had a unique way of summing things up, but he was right. These were choppy waters they were treading

on. He couldn't urge Laura to trust them and press her
for information on her research and expect to get it. He
saw only one option: Bring her into their circle and do
it now. She was only dangerous if she ended up in the
Beasts' hands, and he wasn't going to let that happen.

It was time to get up close and personal—to talk.
He just wanted to talk. Right. Just talk. Maybe if he
told himself that enough times, he'd make himself
believe it.

Walch sat behind a steel military desk deep beneath
the ground, inside the hidden cavern that housed his op-
erational center, a room he alone entered. It was here
that he monitored the island, and here that he now
waited for communication from his master, Adrian, the
leader of the Darkland Beasts. Cameras lined the walls,
as did an array of telecommunications equipment. He
eyed the clock, realizing Rinehart and his men would
be joining Laura right about now. He kicked his heels
up on the wooden surface and reached for a remote,
flipping to the latest feed from just outside the lab, not
more than an hour ago. Instantly, images of Rinehart
and his men appeared on one of the two dozen monitors.

He listened as they discussed their situation, grinding
his teeth as Rinehart demanded that his man, Max, strip
Laura's room of the surveillance equipment. Watched
as Rinehart stared into the camera and spoke: "Walch
can kiss my tight, white ass."

Rage rose in Walch as he heard those words. He
dropped his feet to the floor and slammed the remote
onto the desk. "We'll see about that," he muttered

between his teeth. Rinehart didn't know who he was dealing with or he wouldn't dare cross him. Walch had become more than a man, more than a simple soldier in the United States Army trying to fight his way to a promotion. He was a leader of something bigger now, a ruler of the Demon foot soldiers that lived among the unknowing humans.

Walch flexed his fingers, feeling the supernatural grip of his hand. He longed to shift to his Beast form, to feel the surge of adrenaline it delivered, the added rush of strength that the change accommodated. Yes. He wanted more power. Much more. And he would have it. Adrian had said so. More power, more rewards. All he had to do was deliver Super Soldiers for conversion into Adrian's new Dark Knights—an Army that would defeat the Knights of White. Then humanity would fall to the Beasts.

Resolve filled him and he grabbed the remote, bringing up the lab on one of the screens. Laura's patients had arrived and she was tensely interacting with Rinehart's men.

He considered his options. He could control *her* with a simple threat to her patients. Rinehart was another story. He'd have to send him a stronger message.

He hit a button on the desk where he sat and spoke into a mike. "Bring Lucan to me," he said. Walch leaned back in his chair again, lacing his fingers behind his neck. A smile touched his lips. Lucan was the most valued member of their research team, which made him a perfect choice. He wanted no facade that any of them were untouchable. He was going to enjoy watching Lucan's pain. Because that pain would ensure Rinehart's submission.

Chapter 4

Shaking. Laura was shaking inside. How she had managed to hide that fact, she didn't know. Perhaps years of hiding a secret had steeled her to face the challenge before her.

Laura walked down the hallway, away from Rinehart and his men—men who planned to strip away the new life she'd desperately tried to create for herself and her patients. And one of those men did more than threaten her work—he threatened her sensibilities. *Rinehart.* The impact of that man on her senses was downright intense. Everything about the man set her on fire—her emotions, her body, her anger over his research. And she was angry, but it did nothing to dispel the onslaught of awareness the man created in her.

It had been so long since a man, any man, had gotten

to her. So long, she didn't remember the last one. Hiding her abilities had made every relationship a chore, a lie she couldn't bear. At some point, she'd decided dating wasn't worth the effort or the fear of trusting the wrong person.

So why now? Why Rinehart? Her body was betraying her. How could she want a man who was serving Walch's agendas?

Laura entered the office and reached for a lab jacket from the coatrack, feeling suddenly cold. She leaned against the wall a moment, taking a brief bit of solitude and drawing in a calming breath. But there was no calming her hormones, now raging in overload, and that upheaval meant she couldn't manage a good read on Rinehart. Not that she needed anything but the obvious to tell his story, she reminded herself. He was with Walch, hired by Walch, a proponent for Walch's Super Soldiers. Rinehart was nothing but trouble wrapped in a brawny male body that just happened to be hard in all the right places. Like those strong legs that had been pressed close to hers in the Jeep. Her core ached with that memory, and she quickly reprimanded herself. She had much more important things than that man's body to think about!

She had to be strong for her patients, to figure out a way to get them all out of here. She could do this. If there was one thing she'd learned from having a father in special forces, it was the "never give up" mentality. Where there was a will, there was a way. She was a fighter, just as her father had been.

Determination renewed, Laura pushed off the wall

and started toward her supply cabinet. She made it all of two steps when the air crackled with a visitor. She didn't turn. She didn't have to. Her skin tingled with Rinehart's presence. No one had ever affected her this way, and it was more than a little unnerving. If ever there was a time she needed to feel in control of her gifts, now was that time. But she didn't feel in control at all. Were her powers expanding, exposing a new, deeper perception? Or was there something about Rinehart that created this in her? But what would that be?

Laura reached inside the cabinet and pulled out a package of cotton swabs, and steeled herself for the impact of facing him, before she turned. She found him lingering inside the doorway. Big. Tall. Consuming the small entrance. He leaned against the frame, his head almost touching the archway above. The air crackled some more—with electricity, attraction, awareness; those too-blue eyes of his latched on to hers and refused to let go.

She could barely breathe as his gaze seeped through every pore of her body and drew a shiver. Unnerved by her over-the-top reaction, Laura crossed her arms in front of her chest and hugged herself, put on the defensive by the way he made her feel so…touched. But still, she didn't look away, couldn't look away.

"Can we talk?" he asked.

Why did talking seem so dangerous? Why did everything to do with this man feel dangerous? "We have nothing to talk about."

He studied her with far too much intensity for her

comfort, before asking, "Why are you so hell-bent on hating me?"

"I'm not," she declared, denying the truth behind his statement. God, how she wanted to hate this man, how she wanted to feel something other than this crazy attraction to him. "Nor do I have time for schoolroom games of who likes who." Desperate to avoid his scrutinizing stare, she decided she'd try to dismiss him— not an easy task, she suspected. Laura gave him her back and opened a cabinet door to remove a syringe before glancing over her shoulder. "I'm expecting Kresley any minute." In other words, no time for this conversation.

He was quick to counter. "Which is all the more reason we need to talk. Before she arrives and sees you're upset. I don't want her to see me and my team as the enemy."

That set her off. Laura whirled back around to face him again, going on the attack. "Aren't you?" she demanded, the heat of her attraction to this man shifting toward the safer emotion of anger. Unfortunately, as she turned, the syringe she held fell to the floor and rolled to a stop halfway between them. Embarrassment deflated her anger and made her feel clumsy and silly. Good grief, she had to pull herself together.

Laura stared at the syringe for several seconds before moving to pick it up, apparently at the same moment Rinehart decided to do the same. Suddenly they were both bent down, reaching for the syringe, hands colliding. Sparks darted up her arm, and she tried to yank her hand back. He gently but forcefully held it. "I'm not what you think I am."

What was she supposed to say to that? She didn't
know. For the first time in her life, she was speechless—
she, who had dared to challenge professors to prove
theories that didn't quite hold water, who had stood up
to Walch when he demanded she twist her morals for his
gain. Yet she could not find the words to respond to a
virtual stranger. Rinehart considered her a moment, as if
he expected her to speak, then added, "I'm here to help."

She shook her head in disbelief and pulled her hand
from his grip. "To help Walch, not me."

"I have no interest in helping Walch."

That made no sense. Frustrated at whatever game he
was playing, Laura pushed herself to her feet, and he
followed. But he was still close, too close, toe-to-toe
with her. "You *work* for Walch," she said, tilting her chin
upward to glare at him with accusation.

"So do you," he pointed out.

Somehow her attention caught on the firm, sensual
lift of his mouth, which now hinted at a smile. She
squeezed her eyes shut. Good Lord. Why was she even
looking at his mouth? Why was she aware of the heat
of his body so near?

Her lashes rose and she searched his face, probing,
desperately trying to understand the hidden meanings
that seemed to dance between the lines of this conversation. "What is it you want from me?"

His eyes heated, and his reply came slowly, as if he
considered it with care. "Have dinner with me tonight."
The words came out low, husky, full of an erotic
promise she had no business welcoming, even if the
ache between her thighs said otherwise.

Somehow, Laura managed a chastising laugh, directed as much at herself for wanting to say yes as at his gall for asking in the first place. She had patients counting on her. This thing going on between them— whatever it was—had to stop. It had to stop now.

"I don't eat with the enemy," she said, being clear about where they stood—where he stood with her.

A flash of surprise at her directness slid across his face before amusement danced in his eyes. "Haven't you ever heard that saying 'Keep your friends close and your enemies closer'?" he asked. "Friend or enemy, keeping me at a distance can't be a smart move."

Laura tilted her head to the side, studied him again, and considered her next move. Her father would agree with him. Perhaps, she would, too, if being alone with him didn't scare the hell out of her. If he was leaving this island, he could take her and her patients with him. But would he? She doubted that. Besides, this was Friday night—pizza and movie night with Kresley— and she desperately wanted to keep Kresley feeling grounded and safe.

"Laura!"

"That would be Kresley," Laura said, saved from any further response.

"This discussion isn't over," he said, as if reading her mind.

"We'll see about that," Laura countered, irritated by his bossy, arrogant assumption that he decided when their talk ended. But despite that irritation, excitement fluttered in her stomach. Part of her enjoyed his pursuit. Which was ridiculous. Shared attraction or not, he had an agenda, a reason to push—he was after her research.

He leaned closer and she told herself to back away. Instead, she stood there, enticed by the spicy, male scent of him, jolted by the touch of his hands as they came down on her shoulders. His warm breath trickled along her neck, her earlobe. "I've always enjoyed a good challenge," he whispered.

Laura didn't know what impacted her the most, his touch or the absence of his touch. Her gaze followed Rinehart as he distanced himself, taking a casual stance against the wall, one booted foot over the other. Goose bumps slid along her skin, and she barely contained a shiver. He'd awakened the woman in her, the dormant desires that now demanded satisfaction. Her skin tingled; her nipples ached. She wanted this man in a bad way, an unexplainable way that refused to be dismissed despite the dire circumstances and despite every ounce of smarts she possessed telling her he was trouble.

"Laura." Kresley appeared in the doorway, offering a welcome distraction from her interaction with Rinehart.

She looked pale, sick. Guilt twisted in Laura's gut. Once Walch had informed her about Rinehart's team, she'd had no option but to take precautionary measures. She'd injected her patients with a flu bug. She'd create concern that the illness was a reaction to the treatments she'd been giving the patients, a side effect that had to be addressed before any further testing could be done. Certainly the patients' conditions would delay the testing Rinehart's team planned. A tactic to buy some time while she figured out how to get off the island.

Kresley frowned. "Who are those men out there? They—" She stopped midsentence as her gaze traveled to the left, and she noted Rinehart's presence. "Oh. Sorry. Am I interrupting?"

"Not at all," Laura assured her. "This is Rinehart." Laura bent to pick up the abandoned syringe and then straightened. "He's one of the men I told you about, the researchers who'll be involved with our work here."

"Rinehart," Kresley said. Her frown deepened as she crossed her arms in front of her body protectively. "Sounds like a last name, not a first. You're one of *them.*" Her voice held contempt.

"Them?" Rinehart asked.

"Kresley," Laura said, her voice etched with warning.

Kresley ignored the warning. "One of Walch's soldiers," she said, replying to Rinehart as if Laura hadn't spoken. "The last name as a first name is a dead give-away."

"I'm not one of Walch's soldiers," he told her, his voice glinting with steely certainty. "I'm not Walch's anything."

Kresley cast him a disbelieving look. "Then why are you—"

"Enough," Laura said sternly, cutting off her question. She pointed at the chair next to the medicine cabinet. "Sit."

Kresley hesitated, looking as if she might argue, but she reconsidered and quickly claimed the chair Laura had indicated.

Laura pressed her hands to her hips and regarded Kresley. "You look pale," she observed. "Did you sleep last night?"

Kresley cut her gaze from Laura's. "I tossed and turned a bit," she replied evasively, apparently not intending to admit she was sick.

Laura bit back a reprimand. Kresley knew she had to report any illness immediately, to prevent potential complications with her injections. She pressed her palm to Kresley's forehead. "You're burning up." Now she was really frustrated. This wasn't a "maybe I'm sick, I'll wait until I'm sure before I say something" situation. Kresley just plain wasn't going to tell Laura she was sick. "You were going to let me inject you without saying a word. You *know* I have to draw blood and make sure I know what's going on first."

"But I need the injection, Laura," Kresley pleaded. "I can't wait. What if—"

"A few hours' delay won't affect your control," Laura replied, cutting off her objections. "There's a buildup of the serum in your system. You know this. We've discussed it many times. We have some leeway now." Laura reached inside the cabinet and withdrew supplies. "It's critical we ensure you're not having a reaction to the shots before I give you another one." Which was what she wanted Rinehart's men to believe. She would milk this flu bug for all it was worth. Walch wouldn't want to clone her patients' abilities if the soldiers who received those abilities couldn't control them. She needed Walch to fear complications with the serum.

"Why would the injections cause this?" Kresley asked quickly. "I've taken them for a long time now."

"Extra testing is a precaution," Laura assured her, although she thought it might be a good idea all the way around. Carol was showing signs of, well...of something, she didn't know what. Something was off with her. Dark. Unsettling. She shook off the thought and refocused on what she was telling Kresley. "Being cautious is a good thing." She pursed her lips. "Now let me do my job, and don't you dare keep something like this from me again."

Kresley's hands balled in her lap. "I'm sorry. I just...I'm sorry."

Laura hated to see Kresley upset, but had she not known what was going on, Kresley's lack of honesty could have been a serious issue. She didn't comfort her, couldn't. Not about this.

A few minutes later, samples drawn, Laura tossed the used supplies into the contaminated-waste container on the wall. "Now go to bed," she told Kresley. "I'll check on you in a bit."

"All right then," Kresley said. "Laura—"

Laura waved her away. "Go rest. What's done is done."

Kresley nodded and shuffled from the room, head bowed.

Rinehart's cell buzzed, and she glanced up to see him snap it off his belt to read a text message. His expression was indiscernible, his jaw a hard line, his tension palpable. So much so she couldn't help but question him.

"Problem?" she asked, as he replaced the phone on his belt.

He pushed off the wall. "Nothing I can't handle. Is Kresley okay?"

"I need to run some tests on her and the other

patients. Should take an hour to get a preliminary idea of what I'm dealing with." She hesitated, afraid of seeming obvious, but deciding to go for it. "Needless to say, this will delay your plans. I can't allow my patients to be subjected to anything new until I find out what's going on with Kresley."

To her surprise, he made no argument. "Understandable."

Laura's eyes narrowed. She knew she couldn't have bypassed his scrutiny so easily. He simply wasn't fully in the room anymore; his mind was elsewhere. And something about him had changed. He'd taken on a rigid, soldierlike persona.

"I'll check back in an hour," he added shortly. And then he left. Nothing else said. He was simply gone, leaving Laura staring after him. There was more to Rinehart than met the eye, but Laura couldn't put her finger on what—she sensed it though, felt it deep in her gut. Felt it in her heated reaction to him.

Now she had to figure out what to do about it.

For thirty minutes now, Lucan had been sitting at the crappy metal table in the tiny, empty room he'd been left in, pretending to read patient files. But he knew he wasn't here to read patient files. There was nothing here he hadn't seen before. Nothing here that he couldn't have read in his room, or in the lab with the others.

Lucan might be a lot of things, but a fool wasn't one of them. Or maybe he was. He'd known joining this mission had been a risk, but he'd come anyway. He'd come knowing he was too close to the dark side, a weak link in the Knights' armor. And now here he was, alone, about to face a gaggle of Beasts. The minute that Walch's soldiers had shown up at the lab, Lucan had surmised he was headed for trouble. No, this wasn't about files. He was going to get a working over, his gut said, and a good one at that.

There was a time when he would have welcomed the pain that was surely coming his way, embraced it for the humanity it reminded him he still possessed. But now…now, he feared the pain. He feared it because with pain came the rage of his dark side, the Beast that lived inside him. A Beast that could expose him, and his fellow Knights, to these Darkland Beasts. He could get them all killed.

Lucan inhaled, tapped the file that sat open and pretended to read. But inside…inside, he reached for human memories, pleasant times he could focus on when he was being tortured. Memories that were now so stained by time, he struggled to recall them. No images came to him. Nothing. He shut his eyes, squeezed them tightly together, strained his memory banks. He needed something positive in his mind when they tortured him, something human. *Please! Give me something.*

When nothing came to him, he stared down at the picture of Kresley, the firestarter, and imagined that she was his sister. Imagined her smiling and laughing, happy as she had always been. But a mere second later, the vision shifted, turned into the memory of a Beast grabbing his real sister and killing her. And the tortured expression he'd seen on her face as she had died.

And in that moment, the doors opened; two of Walch's men appeared, ropes in hand. Without a word, they charged at him. Lucan grabbed the arms of the chair, willing himself to contain his fury while they tied him down.

Do not fail the Knights.

Chapter 5

"I thought you knew the code to the elevator," Rinehart demanded as he, Max and Rock watched Des punch numbers into the keypad for the fifth time. Des had managed to tune into the place where Lucan was being held. Rock stood guard at the only door in or out of the place—in other words, they were sitting ducks.

"I'm trying," Des muttered, punching in yet another failed code. He ran a hand along the back of his neck. "Obviously I'm not completely in tune with these visions yet. I was right about the elevator."

"It's now or never," Rock asserted. "We got company."

Rinehart tensed. "How many?"

"Two," Rock reported.

Rinehart acted without waiting for input. He stepped

up to Rock's side and grabbed the door, yanking it open and meeting the soldiers head-on. "About damn time," he said. "We've been waiting fifteen minutes. Walch is expecting us down below."

They stopped in their tracks, stared at him. "How did you get here?"

"I followed the yellow brick road," Rinehart retorted sarcastically, instinctively knowing that the other Knights had taken position behind him—their unity always a source of confidence. "How do you think I got here? Walch told me to get my ass down here and I did. I've been standing here waiting for your kind escort services for fifteen minutes. If he's pissed, it's on your heads." The two soldiers exchanged skeptical looks, and Rinehart pressed onward, jerking his cell from his belt and eyeing the names on their shirts. "Rogers and Miller. I'll just call Walch and let him know you two are the holdup."

Miller responded instantly. "That won't be necessary." The look on his harsh features reeked of hatred.

Rinehart hesitated, glanced at his phone and back at the two Beasts. He snapped his phone back onto his belt and motioned them forward. "Lead the way," he said, motioning the Beasts forward.

The Knights followed in their wake, exchanging a few meaningful looks. They sized up the two guns hanging on each Beast's belt. Rinehart and Rock silently agreed to be the ones to act—they were the ones without mates, with the least to lose. Unexpectedly, a voice rang in the back of his mind, a voice that said Laura was his mate. Inwardly, he cursed the distraction. Now was a time for war, for battle, for focus. Not female distractions. He'd gotten his men killed because of that once before, and he wasn't doing that again.

In the elevator, the Knights stood to the back, while the two Beasts stupidly placed themselves in front, in a position vulnerable to attack. And attack the Knights did—the instant the Beasts stepped outside of the elevator, Rinehart and Rock acted. Before the enemy ever knew what happened, they'd lost their weapons. Each Knight held a gun pointed at a Beast in soldier disguise. The two Beasts whirled around to face them. A snarl escaped one soldier's lips, and Rinehart knew the Beast was struggling to maintain his human form.

Rinehart cocked the gun in his hand. "A well-placed bullet will hurt like hell," he said, his voice cutting like the blade he wished he held. A bullet wouldn't kill a Beast any more than it would a Knight, but it damn sure would cause pain. One of the soldiers dared a step forward. Rinehart lifted his gun slightly. "Make my day. Keep coming at me. Give me a reason to shoot." The soldier stopped in his tracks. "That's what I thought," Rinehart said. He cut his gaze ever so slightly to Des. "Lead the way. Where is he?"

Des motioned with a slight lift of his chin. "Third door on the right."

"We'll cover you," Rock said, as he and Max stepped forward, assuming more aggressive stances in front of the enemies.

Rinehart was moving toward the door before Rock finished his sentence. All he could think about was getting to Lucan before it was too late, before they pushed him over the edge. It didn't matter that Lucan might be perfectly fine, bullshitting about nothing with Walch. It mattered that he might not be—that Rinehart would be the reason if he wasn't. It mattered that Des's visions had said Lucan was in trouble.

Rinehart reached the door a second before Des and found it locked. Without hesitation he leveraged his weight on his back foot and kicked in the door, putting every bit of supernatural strength behind the action, determined he would not be kept out of that room. The door fractured under the pressure, and the two Knights stormed the room. They found it empty.

Both Knights rotated around and aimed at the door, fearful of being trapped. "Where is he, Des?" Rinehart demanded.

Des cursed. "This is the room," he insisted. "This is it. He was here."

A television hanging from the ceiling flipped on, and Walch appeared on the screen. "Violence really isn't necessary, gentlemen. Lucan won't be detained nor has any lasting harm come to him." Rinehart glanced at the door and back at the screen in time to see Walch smile. "This time, that is," Walch added. "Next time might be another story. Let Lucan's visit serve as a warning. I will not be crossed, nor will I kiss anyone's ass, most assuredly not yours, Mr. Rinehart. You *will* serve *me* and me alone until you leave this island." The screen went blank.

Rinehart quickly quelled the guilt over his role in whatever had befallen Lucan. He and Des exchanged a look, and in unison, lunged for the door, neither comfortable staying inside a room that could still become a trap. The minute they'd cleared the room, another door opened directly in front of them.

Lucan was shoved forward; his shirt had been ripped open and blood was dripping from several stomach wounds. Wounds that were meant to induce pain, not death. Wounds that induced anger in Rinehart.

Lucan wobbled, his legs unsteady beneath him. No one spoke, no one moved. Tension laced the air with an elastic quality, calm before chaos. But Rinehart didn't feel calm. He felt the Beast inside him rising, felt it pressing him into rage, into action rather than calculation. He inhaled deeply to calm himself and willed his Beast into submission, almost shaking with the effort. Good Lord, he was further gone than he'd thought. Here he was concerned about Lucan snapping, and he himself might well be the threat.

A soldier walked through the doorway behind Lucan, violently shoving him again. Lucan stumbled, crumbling to his knees. Rinehart flexed the fingers of his free hand, an edgy readiness for battle thrumming through his veins.

Seconds passed, the silence thicker now. Silence that brought only one question—who would act first? And then abruptly, that silence was broken, an unexpected sound filtering through the air. That sound was Lucan's laughter. A pained, bitter laugh, laced with defiance.

"Take him," ordered the soldier standing behind Lucan.

Lucan pushed to his feet—when clearly his captors thought he could not—and walked to stand beside the

Knights of White. Together they faced the enemy, staring them down. They wanted to stay, wanted to fight, but Rinehart struggled with the need to walk away, struggled with the darkness that made him burn for vengeance. There was no doubt he was shaking now, shaking from the effort to hold himself in check. There was more at stake than one fight and a few Darkland Beasts, so why couldn't he pull away?

A hand came down on his arm, and Lucan's voice rumbled to his left. "Walk away," he hissed in a half whisper. "Walk away." And with those words, with the realization that Lucan had taken a beating and still had the will to walk away, Rinehart felt a slap of reality.

"Walk away," Lucan repeated. Rinehart swallowed hard and managed a step backward.

And as often they did, the Knights instinctively moved together, taking the next step away in unison. One by one, they took positions inside the elevator. And as those doors shut, and he stood amongst his closest friends, his brothers-in-arms, Rinehart faced his inner Demon. He was in trouble. He was losing himself. But he vowed he would not destroy this mission, though now he had to end it sooner rather than later. No one else would be hurt under his command. No one.

Hours after Lucan's rescue, Rinehart sat in a chair near the Knight's bed. Fortunately, they were now able to speak freely in select locations where Max had rigged a discreet static device that could be switched on intermittently to cover critical conversations. Even so, no one had spoken of the way Rinehart had come close to snapping; it was in the air, an unspoken concern they all held. He was leading this mission. He should be the strongest, the most prepared. Instead, he was a risk to be monitored. And Rinehart didn't know what to do about it. He clung to the hope that Laura was indeed his mate, that she might hold his salvation in her hands. But with that hope came doubt. He'd heard stories about how mates instantly felt more than desire—they felt trust. Laura certainly didn't trust him. Rinehart's plan was to talk to Laura, to try to win that trust he didn't have, that a mate should already have offered.

"We'll check back in an hour," Max said, as he, Rock and Des headed to the door on scouting missions. Rinehart didn't respond, nor did anyone seem to expect him to. Instead, he sat unmoving, lingering by Lucan's side, not sure why. Lucan had long ago given his account of the events he'd encountered, and Rinehart had asked his questions and received his answers. But still, he remained unable to get out of the chair. Guilt seemed to be a weight pushing him down, holding him in place. It had been a long time since Rinehart had relived the past, but tonight it had crashed down on him like a tidal wave and for no apparent reason. Every day, he went to war against the Beasts. Every day, he and his fellow Knights risked their lives, risked each other's lives. Why was the past resurfacing now from the black hole he'd buried it in? And why did he somehow think Lucan held the answer to that question?

Lucan stretched, stifling a moan in the process, his movements pulling Rinehart out of his reverie. A moan slid past the bandages covering Lucan's bare midsection, bandages that served two purposes—hiding the rapidly healing wounds from the cameras while also allowing the medicine, a special formula created by their Healer, to aid his body's regeneration.

Adjusting his position on the pillows, Lucan cut Rinehart a sideways look. "Stop watching over me like I'm dying or something. Because I have to tell you, man, if you hang out by my bed much longer, I won't respect you in the morning."

Another time, Rinehart might have laughed, but not now. Suddenly, he knew what he wanted from Lucan. He wanted answers beyond what was happening in the moment, beyond Walch and this island.

"I know how close to the edge you are," he said, thinking of the flash of red he'd seen in Lucan's eyes during battle, a sure sign his humanity was slipping away. "Yet you kept it together in there. You didn't break."

A long pause ensued before Lucan awkwardly pushed himself farther up the headboard. "I'll make sure I die in battle before I allow myself to turn." His voice was taut, a bit hoarse, and Rinehart wasn't sure it was from pain.

"Is that what happens? You simply turn into one of them?" It was the question every Knight wanted to ask but wasn't sure he wanted answered. Lucan had been among the previous generation of Knights, nearly three hundred years ago, and he had witnessed many of those first Knights turn to the darkness, lost without a mate to bind their inner Beast.

A look of shock registered on Lucan's face at the

question, before his jaw tightened and he barked a bitter laugh. "If you ever saw one of your brothers-in-arms snap, you wouldn't call it simple." His gaze slid into the distance as if he were reliving the past—perhaps also describing his present.

"I've watched far too many Knights I considered friends slip away. Now I know what they went through, man. I know and I wish I didn't. At first, you feel the taint of the Beast slowly begin to grow. It slides inside your soul and eats away at it. You fight to keep it at bay, struggle to beat it down. Then you do anything you can to feed your primal urges. You go looking for battles when you might have waited for them to find you. Sex becomes an outlet. Sex and more sex. But then sex gets dangerous. You begin to feel the Beast hunger for more than pleasure from the woman—it wants to devour her, and you fear you might just let it. Every minute of every day, you fight in this internal struggle between man and Beast, you fight to stay in control or snap. It's excruciatingly intense."

Lucan's attention abruptly shifted back to Rinehart. "But *you* know all of this." He hesitated, then said pointedly, "Those of us fighting the darkness sense when another is doing the same. I feel your struggle. But at least we have something the others didn't. We have a chance to find a mate."

Rinehart digested Lucan's final words with skepticism. Yes, they all wanted a mate to bind the Beast within and set them free of the darkness. But what if that mate didn't want them? What if that mate turned away and just left them to self-destruct? "Some of us are stronger than others," Rinehart murmured, tormented by his own weakness. Lucan was three hundred. He was ninety-two. "I won't make it to three hundred."

Lucan waved off the declaration. "If I can do it, you can, too."

Rinehart wanted that to be true, but he knew he was slipping, knew all the same desperate feelings that Lucan had described. And he knew them centuries sooner. Lucan seemed to read his thoughts and added, "We have to hang on. We're needed."

It was Rinehart's turn to dismiss Lucan's words. "Not if we become liabilities."

"Ever since we got to this island," Lucan mused, "I've felt I was supposed to be here, that I have a connection beyond our duty. I think you and I are both hanging on because of this place and whatever is going to happen here." His brows dipped. "Do you feel it?"

Darkness was all Rinehart felt these days, but he wasn't about to say that. He ran his hands down his pants. "I don't know what I feel." He pushed himself to his feet. "I should let you rest."

"Yeah," Lucan agreed, sliding his way back down the headboard. "I should rest. Besides. Laura needs attention." He smiled. "And from what you've said, you're the man for that job."

Rinehart's gaze dropped to the floor; turbulent emotions he couldn't begin to describe tightened his chest. After consideration, he wasn't so certain he *was* the man for the job. If she wasn't his mate, she was a distraction he didn't need. He'd been down that path with a woman and didn't want to go there again. In fact, if anyone could connect with Laura on her work, it would be Lucan. But Lucan wasn't in a position to act right now, and they couldn't wait to make forward progress with Laura until he mended.

"She'll trust you," Lucan said softly.

Rinehart looked up to find Lucan staring at him. "You're sure of that?"

"Aren't you?"

Rinehart inhaled. No. No, he wasn't. "I'll check in on you later."

He didn't say another word, but turned on his heels and headed for the door. There was no way around this. He had to go to Laura and win her favor. And he had to do it tonight.

Walch walked into his own quarters and straight to the kitchen, where a bottle of brandy and a glass awaited his evening ritual. Alcohol no longer affected his senses, but he enjoyed the warm, rich flavor of an expensive brandy. A flavor that mimicked the richness of his new, eternal life.

He grabbed the remote and punched a button. A monitor lowered from beneath a cabinet. It was pizza night for the ladies—in other words, information night. Laura spoke more frankly about her work to Kresley than she did to anyone else. Walch flipped the channel to Laura's room and found her absent. Another button, a few more channel shifts, and he found Laura sitting on Kresley's bed, talking with her favorite patient. His cock thickened as he thought of having the two of them in that bed; and that day, he vowed, would come sooner rather than later. Laura's spicy defiance and Kresley's sweet innocence—he would devour their bodies and then claim their souls.

"I thought you'd never get here."

The soft female voice coming from the doorway behind him stroked more than his ears, it stroked his cock, thickened it, and pressed him to act. But he despised the idea of a woman, any woman, dictating his actions— hell, he didn't want anyone dictating his actions.

Walch drew a calming breath and forced himself to ignore his guest. He filled his glass and listened in to the conversation between Laura and Kresley as he swished the rich, amber liquid around in the glass. He downed the liquid, its warming bite sliding down his throat, but the brandy did nothing to sate the growing demand of his body. His primal physical needs were more pronounced now, more demanding. He required satisfaction. But now was not the time to find it with Laura or Kresley.

"Come here," he ordered the female.

Though she walked soundlessly, he could feel her approach in the rush of blood charging through his body. She stopped beside him. Still, he didn't look at her. He motioned for her to stand before him. She appeared there in mere seconds, her long, dark hair like a silky veil clinging to her petite shoulders. She wore a light blue dress—he didn't like it. "I've told you, no clothes."

"I know, but—"

He cut her off, realizing the conversation with

Laura and Kresley appeared to be taking an interesting turn. "Wait for me in the bedroom, and be naked when I get there."

She ducked her head and did as he said. Carol was his slave now, her soul in limbo, her body his to possess. She would do whatever he said, when he said. She would not betray him. But Laura would if he let her. He turned up the sound of the monitor and listened closely to a conversation that had become quite revealing. And knowledge was power, and power was the greatest aphrodisiac of all.

Laura stood in Kresley's kitchen and poured hot tea in a cup. The pizzas that one of the mess-hall cooks made every Friday, special order and ready-to-cook, were in the freezer, awaiting another night. Kresley was too sick for pizza or much of anything else. She rested in the bedroom, shivering her way through a fever while watching television.

Rinehart's team had disappeared right after he'd received his text message, which, though a bit odd, had made her life easier. It was hard enough to dodge the lab techs Walch had assigned to spy on her. She used them on a limited basis, mostly for busywork she created just for their perusal. Hiding her relevant research had become a practiced skill, well mastered, but now with Rinehart's team breathing down her neck, that might not be the case anymore. Their absence that afternoon had, at least, given her a chance to run blood tests and document her facade of concerns that the injections might be creating side effects. None of the other patients were sick yet, but their blood counts indicated they would be soon, which would support her notes.

The test results for Carol had been clear, though she'd expected otherwise. Thinking of Carol sent a bolt of stress shooting through her body; she worried about the implications of Carol's change—her new, darker presence. She didn't know what it was, but *something* was wrong—something was very off. Was the serum altering the patients in some way she didn't understand?

Laura gave herself a little mental shake, realizing the steaming mug in front of her wouldn't be steaming any longer if she lingered. She reached for a sliced lemon and squeezed a few drops of juice into the beverage.

She found Kresley sitting against the headboard of her bed amongst a mass of fluffy, white down comforter and pillows. The entire room was white—white lace curtains, white wood for the headboard and nightstands, little ceramic white angels in various well-placed positions. A bit too sterile for Laura, who preferred rich, warm colors to take her away from the sterile box of confinement that guarding her secrets had painted her into. But somehow the color white served Kresley's sense of comfort in a way only Kresley could understand.

Laura settled on the bed next to Kresley, noting her red nose and bloodshot eyes as she handed her the steaming mug. "This should help the sore throat and chills."

"Thanks," she mumbled, sounding more stuffy. She sipped the warm liquid and shivered. "If I could get warm, I'd feel a hundred times better." Laura tucked the blanket around her a bit more snuggly.

Guilt took another stab at Laura. She'd done this to Kresley. "I hate that you're feeling so bad. I'll stay awhile and make sure you get to sleep okay. Besides. I like our Friday nights, and I'm clinging to what little bit of that time we have tonight." Laura kicked off her high heels and pulled the clip from her hair. She sighed with relief as the knot at the back of her head slackened, easing the tension she hadn't realized was there. Leaning back on her hands, she thought of all their Friday nights. "This is like our little escape, a time we can pretend the rest of the world doesn't exist."

Kresley sat her mug on the nightstand and slid down farther along the headboard. "It doesn't," Kresley said. "Walch makes sure of that."

More and more, Laura believed that to be true. They were captive here. Kresley was too intuitive not to figure that out. "We've made lots of progress since we came here," Laura reminded her, trying to sound positive. She smiled and promised, "Dating is right around the corner."

Kresley's mood shifted abruptly; Laura felt the heaviness of the change settle in the air, around her, on her shoulders. She watched as Kresley balled the blanket in her fists, tugging it up to her chin and peering at Laura over the top. "You'd tell me if something was wrong, right?"

"What?" Laura asked, surprised. But then, she shouldn't be. Kresley was far more intuitive than she knew herself to be. "Of course. What are you talking about?"

"All of a sudden you need help. These men are here to help, and suddenly I am sick. Has something gone terribly wrong with the injections and you don't want to tell me?"

"No!" Laura said quickly, rotating around, one leg on the bed to face Kresley and let her see the truth in her expression. "Nothing has gone wrong with your injections." She hesitated, considering how much to tell Kresley.

And Kresley noticed, and sat up again; urgency, and a bit of panic, were in her voice. "What? What are you not telling me?"

"Nothing, sweetie," Laura assured her. "Nothing. I gave you all your shots today."

"Late," Kresley argued. "And you acted as if you didn't want to."

"Running a test is simply a precaution." She hoped. God, how she hoped. The Carol situation kept creeping into her mind.

"You're worried."

Kresley knew her too well. "I'm cautious," Laura assured her. "There's a huge difference."

Though her words came out steady and calm, Laura's thoughts raced—with worries over Carol and the serum, and with the secret of the effort to escape. Maybe it was time she told Kresley what was going on. Maybe it was time to talk to each of them one-on-one. But still, she hesitated. Her instincts had been to form a plan and keep everyone acting normal in the meantime. But right now, she wasn't any closer to a plan, and Kresley was sensing that things weren't as they should be. Yet the feeling of urgency, of a need to escape this island, escalated every second of every day. Her patients were not children anymore. They were bright, gifted adults. They could help. And she needed help. It was time to admit that and ask for it.

Chapter 6

Laura opened her mouth to reveal the truth to Kresley about her plan to escape the island, when unease prickled along her nerve endings. *The shadows have ears.* The warning rang in her head, and she wasn't about to ignore it, not when a lifetime of living had proven her senses were rarely wrong. She considered her options. She could turn the sound up on the television, and they could climb under the blankets and cover their heads. That should muffle their voices.

"Laura!"

Kresley's panicked reaction drew Laura from her internal debate. She was about to reach for the remote when a knock sounded on the front door. Her gut clenched uncontrollably, the knock thundering at her as if it held an urgent warning: *Stay silent.*

Laura inhaled and narrowed her gaze on Kresley. "You expecting someone?"

Kresley shook her head. "Everyone knows this is our night." Laura started to get up and Kresley grabbed her hand. "I want to know what you were about to tell me."

Laura grappled with her thoughts, chasing down an answer Kresley would accept. "I simply wanted to ask a question."

Kresley frowned. "A question?" she asked, her expression saying she didn't quite buy that explanation.

Another knock sounded, more urgent this time. Maybe someone was sick. "I better get that." Laura squeezed Kresley's hand and stood up. "I'll be right back," she promised, and turned away.

Walking toward the other room, her hand kneaded the tension suddenly building at the back of her neck. She had spent a lifetime hiding her secrets, a lifetime with that burden. She was so damn tired of secrets and lies, yet they would always be a part of her world. She and her patients would escape this island, but she'd never escape the lies.

She reached the door the moment the knocking began again and pulled it open, half-expecting another sick patient on the other side. But it wasn't a patient. In stunned disbelief, she found Rinehart standing before her. He wore well-pressed jeans and a crisp button-down white shirt, his rugged good looks screaming Texas cowboy.

"What are you doing here?" she demanded, unsettled by his presence, but more so by her own reaction.

A smile played on those sensual lips she somehow kept noticing. "Picking you up for dinner."

She blinked. "What?" The man was bold if nothing else. "I never agreed to dinner, and this isn't even my apartment." Laura stiffened, suspicion seeping into her mind as surely as his woodsy, fresh scent did into her senses. Was he trying to question Kresley without her being present? "How did you find me?"

"Your Friday pizza nights are legend around here," he said. His blue eyes were unnervingly hypnotic as they met hers. "It didn't take much to get pointed in the right direction."

Laura took in that answer and decided she believed him. That didn't mean she was going to dinner with him. "If that's so, then you know I have plans tonight. I never agreed to dinner for a reason."

"Because of your dinner with Kresley?"

He was trying to put her on the spot. "One of many reasons," she agreed, making it clear she wouldn't be easily cornered.

The instant glint in his eye said he wanted to press more, but decided against it. "Have Kresley join us." His voice lowered to that intimate, sexy tone he'd used earlier in the lab. "But I'd also enjoy stealing you away afterward for dessert."

His suggestion took her off guard. Her breath lodged in her throat, and her chest tightened with unexplainable emotion. He was playing on the importance Kresley held in her life, and she knew it; but still it got to her, calling out to her on some level she couldn't quite identify. She had to remind herself the man was an incorrigible flirt who wanted her just for her research, who was manipulating her. She shouldn't have to struggle to remember this, not when she had such sensitivity to people. But the heat he generated in her appeared to suppress her ability to read the underlying malice that his involvement with Walch suggested.

Stiffening her spine, she reminded herself of why she couldn't do something stupid and actually say yes to dinner. "Kresley's running a fever," she stated flatly. "I don't want to leave her."

His brows dipped, the playful jesting of moments before gone. "How seriously ill is she?"

Laura responded with careful consideration. Over-reaction would look suspicious. "Right now, it amounts to flulike symptoms."

Concern etched his handsome features. "Are you still thinking the illness could be a reaction to her treatments?"

He seemed so sincerely worried about Kresley's well-being. But of course he was worried, she thought. Sick patients put his research on hold, which was what she wanted. So why did she feel guilty lying to him?

She cut her gaze from his, uncomfortable looking into Rinehart's eyes as she twisted the truth. "I can't rule out that possibility." She was doing nothing wrong, she reasoned silently. Her father had long ago taught her that lies were a necessary, though distasteful, part of protecting the innocent from power-hungry people. Laura snapped her eyes back to Rinehart's face. "Unfortunately, the blood work I drew this afternoon indicated that the entire test group is getting sick. Kresley is simply the only one symptomatic."

He studied her for several seconds that felt more like a lifetime.

"Well," he said. "Until you know, we will, of course, put our work on hold."

Laura frowned, confused by his response. He'd been distracted in the lab when she'd first announced her concerns, so his lack of concern earlier about the delay hadn't seemed odd. But that wasn't the case now. He was focused, lucid, but he wasn't displaying the expected frustration. It made no sense.

"Thank you," she finally said. "I worry about these kids. They are family to me, my kids. I don't want them hurt."

He chuckled at that, a low rumble that danced along her nerve endings with stimulating effects. A sensual sound that sent goose bumps up her spine and told her she was in deep trouble. Something about this man had taken her sensitivity levels and pushed them over the edge. "Your kids," he said, a smile lighting his eyes. "By my best judgment, you've barely got ten years on the oldest in the bunch. I'd guess you're thirty-five at the most and only because you'd have to be at least that old to do all that you've done."

"Thirty-four, and didn't my file tell you all of that?"

"I'd rather *you* tell me," he countered, not bothering to deny he'd seen her file. If he had tried to say he hadn't, she would have slammed the door in his face for taking her for a fool.

Instead, she stood there, chin tilted upward to look into those brilliant blue eyes so alight with interest, so full of simmering heat. There was no question he desired her, and no question that desire went beyond manipulative reasons. Genuine attraction danced between them. She wanted him. What was it about this man that appealed to her? But he wasn't just a man, she reminded herself. He was with Walch; he was the enemy.

"Invite me in, Laura," he urged softly.

"Yes. Invite him in." This time the words came from behind her, from Kresley.

Laura glanced over her shoulder to see her standing in the hallway, shivering inside the fluffy, pink robe Laura had bought her for Christmas just months before. "You should be in bed."

"I'm fine," she insisted.

"You're not fine," Laura argued, shaking her head as she turned back to Rinehart. "I need to attend to Kresley."

"He can come in," Kresley stubbornly inserted in a voice meant to be heard.

Rinehart's eyes sparkled with mischief. "The young lady wants you to invite me in."

Laura pursed her lips. "You could get sick."

"I know a good doctor."

God, the man was impossible to dismiss, as was the sexy little dimple in his right cheek. "You're devious," she accused, a second before she eased back to let him through the door.

He stepped forward and paused when he was directly beside her, his shoulder brushing hers and sending electricity darting through her body. His head tilted downward, close, and his cologne nipped at her senses with dangerously hot results. "And I do believe you like it," he accused in a velvety smooth whisper meant for her ears only. He didn't wait for a reply, sauntering farther into the apartment and claiming a seat on the couch directly in front of the wingback chair Kresley had just chosen.

Rinehart spoke to Kresley as Laura sat on the opposite side of the couch. "You're pretty sick, I hear," he commented.

Kresley nodded and curled her legs in the oversize chair she'd claimed. "I pretty much feel like death warmed over."

Rinehart chuckled. "That sounds serious."

"Which is why I can't go to dinner," Laura replied.

Kresley frowned. "I don't need a babysitter. It's the flu. I'll live. Unless there's something both of you know that I don't."

Laura grimaced. "There's nothing you don't know. I've told you that." She glanced at Rinehart. "Kresley has it in her mind that she's sicker than I'm telling her she is."

"Really?" he inquired. "Why is that?" he asked Kresley.

"You're here," she said. "You and all those other men." Abruptly, Kresley sat up, her hands digging into the cloth sides of the chair.

"I'm sick. I never get sick. And Laura has never needed help with our treatments, but all of a sudden she does."

Laura's chest tightened with emotion as she pushed to her feet. She'd intended to talk to Kresley in private, not sure she could possibly feel any guiltier than she felt in that moment. Despite the warning in her head, it was time to tell Kresley the truth. Soon. The minute she could find privacy.

But before Laura could decide how to respond at present, Rinehart interjected. "I didn't come to the island because you're sick, Kresley. Quite the opposite. I came because Laura's work is such a success. I'm hoping I can learn something from her. Hoping to bring good luck along with me." He looked dubious. "So far it looks like I didn't do so well. You're sick and worried."

Kresley blushed. "No. I didn't mean to blame you." The tension in her body eased ever so slightly. "I guess I'm just not used to having other people around."

"You're worried for nothing," Laura added, her hands going to her hips, amazed at just how smoothly Rinehart had handled Kresley. But she was also hurt that Kresley had doubted her enough to ask Rinehart for answers instead of her. "You should know I'd tell you if something was wrong."

Kresley smirked at that. "You're protective. You wouldn't tell me what was wrong until you'd ruled out making it right first. I know you, Laura."

Laura let out a frustrated breath. Guilty as charged. What could she say? Wasn't that what she was doing about escaping the island? "Well. I'm not doing that now."

"So you admit you're protective," Kresley said, a teasing glint in her bloodshot eyes. She really needed to rest.

"Yes, I admit it," Laura said. "Which is why I say you need to go to bed."

"Only if you let Rinehart take you to dinner. I heard

him ask you, and I won't be responsible for starving you." Kresley glanced at Rinehart. "Her stomach was growling right before you got here."

Rinehart cast her a sexy half smile. "Is that right?" he asked. "Sounds like dinner might be a critical mission."

"I'll survive," Laura snapped back, arms folding in front of her again. Good grief, Kresley was working against her with Rinehart, perhaps bitten by the matchmaker bug. They definitely needed to have a talk about why he was trouble.

Kresley acted as if she hadn't heard Laura decline, her attention still locked on Rinehart. "Oh my God," she proclaimed. "Now I *know* you're military. You called dinner a 'mission.'"

Rinehart leaned forward and rested his elbows on his knees. "My father was army, and I did a short stint in the army and the FBI. But that was a long time ago."

"Laura's father was a ranger," Kresley pointed out.

Laura barely heard the words, her attention suddenly snagged by Rinehart's hands—hands both strong and gentle. Hands she sensed had touched danger and death, hands that possessed the ability to kill. But she also felt the honor behind his actions, felt his desire to protect innocents. Not so unlike the way she tried to protect her patients.

"Laura?" She blinked at the sound of Rinehart's voice, bringing his features into focus, uncomfortably aware that she was staring at him, her eyes now locked on his face. "Are you okay?" he asked.

"Ah, yes," she lied, her voice creaking out. Finally, she'd sensed something other than her own hormonal overload where Rinehart was concerned, but she was more confused than ever. If her senses were right, and they usually were, he was nothing she'd assumed him to be. Delicately, she cleared her throat and added, "Sorry. I started thinking about my research." She laughed nervously, fingers touching her forehead for a moment. "My mind went elsewhere." Trying to regain her composure, Laura fixed Kresley in a warning look. "You need to go to bed," she said firmly before refocusing on Rinehart. "And no, I am not going to dinner. I won't leave her alone."

"I can pick up something for us," Rinehart offered.

The man wouldn't give up. "The mess hall is closed, and everything else is too far away."

"You can make our pizza," Kresley suggested, and pushed to her feet.

Now Laura *knew* Kresley was matchmaking. She had never allowed anyone near their pizza. "I thought that was our special dinner."

"It is," Kresley agreed, "but it's going to waste anyway because I am too sick to eat."

"Am I such bad company that you can't share a pizza with me?" Rinehart asked, his voice demanding her attention.

Laura's stomach fluttered as she met his stare. No man had ever given her this fluttery feeling in her stomach. Normally, she was too edgy and on guard to feel anything but stressed. Working for Walch, Rinehart should be outside the walls she had long ago erected. But he'd gotten inside them and reached places others couldn't find. And suddenly, she had to know why.

"Pizza it is, then," Laura said, and for the first time since meeting Rinehart, a genuine smiled touched her lips.

Kresley pushed to her feet and grinned, satisfaction twinkling in her eyes. "Now I'll go to bed." She didn't wait for a reply, darting away with far too much agility for someone so sick, the bedroom door shutting with a resounding thud, meant, no doubt, to tell them they were alone.

Laura and Rinehart stood there facing each other, their eyes locking, neither moving, neither speaking. The temperature in the room spiked; the intense attraction they shared blossomed with each passing second. She'd never experienced anything like this, never had a man get past her fear of being exposed. How ironic that *this* man could—a man who was so close to those she considered dangerous. That he could reach beyond the emotions that kept her shielded and even create excitement inside her.

"I'm glad you changed your mind," Rinehart finally said, breaking the silence that should have been awkward, but somehow wasn't.

So am I, she realized. But she knew better than to let down her guard. "Don't make me regret it."

Those blue eyes darkened, the message in them darkly sensual. "Regret is the last thing I intend to make you feel."

Her pulse leapt with the question he invited and knew she wouldn't dare ask. If not regret, then what exactly did he intend to make her feel? And why was he so sure she would let him? And why did the idea of finding out thrill her to the core?

Chapter 7

The temperature in Kresley's apartment had gone from icy to distinctly warm and inviting.

Rinehart leaned against the archway leading into the kitchen and watched Laura pull the second of two pizzas out of the oven. Finally, he had her to himself and not soon enough for his liking. She'd spent most of the last fifteen minutes behind closed doors with Kresley—no doubt talking about him. He didn't know what was said, and at this point he didn't really care. The heated looks she'd cast his way were proof enough that the conversation had gone his direction. In fact, Laura appeared less tense, softer and more comfortable in his presence. He could see a glimpse of the woman beneath the rigid doctor, see who existed inside the wall she'd placed around herself, and he liked what he saw.

"All set." She turned to him, one delicate little hand curled around the oven handle. "We can eat."

"Good," he replied. "I'm starved." *But not for food,* he silently added. *For you.*

She laughed. "Me, too." Her hand pressed to her stomach. "For at least an hour now. I thought we could sit in the living room and watch television or something." He nodded his approval, and she grabbed a couple of plates from the cabinet and motioned him forward as she deposited them on the counter. "Go ahead and load up a plate before it gets cold. Try the pineapple and peppers." She smiled—a beautiful smile he felt all over—and picked up the tea glasses she'd filled a moment before. "Unless you're one of those picky eaters afraid to try new things?"

"Adventure is my middle name," he declared. "A pineapple and pepper pizza isn't going to scare me away."

Her smile widened, her expression alight with pleasure, her teeth perfect, white. Her lips full and inviting.

She motioned toward the other room. "I'll put our drinks on the coffee table and come back for a plate."

Rinehart pushed off the wall right as she reached his side. She stopped beside him, her mood sobering as she tilted her chin up to stare at him. They were close. So close he could lean forward and touch her—and damn, how he wanted to. "Thanks for what you did for Kresley." Her voice was low, sincere, hinting at emotion.

Her soft floral scent floated in the air, touching his nostrils with a rousing effect. He stiffened against the impact, the jolt damn near making him tremble. *Damn it.* He. Didn't. Tremble. He'd faced death and Demons a hundred times over and remained as stoic as a statue. Yet, this sexy, petite woman had him shaking in his boots.

Somehow, Rinehart retained his composure. He'd protect Kresley for more reasons than his duty and honor; he'd protect her for Laura. And knowing she read those things on a level beyond simple perception, he funneled those emotions into the words he spoke, into the vow they held and the conviction he felt for that vow. "She'll be okay."

The statement was simple, but there was nothing simple about the way their eyes locked after its delivery. Nothing simple about the connection ignited between them in that moment.

Laura tilted her head slightly, her eyes alight with realization. And he knew from her expression that she'd read the sincerity and conviction lacing his words. She'd felt his emotions as he had several times felt hers. She sucked in a slow, labored breath, appearing a bit rattled by what she'd experienced.

"I…" she started to speak, then hesitated and cut her gaze for an instant. A weak smile touched her lips as her attention turned back to him. Confusion lurked in the depths of her eyes. It was clear she'd changed her mind about whatever she was going to say. On an intellectual level, Laura considered him the enemy, and he knew that. But he also could see now that emotionally she wanted to trust him. And based on what had passed between them in those past few moments, he believed that deep down she already did—she simply wasn't ready to admit it.

Laura motioned with a slight lift of the tea glasses she was holding. "My hands are getting cold." The weakly delivered excuse offered her an escape and she rushed away. Actually, she was running from him—something else they both knew and knew well.

And maybe she should, he thought. He *was* dangerous, on edge. Afraid he could hurt her if he wasn't careful. The mating process walked a fine line between erotic and deadly. His teeth would sink into her shoulder, her blood seep into his mouth. No matter how many times the other Knights swore a mate could not hurt the other, he wasn't so sure. At times he barely felt human, let alone in control.

Rinehart walked to the stove and grabbed the handle, fingers curling around it as Laura's had, and he forced himself to take deep breaths, to calm the rage in his body. *Mine.* The word rang in his head over and over as clearly as a new day. His mate. He felt it in his core. That should be a good reason to get close to her, to ensure she would aid their efforts to get off the island. But if he tasted her, if he touched her, would he hold back? Or would he lose control and claim her without her knowledge of who, and what, he was? Just thinking about sinking his teeth into her shoulder and marking her with his immortality had blood coursing through his veins like liquid fire.

Slowly, he let out a breath that had lodged in his chest and reached for a plate, shocked to see his hand shaking. He reached out and grabbed it, cursing under his breath. He had to be strong. Lucan was right. They were needed. He was needed. His link to Laura might be the only thing that could avert the disaster her research could create in the hands of the Beasts.

He filled his plate and didn't give himself time to think—he headed toward the living room, where Laura was flipping the channels on the television. "I put on the news for now," she said, and set the remote on the coffee table. "I like to see what's going on in the real world at least once a day. But feel free to change it if you like."

The real world. That statement kicked him in the gut, and he was thankful she rushed away to fix her plate. He claimed a cushion on the couch and settled his plate beside the remote on the glass top of the coffee table. His eyes fixed on the small television screen, which was nestled inside a black entertainment center, without really seeing the images being played. Reality seeped into his mind with bitter results. Laura wanted to live in the real world. That was what all of this was about to her, what her research was trying to achieve. She wanted her patients to control their abilities in order to hide them, just as she did with her own abilities. She wanted them to have that gift—that ability to pretend to be like everyone else. And he knew that to claim Laura as his mate would be to take her away from the very thing she was working so hard to find—a way to stop hiding, to stop living in fear. Not that he thought she could ever have that, but if he read her right—and he believed he did—she thought that one day, she could.

"What's the verdict?" Laura said, approaching from his left. "You like the pineapple and peppers?" She sat down on the other side of the couch, knees angled toward him and frowned. "You haven't touched your food. I thought you were hungry."

Inwardly, he shook himself. He had a mission and lives were on the line. If the Beasts fulfilled their goal of making super-soldier Beasts, a lot of lives were on the line. "Lost in thought," he said. He reached for a slice of pizza and took a bite. A combination of sweet pineapple and tangy peppers touched his tongue.

"Well?" she asked, watching his expression.

"It's different," he said and took another bite, the taste growing on him.

"Which is a nice way of saying you don't like it," she said, laughing. "Liking my pizza choice won't make me like you more."

"Too bad," he said, "because I do like it." He proceeded to prove his point by taking another bite.

Laura snagged a pepper with her fingers and said, "You don't have to be nice," a second before she popped it into her mouth.

"I doubt too many people would call me nice, period, so you don't have to worry in that area."

"A hard-ass, are you?" she asked, sipping her tea.

He shrugged. "If wanting things done right the first time makes me a hard-ass, then yeah, I guess so."

Laura rolled her eyes and shook her head. "You might not be military now, but good grief, you sound like my father."

He forgot his pizza and turned to her, his gaze brushing her pink-painted toes in the process. His cock twitched, and he decided he was truly losing his mind. Since when did feet turn him on? "Your father was special forces?"

She set down her pizza and drew a breath. "Yeah. I was a military brat. He was gone a lot and never home enough. And though that sounds like the same thing, it's not. I had friends who looked forward to their fathers' absences. I looked forward to mine coming home. He was a hard-ass." She smiled lightly at the reference, but her eyes glistened with sadness, as if the loss were still raw. Her gaze dropped to the floor. "It's been years, but I still remember his spicy, safe smell."

"And you haven't felt safe since he died."

Her gaze ripped upward to latch on to his, probing, searching. She opened her mouth to speak, hesitated, then, "There's a feeling of security we all get from our parents, no matter what our age. That's the security I try to give to my patients—a feeling of belonging and safety. Most of them were deserted, left on their own because their families turned away from them."

"Because they're different," he stated softly, prodding her cautiously, afraid she would clam up at any moment.

"Different isn't easy," she said, not confirming or denying what he'd said.

"I know."

"Do you?" she asked, her voice full of hope, the air full of simmering heat.

He was afraid to move, afraid to say the wrong thing. "I do." And he did understand. All the Knights dealt with the reality of standing outside, looking inside, not a part of humanity, but still playing a critical role in how it survived.

She studied him, probed, considered. Finally, "Then

why are you here, trying to make them into some sort of guinea pigs?"

Her bottom lip quivered, and he wanted to kiss it into stillness, wanted to kiss away her pain. Because she *was* in pain. He could feel it biting at his gut, feel the deeply rooted ache she carried inside her. "I'm not, Laura. I wouldn't do that to them or to you."

"You work for Walch," she countered with gentle force.

"So do you."

"You keep saying that," she pointed out, a hint of frustration in her voice that did nothing to douse the crackle of fire between them. Somehow they were leaning close, the distance closing.

"Because it's true."

"Why should I believe you don't want what he does?"

"You know I don't."

She shook her head in a barely perceivable way. "How? How could I know?"

His voice held confidence. "You know."

She opened her mouth, shut it. A charge darted through the air. Warmth wrapped around them. "If you don't want what he does—then what? What *do* you want, Rinehart?" Her voice came out husky, laden with the sexual tension flowering between them.

There was only one answer to her question, only one way to respond. "You," he whispered hoarsely, reaching for her even as she moved toward him.

Suddenly, they were in each other's arms, no barriers, no questions. No Walch. No island. An invisible force, a mating bond, pulled them together, dissolved logic and reason. Lips melted together and time stood still. Gently, he prodded her mouth open, his tongue finding hers in one long stroke that shook him from head to toe. Another slow stroke and she shivered. He slanted his mouth over hers, deepening the kiss, losing himself in the sweetness of her taste. Loving the way she met him stroke for stroke, the way soft sounds of pleasure filled her chest. God, how he wanted her. How he needed her. Passion welled inside him, turned hotter, more intense. Expanded into something he'd never felt before and barely understood. Sex and battle—those two things were the places where he, and all Knights, directed the dark side of their existence, the primal side that still felt the touch of the Beast. But those things never took away the emptiness, never stole away the black hole that seemed to poison their existence.

But kissing Laura, holding her, feeling her next to him, touched that place inside him that he thought couldn't be touched. Made him believe it could be filled. Made him burn to make it happen. Made him wild with need. It seemed to do the same to Laura. She squirmed against him, her hands traveling his body, tracing his flexing muscles, his clean-shaven jaw.

Somewhere in the far corner of his mind, he knew the intensity of their reaction was hypnotic, that it peeled away logic and reason, and consumed beyond thought. But for now, for this red-hot period of time, all he could think about was wanting more. More of this kiss, of her taste, of the sense of rightness kissing her filled him with.

Their tongues tangled in a rush of tantalizing strokes. Her leg was somehow across his thigh. His hand slid

upward, under her skirt, over the softness of her bare skin
and under her backside. She moaned as his fingers
skimmed the intimate flesh. Rinehart pulled her toward
him, and she didn't resist. Instead, she arched into him,
her hand sliding to his jaw, her breasts pressing into his
chest.

Her fingers touched his lips. "I never do things like
this." Her lips grazed his. "I can't seem…to stop myself." There was emotion in her voice, a bit of turmoil,
maybe even a hint of accusation. "What are you doing
to me?"

She didn't want to be out of control; he got that from
her words. Well, neither did he. "Sweetheart," he murmured, "I could ask the same of you." His mouth came
down on hers in a punishing kiss that said he didn't want
to need her. But he did. Plain and simple, he did. And
she did.

He pressed her onto her back, impatient with the
sitting position that didn't allow him to feel her fully.
That didn't allow him all he craved. His hips settled firm
against hers, and her leg wrapped around his calf. Ah,
yes, he thought as his cock nuzzled the sweet V of her
body. His free hand swept her side, her hip, her breasts.
Laura moaned into his mouth, her scent sensual and
aroused, touching his nostrils and making him groan.
God. He wanted inside her. He wanted—

A knock sounded on the door. Damn it! It didn't
matter. He blocked it out. He wanted her and nothing
else mattered. He kept kissing her, touching her.

Laura moaned and pressed her hands to his cheeks.
"Door. Someone—"

He kissed her. She kissed him back. Another knock. She tore her lips away from his, her breath coming in heavy gasps. "Door." Her chest heaved. He tried to kiss her, and her fingers covered his lips. "No. It's...it's Blake."

Instantly, he frowned and she paled, her eyes wide with the abruptness of sudden shock. She knew who was at the door without answering it. How could she know it was Blake knocking and not someone else? With willpower, Rinehart reined in the rage of desire, burning him inside out, enough to register that question. And then he knew one of her gifts: Laura sensed things others could not.

"Oh, God," Laura murmured, dread in her words. She'd slipped and shown him a side of herself she showed no one. Her reaction only made that mistake more evident. And by the look on her now-pale face, she was afraid he would betray her, that he would be an op-portunist who used that information against her. That realization twisted his gut, and anger started to form. She sensed things, but she couldn't manage to give him her trust? Was she his mate or not?

Rinehart raised up on his elbows and stared down at her, and the terror he found there cut him like a knife. Terror of him, because he knew something no one else did. He reached for calmness and clear thought. Inhal-ing, he reminded himself she'd been running from her secrets for years. He exhaled the breath he was holding, realizing that her reaction wasn't about distrust as much as it was about survival. But somehow, some way, she had to find a way past that. Because now they had a bigger issue to be dealt with—Walch was taping every-thing that was going on. He had suspected Laura had gifts. Confirming it to be true would only make her more of a target. He couldn't risk Laura being any more on the radar than she already was. What if Walch confined her in some way?

And Jag had been clear—Laura would be dangerous if she fell into the Beasts' hands. Rinehart had no intention of letting that happen. She was in his hands now, and that was where she was going to stay. Whether she liked it or not—Laura was about to learn to trust him.

Chapter 8

"Laura! It's Blake."

Laura squeezed her eyes shut at Blake's announcement. Now, Rinehart knew her secret. She had known who was on the other side of the door before she should have. She hadn't made a stupid slip like this one since the fifth grade when she'd told her teacher, Ms. Wilkens, that her husband had been in a car accident only seconds after it happened. She remembered that day clearly, and not because of the shock on her teacher's face, but because of her father's wrath when he'd come to clean up her mess.

Since then, not one slip had occurred—until now. And, damn it, Laura didn't know how to explain her screwup any more than she knew how to explain why she had not only let Rinehart kiss her, but damn near invited him to strip her naked.

Another knock jolted her out of her reverie. "Coming!" she shouted automatically.

Rinehart stared down at her, his arms framing her upper body. "Can you have him come back later?" he asked, no doubt because he wanted to discuss her slipup. Or maybe he wanted to get naked. Neither seemed a smart choice at this point, though the idea of being intimate with this man certainly had her body sizzling.

She rejected his suggestion as firmly as the heat swirling in her core would let her. "He'll think something is wrong. I never send my kids away." He nodded his understanding, but made no effort to move from on top of her. He was making her insane, messing with her head. Stealing her sense of control! She shoved at his unmoving rock wall of a chest and glared up at him. "Get up," she ordered.

Piercing determination glared in his eyes. "Not without one last kiss." And before she'd registered his intention, his lips brushed hers, a fleeting moment of fire before his mouth was near her ear. Wickedly warm breath tickled her neck before she found out his true intention, which was not the kiss—it was a message. "Don't respond to what I am about to tell you," he warned, his voice low, barely audible even spoken this close. "Walch has the place bugged. I'm here to get you off this island, Laura, but you must do exactly *what* I tell you, *when* I tell you. Meet me at the north docks in an hour. We can talk there."

His head moved away, eyes latching on to hers, a silent question bordering on demand in those rich blue eyes. His steely body unmoving, telling her without words he would not let her up until she agreed to his request—or rather, demand.

With a sudden claustrophobic need to be free, she nodded, her voice lodged in her throat like her breath, the implications of his words rattling her inside and out. Only minutes ago, she'd nearly told Kresley of her escape plan—thank God she'd followed her instincts.

The instant she signaled her agreement, Rinehart's big, warm body lifted off of hers. He towered over the couch, offering her his hand. His eyes brushed her bare legs; her skirt was still practically at her waist.

She shoved it down and pushed to her feet, ignoring his hand and the hot look on his handsome face. Her mind raced and her heart pounded as if it might explode from her chest. Who was this man? And did she dare believe he was here to help?

Smoothing her palms fretfully over her wrinkled skirt and wild hair, she realized there was no hope of figuring out answers to the millions of questions in her mind before answering that door, nor was there any way to fix her frazzled attire. "He's going to know that—"

"—you're human?" Rinehart offered softly, standing beside her, far closer than she expected. Her chin tilted upward, her skin warmed where it already tingled from his touch.

Another knock, but she didn't respond. She stood there, feet planted, staring at Rinehart, seeing an offer of support and comfort in his expression—comfort that he didn't understand couldn't be found. Not by her. Was she human? Yes. Average, no. And that changed things. But he wouldn't understand what that meant. How could he? Only a short time ago, she'd almost confessed her escape plans to Kresley. She'd slipped and shown one of her abilities to Rinehart. She was losing her edge, and it was going to get them all hurt. And the only common denominator to all this mess was Rinehart. The faster she got away from him and cleared her thoughts, the better.

She inhaled and rushed to open the door. The minute she pulled it open, Blake started talking. "I was starting to worry. You took forever."

"Sorry. I was loading the dishwasher, and my hands were wet." It was a lie, but a well-intended one. An idea dawned on Laura. "I know you worry about Kresley, but she's fine." She forced a smile. "I knew it had to be you before you said it was." She'd long ago figured out his schoolboy crush on Kresley.

Blake blushed. "Oh, ah, yeah. How is she?" He stepped forward as she eased the door back. His tennis shoes moved soundlessly forward, his blue sweats, T-shirt and rumpled dark hair accenting his youthful, frazzled appearance.

"She's sleeping and she's fine," Laura reported, hopeful that Rinehart was buying her trumped-up reason for expecting Blake at the door.

"Good," Blake said, sounding distracted. "I… Good. That wasn't actually…" He stopped talking, pausing inside the door, his gaze catching over her shoulder where she knew Rinehart waited. "You have company." His gaze swept her bare feet and rumpled attire.

Laura ground her teeth against the embarrassment seeping through her. Were her lips swollen? Her makeup smudged? How obvious was it she'd been lip-locked with a man Blake knew she'd met only hours before?

"I do," she said, trying to sound lighthearted as she sidestepped to motion to her "company." "You remember Rinehart?"

Blake looked exceedingly awkward. "Yes. Hi." He lifted a hand to wave at Rinehart. "I didn't mean to interrupt." But he didn't offer to leave, either. In fact, he stepped farther into the room, his fingers flexing, his demeanor wired, edgy.

Laura was aware of Rinehart studying Blake, could feel tension curling in the air around him.

"You're not," Rinehart said, his tone friendly, free of any signs of the concern she sensed in him. "And regrettably, I was just paged. I need to take off."

He turned to Laura, the placid expression on his face a well-worn facade of indifference in the midst of awkwardness. "Thanks for saving me from the mess hall," he cajoled. His voice lowered slightly, hinting at discreet intimacy. "I enjoyed the pizza. It was different." The corners of that sensual mouth lifted a second before he surprised her by saying, "Different is good."

She blinked at those words and wondered if he was talking about pizza or about her. Was that his subtle way of telling her he knew she was different, no matter how hard she tried to cover up her slip? Damn it, she hated the way he had her dancing on eggshells. She did enough of that with Walch.

Rinehart turned to Blake, wished him a good-night and then nodded to Laura, the magnetic pull of his eyes latching on to hers with simmering results. And in that moment, years of skepticism, of worry over people manipulating her, drew forth another suspicion: What was creating this almost hypnotic effect between them? Did Rinehart have some kind of gift? Could he create this heat in her using that gift? Was he truly here to help her escape, or was he here to manipulate her into submission? And as she closed the door behind Rinehart, she decided that these were questions she would have only a short hour to debate. Because friend or foe, she was meeting him on that dock—and because the one thing her instincts were telling her with complete clarity was to get off this island.

The minute the door closed behind Rinehart, Blake went on the attack. "You don't trust him, do you?"

"I just met him," Laura countered. "Why? What is wrong with you? What's happened?"

"I was outside when two of his men came out of the building talking about—"

"Stop!" A alarm was going off in Laura's head. The bugs. Anything he said would be recorded.

His eyes went wide. "What? Laura, I—"

"What's going on?"

Laura looked up to see Kresley standing in the doorway. *Great.* Another obstacle. "Nothing important," Laura said quickly.

"It *is* important!" Blake declared in disagreement. "I heard—"

"Blake!" Laura ground out sternly. "Stop." His pale face was turning red, and this time it wasn't from embarrassment. It was from anger.

"Look," she said softly. "I want and need to hear what you have to say, but Kresley is sick. Let's make sure she is okay first. Okay?" He drew a breath and nodded, but it was clear from his grimace that he wasn't happy about it.

"What is going on?" Kresley asked. "Where's Rinehart?" She frowned. "Did you kick him out already?"

Laura put her hand on her forehead, trying to figure out how to handle this. "He got paged."

"And I bet I know why!" Blake said.

Laura cut him an irritated look as Kresley swiped her hand through the air. "*What* is going on!"

Ignoring the question, Laura focused on the important issue of the moment. Kresley looked better, less washed out. "Are you feeling any better? Are you up because something is wrong?"

"Nothing besides that you two were loud," Kresley chided. "And yes, I feel better. My fever broke."

One good thing, Laura thought. "So you can stay by yourself?"

"I'm fine by myself, except that I really want to know what's going on."

"I'll explain when I know myself." She considered that answer, and added for clarity, "And that will be in the morning. So go to bed."

Her attention turned to Blake. "You. Come with me." Laura pointed to the door and started in that direction, but then hesitated. "After I get my shoes."

Several minutes later, Laura stopped on the beachfront with Blake by her side, her shoes off again and dangling from one hand, sand squishing between her toes. This well-lighted area of the beach that sat directly behind the lab parking lot offered the quickest solution for privacy. Close enough to call for help, but far enough away to avoid listening devices. The water was calm, soothing; the breeze, cool. Laura, however, remained rattled and out of sorts, her skin hot everywhere Rinehart had touched.

"Why are we here?" Blake asked, a hand sweeping the wide-open space of the beach.

"I needed a walk and some air badly," she explained, knowing the answer wasn't going to be enough for him, but it was all she had to give. "And I didn't want to keep Kresley awake."

He glared at her, arms crossed in front of his chest. "Sixteen does not translate to stupid, you know. I see what's happening. You think someone is listening in on our conversations." It wasn't a question. "You think someone is bugging our rooms."

Laura laughed, a choked sound that mocked her for the attempted lie. But she couldn't tell Blake her fears, not Blake. His youth made him impetuous, and she couldn't risk him doing something rash. "You've been watching way too much television. Now. Tell me who and what you overheard."

His lips thinned and he looked like he might argue. Instead, he said, "Those two men who work with Rinehart—Rock and Max. They came out of the building and walked onto the beach as I was coming in from a run." He paced back and forth, and then turned to her. "It's not good, Laura. Not good at all. They said they were going to take us off this island. I think they plan to kidnap us."

Or help them escape, but she couldn't say that. Not yet. She had to reason him into letting this go. "Let's take a deep breath and backtrack, kiddo. Why would they say such a thing in front of you? That makes no sense." His gaze dropped, and she grimaced. "You were invisible." Time and time again, she'd warned him about doing that.

"Yes, but—"

"No buts!" She sliced a hand through the air. This was why she couldn't let Blake in on what was going on. He did rash things without thinking. "What if you would have lost control of your powers and suddenly appeared standing beside them? What then?"

"That hasn't happened in months!"

"Kresley's sick. Your blood work says you will be, too. It could have happened."

"I'm sick?" His eyes were wide with worry. "What's wrong with us?"

"The flu, Blake, but you can see from Kresley how bad it is. And you know when you get sick, you lose control over your invisibility."

"Not since the shots, and Kresley hasn't started a fire since she's been sick."

"There hasn't been enough time to be certain the illness won't impact control. We can't take risks."

"If these men want to kidnap us, what choice do we have?"

Out-of-character impatience bit at her nerves. Time was ticking away to her meeting with Rinehart, and it appeared she would have no opportunity to think through her options before meeting him. But that wasn't Blake's fault. He was a kid, caught in a firestorm that he didn't understand. A kid growing up fast. Too fast. She wanted him to live without having his ability controlling his every move. She wanted her research to matter to him.

She steadied her voice. "Don't take risks without talking to me first."

"I didn't mean to," he countered. "I took a run, timing myself to see how long I could maintain my control. The next thing I knew, they were just there, talking. I couldn't help but listen. And besides—" he flung his hands in the air "—you're missing the point! They want to take us off the island."

God, she hated lying, so she tried to be as truthful as possible. "I talked to Rinehart about this very subject over dinner. He's old-school military, like my father was. Has to be prepared for anything and everything." She rolled her eyes. "The man brought his own security people to a military facility. What does that tell you?"

He looked relieved. "You talked to him about us getting off the island?"

She nodded and sat down on the beach, patting the sand beside her, pleased when he joined her without hesitation. She could feel him beginning to calm down. "Our program is top secret," she continued, "so clarifying an evacuation plan makes sense."

"I guess it does," Blake said, digging his name in the sand with a shell. "It still felt like more than that."

"Paranoid is *my* job," Laura said. "Leave it to me.

Leave this alone, Blake. I don't want anything to go wrong right now. I am close to perfecting your serum. Let me do that for you. Let me give you a life that won't be in confinement." He didn't respond instantly, and she prodded, "Blake?"

His gaze lifted to hers. "I do appreciate all you do for us, Laura."

"You aren't going to let this go, are you?"

"I didn't say that."

"You didn't say otherwise, either." Blake would act rashly and end up in trouble. Everything was spinning out of control. She had to think. "Head to bed. Your morning tutoring will be here before you know it." There was no softness to her voice, no understanding. She was trying to help him, and he was going to work against her. She could feel it in every inch of her being.

"What about you?" he asked.

"I'll be there in a few minutes." Her tone was short, and she could see from Blake's expression that he was surprised.

He hesitated, but pushed to his feet. "Just be careful out here alone, okay?"

"I'm always careful," she said, tired of how true that statement had become. She lived in a shell that was quickly becoming a jail cell. He stared at her a moment longer, then turned toward the parking lot. Over her shoulder, she watched him walk toward the building before her vision drifted across the water, to the twinkling stars in the clear, black sky. When they had first arrived on the island, she had thought it was heaven. Now, it felt like hell. A hell they had to escape.

And she needed help to do that. She'd already decided that when Rinehart had appeared at the opportune moment. Maybe too opportune. Her father's warnings of caution replayed in her head. Laura leaned back on her hands, sand sliding through her fingers, cool and grainy. And she reached deep, trying to sort through what her instincts told her about Rinehart, and what life and her father had taught her about protecting herself. But there was a potent new piece of the puzzle clouding her judgment—desire. Her attraction to Rinehart was fire in her veins, unnaturally compelling—hypnotic, even.

And that made him dangerous. That made her instincts impossible to interpret. And if she couldn't trust her senses, she couldn't trust him. No matter what promises he made tonight, she had to be cautious, had to keep her guard up. And yet, as it stood, he was her best shot of escape from this island.

Chapter 9

Deep in the Mexico mountains, home of the Darkland Beasts, a battle between two Beasts was taking place. Adrian, ruler of the Darkland Beasts, sat in his silk-covered chair on the podium that overlooked the center of the massive underground coliseum he'd built for his amusement. At his feet lounged two gorgeous women, one blonde, one brunette—variety being his favorite flavor.

Beneath them, inside the war zone, two soldiers were circling a bonfire, maneuvering to defeat one another. They wore nothing but buckskin pants—no shirts, no magical armor, none of their standard attire.

Unlike the other Beast in the battle, Tezi, Adrian's secret weapon against the Knights of White, retained his human form, his weakest side—no doubt to prove a point: that he could destroy his enemy with ease, without ever breaking out his beastly strength. Tezi's long raven hair was braided at the back of his neck, and his thickly roped muscles were painted in war colors of red and black. His eyes, even from a distance, held a predatory gleam that said he enjoyed killing.

With a quick jut of the knife he held, Tezi sliced the enemy's arm. The soldier snarled through his fanged teeth, his half-Beast, half-human face twisting in pain. He lunged at Tezi, and the crowd of Beasts, hundreds of them, roared to life around the coliseum.

Tezi easily avoided his opponent's action, as the Beast he faced had little experience with this gritty hand-to-hand combat. In this battle, there were none of the long sabers normally used to behead and kill the immortal Knights of White. Tezi had convinced Adrian they could no longer allow the Beasts to battle in the expected fashion. Instead, they must attack in ways that would tear down their guard—a plan that well suited the other strategic moves Adrian had put into play.

Adrian had forgone his brutal approach of simply attacking humans in the dark and converting them. He had implemented programs to infiltrate the human society, to live among them as the Knights were able to do. The first move in this direction was Walch and the military facility he operated. They'd choose people like Walch, with stature in the human venues that served their needs, and then convert them. They'd take over humanity little by little in a big way.

Adrian grimaced, his attention fading from the battle below. This new strategy meant giving his Beasts more power, more identity, than he preferred. He drew a breath, and the air around him crackled with energy, with the tension this prospect created in him. He reminded himself of the greatness he possessed, the magical gifts. His Beasts feared him, and rightfully so. He'd simply make fast examples of any that crossed him. After all, his ultimate goal had to be considered: He wanted rank in the Underworld and for Cain, his master, to offer that freely. If he would not—Adrian would take his power.

Adrian refocused on the battle below. His Beast soldier was barely keeping his footing at this point. Tezi was demolishing him; the Beast deserved to die. Adrian shook his head. To achieve these new goals, his Beasts could no longer rely on armor and darkness to cloak their existence. And Tezi, a vicious killer and manipulative thinker, was, without question, the perfect Second to aid their transition into a new way of operating.

With another vicious punch of his knife, Tezi landed his blade in his opponent's stomach. A second later, the Beast was on his back, Tezi on top of him. A few sharp cuts, and he held the Beast's heart in his hand. He let out a fierce battle cry—the Aztec warrior of his past still linked to his current battle tactics. Pushing to his feet, he flung the flaming heart aside, seeming more irritated by its existence than bothered by the fire.

He dropped to his knees then and bowed to Adrian. The other Beasts followed his example. Adrian smiled. Tezi knew who had the power, who could give him what he ultimately wanted—and Tezi showed his respect, unlike so many of his past Seconds. Beasts he'd destroyed or tortured for crossing him.

Tezi pushed to his feet, but the other Beasts remained on their knees. He flashed out of sight and orbed through space, a gift he'd retained from a prior life. A second later, he kneeled before Adrian.

Adrian inclined his head at Tezi and allowed him to stand, something he rarely allowed his followers. And never before had Adrian allowed a Second to retain a name. They had been called only Segundo, his second. But then, Tezi had no desire to overthrow Adrian's empire or to threaten his power.

As the first leader of the Knights of White, Tezi had come to him with the darkness of his tainted soul tearing him up inside. And he had given himself to Adrian on one condition—he would be given a chance at revenge, a chance to make the higher powers pay for what they had done to him and his circle of Knights. Now, with his soul stripped from him, as it was from all Beasts, evil flourished in Tezi—all the good in him destroyed. And that evil drove the violence that had tracked his life, the violence he'd lived as an Aztec warrior and then as a Knight of White. He was a killer, a perfect, deadly Beast.

"When do I get my new soldiers?" Tezi asked, his voice thick with a Spanish accent, and betraying a slight hint of demand that he clearly worked to keep in check. "I cannot defeat the Knights like this." He gestured toward the Beasts below them. "Not with these pathetic excuses for soldiers. No wonder you need hundreds to battle so few Knights."

Anger coiled in Adrian's gut at the insult. Disgust and disappointment, as well. The respect he had come to expect from Tezi was nowhere to be found. "You dare to insult my army and make royalty of the Knights?" he demanded. "Be warned, Tezi." His voice dropped, a lethal warning clinging to his words. "I can rip out that Aztec heart of yours with a snap of my fingers. And I don't require a knife to get the job done."

Tezi stared at Adrian, his dark eyes fearless. "You cannot defeat the Knights if you fail to understand their strengths." His voice took on a gravely, intense quality, one of pride. "As for ripping my heart out, when the time is right, and my duty complete, I will gladly let you have it. It is an honorable way to die," he added, referring to the sacrifices his people had made to the gods.

Adrian laughed, always eager to remind Tezi of the many reasons he should hate Raphael. "How ironic to hear such a thing from the noble Aztec prince who tried to convince his people to believe in a god who didn't require human sacrifice."

"I know now what I didn't then," Tezi ground out between his teeth. "That sacrifice is demanded by all those above and below." Tezi believed that his generation of Knights had been unfairly sacrificed after being given a hope of life the Aztecs had never given those they'd imprisoned. He crossed his arms in front of his chest, his legs shoulder-width apart—unmoving, determined. "And so they will see the sacrifice and destruction of all of their Knights."

Adrian looked down upon his Beasts, passing along disturbing news delivered by Cain. "There are rumblings in the Underworld about our plans. Someone may sell us out to the Knights. We must consider our options."

"Walch must be managed," Tezi said instantly.

"Walch is the recognized human leader on that island. He stays."

"He has acted too slowly."

"Confined by human scientific limitations."

"Because he's walked around the female doctor's sensitivities. If the cloning process already exists, which you say Walch declares to be truth, then we must press it to completion. This female has been his problem from day one. It is time she be dealt with appropriately. I can achieve what Walch cannot."

Adrian arched a brow at him. "Which is what?"

"Immediate cooperation," Tezi replied, his voice steely confident.

Adrian did not like where this was going. "If your existence slips out to the Knights before your army is ready, what then?"

Tezi snorted. "Then they will know I am coming for them. I am tired of hiding."

Adrian shook his head at this new position, irritated that Tezi had lost touch with the bigger picture. "Your vengeance serves my agenda, Tezi, or you would not be here. But do not forget this is indeed *my* agenda. You will not expose yourself until I say it is time. That island is to be our first military post. We will not do anything to risk alerting the humans they are in danger."

"Nor can we risk moving too slow and having the Knights destroy our plans."

"And what of Walch's opinion that the doctor will hold back information if she is forced into submission?

He believes that her free-will consent is critical to our success."

The corner of Tezi's lips hinted at a smile. "I've found that pain creates free will."

A short-sighted answer. Disdain filled Adrian's voice. "You cannot defeat humans if you do not understand them," he said, a bite to his voice as he used Tezi's own words about the Knights. His prior doubt slid away. "That is exactly why Walch is needed. His recent humanity is a tool we must use as a strength, not a weakness. He knows that what breaks humans is emotional, not physical. Their own pain is not as motivating as the pain of someone they love."

Tezi balled his fists by his side. "Yet he has done nothing but coddle this female doctor and hope for her cooperation." Anger eroded his features. "I've been patient, Adrian, waited until the right time to seek my revenge. I cannot stand by and watch my perfect army fall apart. The time to end the Knights of White is now."

Adrian leaned back in his chair, hands resting on the jeweled arms. Walch was, indeed, moving too slowly; on that point, Tezi was accurate. But Adrian had coveted the demise of the Knights for far too long to falter now. If Cain would not grant him power in the Underworld, then perhaps with the Knights gone, Adrian would claim the earthly realm instead.

Action was needed. "Hold your hands in front of you," he ordered Tezi.

Without hesitation, Tezi fearlessly did as ordered. Two silver snakes appeared around his wrists, slithering around until they took solid form. A menacing smile slipped onto Tezi's lips. He knew what gift he had been given, what power those bracelets delivered to him.

Tezi kneeled in front of Adrian, respect offered fully once again, as his ruthless quest for vengeance was now closer to becoming reality. "I will not fail you, master." And then he disappeared.

An hour after watching Rinehart tear down Laura's prickly exterior with a long, hot kiss that turned into erotic foreplay, Walch lay in the center of his bed with Carol's naked body curled up next to him, her hand trailing his biceps. She wanted him again. He could smell her desire, her need. She was transitioning from human to Demon; her primitive urges were more pronounced now, and her willingness to do whatever it took to find satisfaction was becoming her nature. But then, Carol had tasted evil from the beginning; she had never been pure. It had been easy to take her deep into the darkness of conversion with no hope of turning back. In the past, females were killed before full conversion, but not Carol. He had plans for Carol—she was his insurance policy, his army of one who would use her gift, and newly found Beast strength, to take on Laura if need be.

He smiled, enjoying the knowledge that he alone held Carol's and Laura's destinies in his hands. Carol smiled up at him, her gaze holding his as she nibbled at his naked chest, the silky feel of her hair teasing his skin, her lips and tongue teasing his nipple. His cock thickened, the pleasure of possessing his first convert as intense and potent as it had been on day one. A pleasure all the sweeter with the night's success.

He'd gambled and won, hedged a bet while recruiting Carol as his backup plan. Rather than force Laura's cooperation and risk her working against him, he'd looked for a way to manipulate her submission and found it in Rinehart—a two-for-one deal—a man who could deliver both the cloning procedure and Laura.

Walch's hand slid into Carol's hair, and he kissed her, a demanding kiss fed by the images in his head. Images of Rinehart touching Laura, kissing her, proving that the prickly little doctor could be brought to her knees, and he couldn't wait to watch. Soon. Soon the cloning would be complete—soon he would have the rewards Adrian had promised him.

Excitement flared within Walch, and his hands went to Carol's slim neck, his teeth scraping a soft line down her jaw. He wanted to taste her blood again and, with each crimson droplet, to take more of her soul. He shifted into beastly form, his face half-Beast, the hunger inside too much to ignore. Instantly, his cuspids elongated as greed pulsed within him. He rolled Carol onto her stomach, slid on top of her and pinned her beneath him, though she did not fight. He shoved her hair aside and took what he wanted—he sank his teeth into her shoulder.

Carol stiffened and gasped in one instant, and then sighed the next, pressing her body upward, trying to mold her back into him. The crimson sweetness of her blood spilled into his mouth, and with each drop, another piece of her soul floated into limbo. His mind floated into the euphoria, the taste of her on his tongue pure bliss—bliss that ended abruptly as he was yanked upward and away from Carol, thrown across the room with superhuman force.

Walch landed against the wall with a thundering force, his head snapping back and hitting the hard surface, the sound of cracking wood splintering behind him. The air crackled, charged with a powerful presence.

The soldier in him ignored the pain and reacted. With supreme effort, Walch shoved the weight of his naked body up the wall until he was sitting, facing his attacker, quickly making the three-second assessment his military training had taught him to make.

A single male stood before him, an array of colorful tattoos covering his bulging biceps, trailing over his broad shoulders, down his arms to the thickness of his forearms. Silver snakes twined his wide wrists, and the black leather vest he wore tapered at his midsection to display similar markings on his chest and stomach. Long, black hair hung loose and wild around a square jaw and defined cheekbones that were slashed with red—a human face, though this was no human. Death and destruction clung to him like a second skin.

Walch shoved up the wall, scrambling to get to his feet. The male raised his hand and pointed. Pressure forced Walch's shoulders back to the wall; he was frozen in place by an invisible barrier of some sort.

Carol was standing now, intent on defending Walch with her skills. Using her mental prowess, she sent random items flying at the stranger—a chair, a lamp, a book. The stranger waved a hand, and the makeshift weapons fell to the ground. Another invisible force flung Carol to her back, pressed against the mattress.

"I can't move!" she screamed. "I can't move!" Her voice was wild with panic, her body stiff and straight.

"Who are you? What do you want?" Walch demanded, his tone a deceptive calm.

The stranger's dark, menacing eyes locked with Walch's. "What I was promised," the man said simply. "A reasonable expectation, I believe. I want my army of Dark Knights."

Walch inhaled a shuddering breath and let it out with one word—a name. "Tezi," he murmured, fear tightening his breath in his chest. The former leader of the Knights of White, powerful and dark in all the ways he was once good. The warrior sharply inclined his head to confirm his identity, and Walch launched into an exasperated explanation. "I only need a few more weeks. I will give you your Knights."

"I grow tired of excuses," Tezi rasped angrily, as he walked to stand before Carol. Out of nowhere a blade appeared in Tezi's hand, a blade he sliced down Carol's stomach as she screamed out in pain. Blood pooled on her abdomen, and the knife disappeared into thin air.

Tezi pressed his fingers into the blood on Carol's stomach. He then looked at the tips with disgust in his face a second before he disappeared, seemingly gone from the room until he reappeared in front of Walch.

Tezi held his palm up, exposing his blood-dipped skin. "Black," he spat. "Her blood is black, drying up until she is dead or fully converted. She cannot have her abilities cloned in humans because you stole her humanity." His eyes flashed red and then yellow, his voice hissing in anger. He rubbed his fingers together in the black goo. "Did you intend to let the doctor sample this? Did you not think this would be a problem?" Tezi pressed those blood-tipped fingers into the center of Walch's chest and began drawing a black circle around his heart. Walch cried out, feeling as if his heart were being ripped from his chest, like an invisible, lethal blade hacking his flesh. Long, excruciating seconds passed, and then, as abruptly as the pain had started, it ended. Tezi's red stare came back into focus. "Any chance you had of convincing me of your capability is gone," he said. "Carol is now a potential exposure I cannot allow. You force me to take immediate actions."

The vise holding him against the wall abruptly disappeared. Walch fell to the ground, his legs unable to hold him up, his breath heaving from his aching chest.

Walch opened his mouth to explain his plan, to explain why he'd started Carol's conversion, but what appeared before his eyes silenced his words and sent a shock wave of terror through his system.

Tezi extended his arms level with his shoulders, and the silver bracelets on his wrists slithered off, suddenly alive. Two silver-bodied snakes settled at Tezi's feet and began to grow. They curled into full-size serpents, each two feet long and four inches thick, their beady eyes pinning him in a trance as they hissed through huge fangs. Another moment passed, and they changed, yet again, growing, shifting, taking the form of two beautiful dark-haired females dressed in silver bodysuits—twin deadly beauties.

Tezi smiled as the twins nestled close to his side,

each placing one slender hand on his chest. "Meet Lithe and Litha, guardians of the Underworld's serpent pits, special friends of Adrian's whom I've become quite fond of. I brought them along to aid your efforts to complete your duty." He paused, as if intentionally forcing Walch to wait for more detail, torturing him with what might come next. "As you will soon learn first-hand, receive the Serpent's mark, and you belong to her for all of time." He smiled and covered their hands with his own as if embracing their touch. "They live in your dreams, track you through your sleep. They can deliver you to lush fantasies or the most horrendous of hallu-cinations. They can make you go insane from both pleasure and pain." He paused, inhaled and let it out. "I had meant them as a simple incentive for you alone, Walch, a punishment-reward system. But now, the guar-dians will be doing what you have not. They will seek out these patients and mark them before you manage to get us all discovered. Once the doctor witnesses her patient's hallucinations, she will cooperate and she will do so in silence."

The guardians started a sensual slither of a walk toward Walch. There was nowhere to go, no place to run. They embraced him from either side, just as they had Tezi, their full breasts pressed tight against his shoulders. Their silver-tipped fingers explored his chest, his body. He moaned, pleasure ripping through him in an unnatural way. And despite the sensual release that the touch promised, his mind raced with the promise that hell was coming.

Tezi seemed to read his mind. "Lithe and Litha have

been instructed to meet your pleasure needs until I say otherwise." He paused. "Until you dissatisfy me." Walch barely heard his words. Lithe and Litha were touching him, magically touching him in a way he didn't understand, but it didn't matter. Pleasure came with each brush of their hands, each rasp of their breath against his skin. "But if you fail me," Tezi said, "they will no longer be required to offer such pleasures." Suddenly Lithe and Litha shifted again, leaving him gasping with the loss of their touch. Two silver snakes curled on the ground at his feet and then slinked up his calves, wrapping them as tightly as rubber bands.

"It is time for you to see what belonging to Lithe and Litha means," Tezi declared. "How else will you explain to that little doctor of yours the fate of her patients, if she does not give me what I want?"

Suddenly, Walch was in a pit, snakes everywhere. He tried to tell himself it wasn't real. He knew it was his imagination. But their suffocating touch said otherwise; above him, below him, on top of him, snakes biting at his arms, his legs, his feet. They were feeding off him.

"Tezi!" he screamed. "Tezi!"

But no answer came.

Chapter 10

The Knights gathered on the dock several miles from the research facility, with the exception of Lucan, who still had plenty of healing to do. As expected, there wasn't a boat in sight. No one came to or left this island without Walch's knowledge.

"We all felt it," Des said, explaining why Rinehart had been paged. "A punch-in-the-gut sudden rush of evil."

"It has to be Beasts," Rock added, leaning against the wooden railing next to Des. "And lots of 'em. More than I've ever sensed in one place."

Rinehart grimaced. "Like we weren't dodging enough of those bastards as it was," he grumbled, rubbing the tension balling in the back of his neck. "Walch couldn't convert the remaining humans on the island until they were given a power, so maybe he brought in reinforcements."

Max's attention flickered to Rock. "All jokes aside kid, but...you're young, and I'm older than dirt. I read things differently." He shrugged, his hands shoved in his jeans pockets. "This felt more like one powerful, malicious presence."

Des lowered his gaze. "I got the same read as Rock."

"As far as I'm concerned," Max said, "it's one more reason to kick up the pace on this mission. Get these patients off this island before whatever it is gets their hands on their powers."

"Three days," Rinehart reasoned, thinking this through logically despite the foreboding circumstances. "I need that long to prepare Laura and her group. We can be gone by sunup Monday morning."

"Sooner would be better," Max added. "Have you told Laura what is going on?"

"I was working on it when you paged," Rinehart said, reminding them that they'd cut short his encounter with Laura. "She's meeting me here any minute."

Des snorted and flashed a grin. "She's a hard sell, R. Better polish your charm." His humor faded. "We need her on board. Trying to take that group of kids off this island if they see us as the enemy will be a slippery slide I don't think we want to ride. And we have enough to worry about with Carol. That chick had that deep, soulless look in her eyes. She's not playing on the right team anymore."

Rinehart hated the truth of Des's statement, and his heart was heavy with the thought of telling Laura. "We'll have to sedate Carol for the extraction and hope she's not too far gone for Marisol to pull her soul back."

The Silhouette Reader Service — Here's how it works:

Accepting your 2 free books and 2 free gifts (gifts valued at approximately $10.00) places you under no obligation to buy anything. You may keep the books and gifts and return the shipping statement marked "cancel". If you do not cancel, about a month later we'll send you 4 additional books and bill you just $4.47 each in the U.S. or $4.99 each in Canada. That is a savings of 15% off the cover price. It's quite a bargain! Shipping and handling is just 25¢ per book. You may cancel at any time, but if you choose to continue, every other month we'll send you 4 more books, which you may either purchase at the discount price or return to us and cancel your subscription.

*Terms and prices subject to change without notice. Prices do not include applicable taxes. Sales tax applicable in N.Y. Canadian residents will be charged applicable provincial taxes and GST. Offer not valid in Quebec. Credit or debit balances in a customer's account(s) may be offset by any other outstanding balance owed by or to the customer. Please allow 4 to 6 weeks for delivery. Offer available while quantities last.

If offer card is missing write to: Silhouette Reader Service, P.O. Box 1867, Buffalo NY 14240-1867 or visit www.ReaderService.com

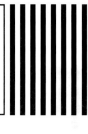

NO POSTAGE
NECESSARY
IF MAILED
IN THE
UNITED STATES

BUSINESS REPLY MAIL
FIRST-CLASS MAIL   PERMIT NO. 717   BUFFALO, NY

POSTAGE WILL BE PAID BY ADDRESSEE

SILHOUETTE READER SERVICE
PO BOX 1867
BUFFALO NY 14240-9952

GET FREE BOOKS and FREE GIFTS WHEN YOU PLAY THE...

Lucky 7

Just scratch off the silver box with a coin. Then check below to see the gifts you get!

SLOT MACHINE GAME!

YES! I have scratched off the silver box. Please send me the 2 free Silhouette® Nocturne™ books and 2 free gifts (gifts are worth about $10) for which I qualify. I understand I am under no obligation to purchase any books, as explained on the back of this card.

338 SDL EXGU   238 SDL EW5U

FIRST NAME

LAST NAME

ADDRESS

APT.#	CITY

STATE/PROV.	ZIP/POSTAL CODE

7	7	7	**Worth TWO FREE BOOKS plus 2 BONUS Mystery Gifts!**
🍒	🍒	🍒	**Worth TWO FREE BOOKS!**
♣	♣	♣	**Worth ONE FREE BOOK!**
🔔	🔔	🍒	**TRY AGAIN!**

www.ReaderService.com

(S-N-05/09)

DETACH AND MAIL CARD TODAY!

© 2008 HARLEQUIN ENTERPRISES LIMITED ® and ™ are trademarks owned and used by the trademark owner and/or its licensee.

The longer that a Beast controlled a soul, the harder it was to salvage. He eyed Max. "Can you get a message to Jag about all of this?"

"Will do," Max confirmed. Rinehart's gaze caught on the distant silhouette of Laura, shoes in hand, hair loose and lifting gently in the wind. Max's attention followed Rinehart's, and he added, "Looks like our invitation to leave." Rinehart didn't respond immediately. He couldn't seem to tear his eyes from her. His chest was tight with the reaction he had to seeing Laura. "Watch your back," Max ordered gruffly, heading down the wooden dock with Rock by his side.

Des lingered. "I know you know this, man, but I have to say it." The out-of-character seriousness in Des's voice jolted Rinehart from his trance. He arched a brow at Des. "No matter how she responds to what you tell her," he said, "no matter how much she might resist, you have to take her under your protection. There's no time, not after what Max sensed out here tonight. Whatever or whoever it is, we both know this is about Laura and her research. And this isn't just about her being in danger. This is about the danger that her research represents in the wrong hands."

Rinehart inhaled a shaky breath, Jag's words coming back to him. *At all costs,* he was to keep Laura out of the hands of the Beasts. "I know," he confirmed, his voice steely edged. "Believe me, Des, I know."

Des studied him a moment, and then clapped a hand on his back before walking away. Rinehart's gaze traveled along the wooden dock, over the railing, and latched on to Laura. She stood several feet away in casual conversation with Max and Rock. As the Knights departed, she whirled around to face the docks.

Instantly, their gazes collided, and a punch of emotions hit him smack in the center of his chest. Their bond was inevitable, but their mating was not. Both of them had shown the courage to help others at all costs, and the willingness to sacrifice to protect those in need— to serve the innocent. But there was a need she possessed that he did not—the need to be normal. He'd never been normal, nor would he ever be normal. Nor did he want to be. All his life he'd fought the battles no one else would.

Emotion tightened his chest as he thought of Jag's orders—orders that could force him to sacrifice his mate in the war against evil.

The injustice of what he faced tortured him, twisted him in knots. He jerked around, stalked down the walkway toward the shadowed end of the wooden dock to the edge of the water.

He was hanging by a string *now,* barely clinging to his human side. His gaze lifted upward. Surely those higher powers who ruled the Knights knew he couldn't live through her termination, and certainly not without himself becoming a sacrifice, as well. He ground his teeth. Or was that what they were counting on? Maybe they considered him a lost cause.

The creak of wood behind him told of Laura's approach. He reached deep, struggled to rein in his emotions, his dark side. Slowly, he sucked in air and beat back his Beast. Damn it, he would not fall to the same darkness he'd been hunting for damn near all his life, no matter how certain the higher powers might be that he would. Nor would he allow Laura to.

This war wasn't over until it was over. Whatever it took, he'd complete his mission, and he'd fulfill his resolution to save her. And if there had to be a sacrifice in this, it would be him and him alone.

Laura stood at the end of the wooden dock, her shoes left behind in the sand.

Only minutes before, she had been full of bravado and determination. But now that the moment of truth having arrived, she hesitated. Cloaked in shadows, Rinehart stood at the end of the dock, wrapped in a darkness that reached beyond the night. Turbulence rolled off of him as rapidly as the ocean's waves poured over the shoreline. Even from a distance, he was a big man, his shoulders broad, his waist tapered, his presence forceful. Danger trickled off of him, a second skin, an edge that radiated a willingness to kill. Yet oddly, she felt no risk from him.

She focused, inhaled, reached out to Rinehart using the psychic link she had to anyone near her, trying to understand his troubled state. Feeling pain and torment like a twisting knife in her gut, Laura's hand went to her stomach. Suddenly, it didn't matter that this was a man who knew her secrets, didn't matter that he could tear down her barriers with a mere touch, a kiss. Urgency pressed her forward.

Soundlessly, she closed the distance between them, one step, two. Her senses told her he knew she was there, that he was aware of each footfall of her progress toward him. And that he was aware of the moment she paused not more than a foot behind him.

Confirming as much, he turned to face her, moonlight casting light on his stark features. On a face so fraught with turmoil, it tightened her chest. "What is it?" she whispered hoarsely, fearful of what he knew that she did not yet know. "What's wrong? Has something happened? My patients—"

"—are fine," he said, narrowing his gaze on her. "But you can sense the danger to them and to yourself. I know you can." He didn't give her time to respond, to deny, and Laura grabbed the railing, somehow needing the extra support as he continued, "Walch isn't operating under army directive any longer, Laura. Frankly, Walch isn't even Walch anymore."

"What?" she asked, blinking at the odd choice of words. He spoke them as if he meant them in a literal sense. And yes, Walch had somehow been corrupted, but he was still Walch. "I don't understand."

"The group Walch is involved with is capable of things most humans can't begin to comprehend. Once someone is inside their circle, there is no turning back. They become lost in that world."

"As in brainwashing?"

He hesitated. "Something like that."

She wasn't satisfied with that answer, but she had to prioritize her need for information, get as much as she could while he was still talking. "This group…who are they?"

"*Who* they are isn't as important as *what* they are capable of and *what they want*. They have special abilities already—they're stronger, faster, able to do things other humans cannot. But it's not enough for them. They want more. They want you, Laura. They plan to use your research to create killing machines, soldiers who can't be stopped. Soldiers who can be converted to their kind."

She swallowed hard; his statement was ominous and far too coded for comfort. "Their kind?"

"They aren't what most would consider human."

A sensitive spot inside her flared into defense mode. "Meaning anyone who has a special talent isn't human?"

"It's not like that," he said, taking a step toward her, his hand lifting, reaching. She countered his move, backing up, a spark of anger charging through her body. He hesitated at her retreat, frustration etching his features, his arm slowly lowering. "We are talking about abilities born with one purpose—destruction. Evil in its purest form. Evil that isn't human. You aren't anything like them, but if they can change that, they will. I have to get you away from this place before they get to you, but you have to do exactly as I tell you when I tell you. That means you have to trust me."

She shook her head, confused by his coded responses, afraid to trust him despite her instincts telling her that she could. Afraid because his presence overwhelmed her. Even now—angry, scared, on edge—she could almost feel his body against hers.

She'd been wrong about him being dangerous to her. She had no control over her reaction to him. Taking another step backward, she shook her head, rejecting his appeal for trust. "How do I know you aren't one of them? How do I know any of this is true?"

He pinned her in a potent stare. "You know, Laura. You trust me. It scares the hell out of you, but you trust me. What happened back at that apartment wouldn't have happened if you didn't."

"Maybe what happened is exactly why I shouldn't trust you. You…you make me act crazy. You make—"

He cut her off. "No more than you do me. And it's a distraction I don't want, but I can't make it go away any more than you can. Instead, we need to make it work for us, Laura. We have to come together, and get you and your little surrogate family off this island."

She inhaled and shoved her trembling hand through her hair. Trying to rein in her whirling emotions, she turned away from him, hugging herself against the gust of cold fear that tore through her insides. Not since her parents' deaths had she fully trusted anyone. And Lord help her, she desperately needed a confidant again. But she couldn't let it be him, not a military man. Not a man with orders he had to follow, orders that most likely would take her to a place she didn't want to go. Her father's warnings echoed in her head. *The military will make you into a science project.* And it was true. The deciding factor that had brought her to this island was seeing the kids trapped here, treated like prisoners. She'd hoped to deliver them to freedom. Now, she had turned herself and Kresley into captives right along with them.

"Rescue us and take us where?" she asked, not turning around. Not yet. "Another research prison?"

"We're offering you protection," he said softly. "Nothing more."

She whirled on him then, giving him a condemning stare. "Protection," she said flatly, sensing his tension, that he held back details out of fear of her reaction. "*Protection* is a nice way of saying 'prison.' I know how the military operates. My father was part of the exclusive group who knew the down-and-dirty of it all." She inhaled sharply, and then slowly let it out, calming herself, forcing her voice lower. "You want trust? Then do that 'earning' you mentioned back at the lab. Talk straight."

He studied her, and she could tell he was weighing his words. His jaw clenched, flexed. "I never claimed to be with your military. The military doesn't have any idea we are here. They have no idea we exist."

She blinked at the unexpected declaration. "Then who sent you?"

"Consider us a covert special-interest group. We will never expose your secrets. We prefer that you stay off the radar. So while your objective is to avoid becoming a lab rat, ours is keeping you away from those who would misuse your research and your abilities."

His gaze shifted suddenly, rushed around the perimeter, toward the dock and the seashore, then back to her. At the same moment, another chill chased a path down her spine, but this time it wasn't from emotion, but warning. Rinehart's gaze slid back to hers. His voice was lower now, raspy and intense. "They'll take you if I let them, Laura, and I can't let that happen."

The protectiveness lacing his words wrapped around her, a warm blanket in the midst of the coldness of reality. Because something *was* out there; something was watching. And it did want her. Wanted her in a greedy, dark way. She flicked a nervous glance at the sandy shore and stepped close to Rinehart, pressing close to his side. Why, she didn't know. She had powers beyond what any of her patients possessed. Powers that could protect her from almost any danger if she dared expose herself by using them. Yet, right then, in that moment, she was experiencing sensations never before felt, and for some reason she needed to feel Rinehart close to her. Her skin was crawling, her nerve endings tingling, with the menace surrounding them.

Rinehart's arm slid around her, his long, muscular thigh pressing against her own, and that closeness comforted her in a way her powers could not, in a way she didn't understand. She stared out into the darkness of the woods beyond the beach. "You feel it, too, don't you?" she whispered, needing to know, for once in a very long time, that she wasn't completely alone.

"Yes," he said. "I feel it, too." His voice was calm, the energy he put off strong and reassuring. He seemed confident, steady, unfazed by the danger present. Gently, he caressed her shoulder, and remarkably the edginess inside her began to ease. Perhaps it was the sense of finally standing with someone rather than alone, as she had for so long. And though standing with Rinehart exposed her in ways best avoided, she saw no other option. Because whatever was out in those woods was far worse than Walch or any military prison. With his other hand, Rinehart reached for the phone on his belt buckle, punching a speed dial number. She could hear the ring, hear the male voice answer. "Code one," Rinehart said, and hung up.

He replaced the phone on his belt and turned her in his arms, his hands going to her shoulders. "Listen to me, Laura. There is more to discuss, much more. Things we can't discuss in a building wired to hear every word we say. But right now, we are getting the hell off this beach."

She nodded her silent approval, ready for action. "Yes," she added. "Let's go. Let's go, now." He said nothing more, but reached for her hand and tugged her forward.

They were on the move.

Chapter 11

Rinehart's hand wrapped around Laura's, offering unfamiliar warmth inside and out. They were running from danger they couldn't see, danger they could almost taste in the air, smell in the breeze. But it was fading as they neared the lab, slowly easing to a less intrusive presence.

Laura tightened her grip on Rinehart's hand, not sure why she felt so compelled to retain this complete stranger's touch, why it made her feel safer. She reminded herself she had well-hidden abilities she could use to defend herself. Those abilities that had caused her a lot of emotional pain in the past, but here on this beach, in these moments of retreat, those abilities offered a sense of security. She knew she could fight if she had to. She didn't need anyone's protection. So why did she want it? Why did she want Rinehart's right now? Her skin prickled with the certainty of being watched, with the touch of callous eyes. Her gaze flickered along the line of the woods, silently seeking out what was there. Who or what was watching them? She trembled with the intensity of that malicious presence. She knew this was no human she sensed, although she had tried to reject that ridiculous perception. But Rinehart's words as he described Walch's group came back to her: *Most wouldn't consider them human.*

As if to emphasize the bite of that memory, a seashell dug into her bare foot, and she stumbled. Rinehart reached for her, caught her. "Are you okay?"

Nodding, Laura murmured a confirmation and launched back into action. She'd seek answers to the questions in her mind when they were safely inside the building again. And they were close. So close she could see the building now. Just a little farther.

But just when she thought they would escape unscathed, Laura's eyes caught on the horizon and she sucked in a breath. Three figures were closing in on them rapidly, three men, their steps deliberate, their long strides seeming as one—a well-tuned fighting machine. These men were soldiers. Were they Walch's men?

Laura would have stopped, would have turned away, but Rinehart tugged her forward. She opened her mouth to protest when her gaze sharpened and she recognized these men as Rinehart's research team.

Soldiers, she repeated in her mind. They were soldiers. How she could have seen them as otherwise before this, she didn't know. Confidence grew with this conclusion. She understood soldiers. If their orders were to get her off the island, then they would. But she also knew soldiers did what they were told without asking questions, without their own agendas. What of the agendas of those they worked for? And who exactly did they work for?

Soon they all communed in the parking lot beside the building. "Give me just a minute, Laura," Rinehart said, stepping away from her long enough to say a few words to his men, leaving her under the beam of an overhead light.

She watched them talking, could hear their murmured voices. Reaching deep, she looked inside herself and tried to connect with them, tried to understand how she had misread them before now. Her gaze traveled along Rinehart's long, muscular legs and settled on his nice, tight backside. She swallowed hard, a flutter of arousal stirring in her stomach. Okay. There was her answer. Her senses were in overload—no, her hormones were in overload, after being dormant longer than she wanted to think about. That womanly need had been dismissed without worry until Rinehart showed up and jolted it to life. And that, coupled with a growing urgency to escape the island, had simply had her in emotional overload. A problem that thankfully seemed to be temporary as she became more comfortable with the feelings Rinehart drew from her.

Only a minute or two passed before Rinehart and his men parted, the others scattering in various directions as Rinehart returned to her side. "Where are they going?" she asked, suddenly acutely aware of his broad shoulders and towering height as she tilted her chin up to look at him.

"I'll feel better if they check the perimeter," he explained, his tone casual, unaffected. A facade. He was tense, on edge. Trying to keep her relaxed—like that was possible. He added, "I just want to be safe. To ensure there's no imminent threat." He motioned toward the building. "But I'll also feel better once I have you inside."

Surprising her, he reached for her hand, laced his fingers in hers and started walking. Heat darted up her arm, a distraction she shoved away as she dug her heels in. "No. You said we can't talk in there. I need some answers."

He hesitated, then half turned to her, his eyes grazing the horizon before settling on her face. Another sign he was far from at ease. "Problem solved," he declared. "Max rigged my room with a scrambler. We can talk there."

She sucked in a breath and let it out as she spoke. "In your room."

"Yes. In my room." The edges of that sensual mouth of his hinted at a smile. "I don't bite." His eyes darkened. "Not unless you ask me to." Laura felt heat rush to her cheeks. His thumb stroked her hand. His voice lowered to a whispered promise, "You're safe with me, Laura."

Laura stared at him, her heart squeezing with reaction to his words. She darted back a reply, quick to hide behind a flip remark.

"The jury is still out on that," she finally chided. "But I'll take my chances with you over whatever is in those woods." She averted her gaze and pulled on his hand to set them in motion.

His promise of safety still played in her head, reaching inside her, touching her deeply. She couldn't dismiss the words as she would if someone else had spoken them. Before Rinehart, she didn't think she'd needed protection, comfort, a confidant. She thought she'd dealt with all those things, thought she'd dismissed what she realized now had only been suppressed.

They had reached the front steps of the building; the darkness of the woods and what lurked between the masses of brush and trees were now behind them. But a new danger waited inside. She was going to Rinehart's room, a man she'd practically undressed once already today. A new risk to be faced: the risk of forgetting that Rinehart was still dangerous—the people he worked for, an unknown; forgetting because she wanted him in a way she hadn't wanted anyone in too long, if ever; forgetting because he made her feel like she didn't have to stand alone anymore. Rinehart tore down her walls. She couldn't let him.

There was too much on the line.

It took far too long, by Rinehart's standard, to get Laura safely inside his room.

They'd taken a detour to check on Kresley's apartment that, while frustrating, had at least allowed Rinehart some time to update with his team. The perimeter was clear; the building was as secure as it could be, considering where they were. Transportation for the extraction was also in place, a helicopter to ensure no one was left behind. The other option had involved Jag and Marisol simply orbing them all out in small numbers, but the risk of leaving anyone behind in danger, even temporarily, had ruled that out. And now, finally, he and Laura could put everything else on temporary hold for a while.

They stepped out of the elevator, completing the short walk to his room. Awareness, sexual heat and a whole lot of tension radiated between them as he unlocked the door and motioned Laura inside.

She eased past him, her shoulder brushing his; his groin tensed with the contact, his desire flaring, the wildness of his Beast clawing at his gut. As if she sensed the darkness in him, her gaze lifted, brushing his with a nervous touch before darting away. Damn it, he had to maintain control.

But control evaded him as he followed her through the door, his attention instantly snagged by the way the clingy black dress hugged her truly stellar ass. He inhaled, desperate to rein in his Beast, fearful she would sense the primal side of him. He had to protect her from more than the Beast outside this room—he had to protect her from the one inside him. She started to turn, and he quickly gave her his back, facing the door under the pretense of locking up, reminding himself of his agenda to save her and the others, swearing to himself that he would not touch her.

He had to get by this, had to make sure Laura and her patients were medically stable and ready to move when the time was right. More important than that,

Laura had to trust him enough to convince her patients to follow the Knights to safety.

He flipped the lock, but still he didn't turn. Instead, he snagged from his pocket the remote Max had passed him on the beach. He green-lighted the scrambler and shoved the device back in his pocket. Then, and only then, he turned to face Laura. Which was apparently all she needed to go on the attack; the delay getting to the room had worked against him.

"Who are you, Rinehart? What do you want from me?"

So he'd been right about her growing discomfort. Their alliance on the beach had been forgotten—she'd created a new wall of fear in her mind.

She was close, not more than two feet away. He wanted her closer, but held his position. "A friend. Someone here to help, Laura."

She shook her head, rejecting that answer, emotion thickening her voice. "How can I know that for sure?"

He searched her eyes, delved deep into their depths and saw the answer he sought. "You know, Laura."

"Stop saying that!" she said. "There is no way I can know. You've given me no proof. I don't even know who you work for."

They were here, in his room. Alone. A million secrets between them ready to be revealed. The sooner they found a path beyond those secrets, the sooner they could start planning an escape to safety.

"You know because you sense things." He decided to go out on a limb, to start easing her into the truth of who and what he was; what the enemy was. "Like we *both* sensed that evil on the beach, in the woods."

A shuddered breath escaped her lips, shock registering in her eyes at his admission. "You're telling me you sense things."

"Only evil," he said. "And even that has limitations, but I put it to good use. I use it to protect people. It's what I am, what I do. What everyone who works with me has dedicated their lives to. We're the good guys, Laura, and I wish like hell I could prove that to you right now. There is so much I could show you, so many amazing things that would astound you." He took a step toward her, relieved when she didn't back away. "But right now, I can't give you an answer beyond faith in your own abilities."

"That isn't good enough when five people's lives depend on me making the right choice." The words came out a raspy whisper.

He forgot about keeping his distance, forgot promising to keep his hands to himself. He closed the distance between them with two long strides, pulled her into the shelter of his arms. She didn't resist, but her body was stiff, her fingers curling in a tight ball around the front of his shirt. She wanted to be in his arms, but feared being vulnerable. He couldn't let her keep those walls up, no matter how dangerous touching her was.

His fingers laced through her hair; his palms framed her heart-shaped face. "It's gotten you this far," he reminded her. "Why doubt now?"

"I can't let anything happen to them. I won't."

"*We* won't," he assured her. "You're not alone, Laura. We're here to help. *I'm* here."

She stared up at him with stormy eyes, turmoil

rolling off of her in waves, crashing into him with forceful impact. Filling him with a need to take care of her, to make it better. "I don't even know who you are," she whispered.

He brushed his lips over hers, and he felt them quiver beneath his caress, her body slowly seeping into his. "You know," he murmured. "Deep down inside, you know."

"It's not enough," she whispered, the tight hold of her fingers on his shirt loosening. "I can't…it's not enough."

Those words hit him like a two-by-four, triggered something inside him. Damn it, it had to be enough. It had to be enough or she might not make it out of this alive, and he wouldn't allow that to happen. *He* had to be enough.

He didn't think, didn't consider the repercussions of what he was doing. His mouth came down on hers, a kiss meant to claim, a kiss laden with fierce passion—with the anger of her resistance to their bond. It was a primal feeling, an unreasonable one, a feeling borne of a deep fear that she would reject him in the end, no matter what. That thought pressed all others away. He wasn't thinking of danger, wasn't thinking of the Beast within him that could flare at any moment.

He deepened the kiss, his tongue sliding against hers with long, possessive strokes. Telling her with his lips, with his tongue, he was what she needed. He was her salvation.

Her body shifted, her hips melting into his. He barely contained a moan. His hand reached behind her, covering that sweet little ass and pulling her tight against him.

She panted between kisses, her arms wrapped around his neck, her lush breasts pressed against his chest. "You're doing…that thing you do to me…again."

He nipped her lips, telling himself he meant the words he was about to speak. "I'll try to stop." He kissed her again, his fingers sliding along her side and brushing the curve of her breast.

"I don't believe you," she whispered, moving her hand to her side so that it covered his. But she didn't stop him; she didn't try to detour his hand as it slid over her breast and kneaded the lush mound. Instead, she arched into the touch, her hand tightening over his, urging him to continue. His thumb stroked her nipple, drawing it to a peak beneath the thin black silk of her dress.

The sweet scent of her arousal touched his nostrils, driving him wild with passion. Rinehart picked her up and started walking toward the bedroom. She gasped with surprise, but made no complaint, her arms sliding around his neck.

Darkness cloaked the room, yet he bypassed the light switch; the cameras were still there, and the idea of Walch watching them, invading their privacy, roused anger inside him. They had nothing but static sound and the absence of light to protect them from those intrusive cameras.

Laura murmured his name; her lips and fingers brushed his jaw. He settled her on the mattress, eased her up the mattress as his knees went down with her. With his palms riding up her thighs, he pushed her skirt upward as he parted her legs and settled between them; his cock nestled in the V of her body. His elbows rested on either side of her head; his lips lingered above hers.

"Laura," he whispered, their breath mingling, the air charged with their desire. She felt perfect beneath him. Right. Right in a way that soothed the roughness in him, pulled back the Beast. "I want you so much, Laura."

Her fingers slid through his hair, over his head. "I want you, too," she answered. "I…" She pulled back, tried to see through the thickness of the darkness, to see into his eyes. "Tell me this is real, that you don't have some ability to control my desire."

Guilt twisted in his gut. They were mates. The passion between them was natural. But he couldn't say that. Not now. Not without scaring her. But he couldn't lie, either. "I can't control you any more than you can me," he answered truthfully. "And right now, you're doing a damn good job of it."

"Promise," she ordered. "Say it."

"I promise," he said, knowing she was reaching inside him, deciphering his emotions, separating truth from fiction.

Her chest rose and fell, the tight peaks of her nipples beckoning to him. He wanted to touch her all over, to taste all of her. His hips slid deeper inside the V of her body, his cock throbbing with the heat radiating off her. His lips brushed hers; his tongue delved just past her teeth.

She started to respond, her tongue flickering against his a second before she tore her mouth away. "No. Not yet. You confuse me, Rinehart. Turn on the light," she said. "I need to see you. I need to see your face."

Reality sliced through his mind. "I would like nothing more than to see you, Laura. To give you the satisfaction of seeing how much I want you." His voice deepened with arousal. "To see your face when you come." He hesitated, a combination of passion and guilt working a number on his judgment as he blurted the truth. "But there are cameras everywhere. Walch can see every intimate moment of our lives."

"What?" she gasped. "No. No. How? Are you sure?" She'd known her work area was monitored, but never considered something as unethical and invasive as what Rinehart suggested now.

Damn it! She was upset, and trying to sit up. He was aroused, struggling for control. He sucked in a breath, willed his body to calm itself, and somehow he rolled off of her. He lay on his back, fighting to restrain the lust pulsing through his body. Trying not to think about how sweet she'd felt beneath him. She was sitting up; he could feel her straining to see through the darkness, staring at him; he could hear her silent demand for answers.

"Walch installed a monitor in my room," he reluctantly admitted. "I guess he assumed everyone is as twisted as he is."

A shocked sound slid from her lips, and she jerked toward the edge of the bed. Instinctively, he reached for her, shackling her wrist.

She yanked at it. "Let go!"

"You think I watched you," he growled between his

teeth, his anger spiking as he recognized that he, not Walch, had become the enemy.

"What do you expect me to think?"

"Why would I tell you if that were the case?" he demanded. "I thought you sensed things."

"Emotions," she spat back, tugging at her wrist. "I don't read minds. I get what you give me and right now, that's a whole lot of guilt."

Guilt? She was convicting him over fucking guilt? He ground his teeth, pulled her flat against his chest, and pressed her close. She made a frustrated sound. "Let go!"

"Not yet," he declared, holding her easily though she was shoving at his chest. "You say I am putting off guilt. You know why? Not because I watched you like some sort of pervert, but because I tried to get rid of those cameras. I tried to protect you. My mistake was that I didn't believe Walch would do anything about it. I thought he needed us too much for the cloning program. But I was wrong. He did do something. He tortured Lucan to make me pay for crossing him. A man who trusts me. One of my men, whom I'm responsible for protecting."

She stopped fighting him. "Oh, God. Oh, God, Rinehart. I'm so sorry. I… Where is he? Does he need medical attention?"

"He'll survive," he said, shrugging off her touch and sitting up. He ran a rough hand through his hair, then shifted his weight up the mattress so he could lean back on the headboard. The need for privacy had passed; the mood had swung from passion to anger in a matter of moments. He flipped on the bedside lamp and blinked into the light.

   Laura's disheveled appearance punched him in the gut: she sank to her knees, her eyes stormy, her hair a wild, sexy, mussed-up silk. Her feet were tucked beneath that perfect ass he'd been touching only minutes before. His cock pressed painfully against his zipper. Why did he still want her? Why? No. He would not be foolish over a woman again.

   "They tortured him because I let whatever the heck it is you do to me cloud my judgment." Those words burned with far too much reality; long ago, he'd gotten his men killed by the Beasts over a damn woman.

   Shock filled her eyes. "Don't say that!" Pain laced her words, washing over her features. He cut his gaze away from her, fighting desperately to remain detached. He could not allow himself to be sucked back into the spell she cast on him. She repeated her words, softer this time. "Please don't say that." She hesitated. When she spoke again, defeat colored her words. "Everything is so out of control. I don't know how to fix it."

   Guilt. More guilt. It rushed through his veins and twisted his heart. His gaze lifted to find her knees curled to her chest, arms wrapped around them, her hair hiding her face. His actions came without thought, driven by pure instinct. He found himself once again moving toward her, sitting beside her, hip to hip so that he faced her. He tilted her chin up; she was fighting tears. There were a million promises he could have made, but not the one she wanted to hear, not the promise of a place called Normal that he knew didn't exist. And she couldn't promise him what he wanted to hear. Couldn't tell him she could leave her fantasy of that normal life behind. So he said nothing, asked nothing. Instead, he eased her into his arms and pulled her down on the bed with him.

Chapter 12

When Rinehart's strong arms surrounded her, Laura melted into him. He was a stranger, a man she had thought was an enemy only hours before. Yet she was warm in places she didn't know could be warm, aching in places she instinctively knew only he could soothe.

Blinking into his hot stare, she searched for the anger she'd seen moments before, the accusation he'd thrown her way, but she saw neither, felt neither. Still, she couldn't let it go without some resolution, not after the conviction his words had held, not when she knew that Lucan had been tortured because Rinehart had tried to help her. She'd spent her entire adult life trying to make a difference, trying to do the right things. But everything seemed to be falling apart. Her kids were in danger. She was in danger. Now it appeared others, too, had faced danger on her behalf.

"I didn't mean for Lucan to get hurt," Laura whispered. "I...wish you wouldn't have tried to help me. Not at someone else's expense."

He squeezed his eyes shut, took a short, hard breath before his gaze fixed on hers, the depths of his stare like dark pools of dire emotion. "It is I who didn't mean to hurt *you,* Laura."

She touched his cheek, her fingers trailing to his strong jaw. The rasp of stubble against her skin sent a dart of awareness through her body. "Yes," she murmured, "you did." She swallowed against the ache he'd created. "And it worked." He started to object and she pressed her fingers to his lips. "But you had good reason. I misread your guilt and judged you. I'm sorry."

He grabbed her hand, curled her fingers around his, and kissed the tips. He stared down at her with so much passion she could hardly breathe. "Laura," he said huskily.

The deep, dark pools of his eyes filled with desire, lust, hunger. Little darts of fire licked at her limbs in response. This was what she needed, this escape. A shelter in the midst of a firestorm that wouldn't stop raging.

It was true, there were still unanswered questions between them, but they were alike in some way she had yet to identify, alike in a way that drew her to him. One night, she told herself. One night. That was all this had to be. One night to let go, to be touched, to be held. God, it had been so long.

"I want you," she confessed, boldly staring into his eyes, boldly asking for what she wanted—and what she wanted was him.

Fire lit his gaze, and a low growl escaped his sensual lips. His head lowered, his mouth slanted over hers, his tongue pressed past her teeth and found her own. Hot strokes of that velvety tongue followed, answering her declaration without words, telling her that he, too, needed this escape. He needed *her.*

They went from slow sensuality to raging desire in all of thirty seconds. His hand rode beneath her dress, beneath the thin strap of her thong. He nipped her bottom lip and gently eased her backward, pressing her shoulders to the headboard. His hot stare stroked hers before he ripped away her panties and spread her legs. Her dress was high on her hips, and remotely she thought of the cameras. That worry was quickly dismissed as Rinehart positioned his big body in front of her, a protective wall hiding her from anyone else who might be watching. She was exposed to him, Rinehart, and no one else. Exposed to the heated inspection he cast upon her spread legs, lust radiating off him with such force she shivered with the impact. The primal, almost animalistic need in him bit at her senses, telling of the depth of his desire and stirring her own. Her nipples tingled; her core ached. Never had she felt so intimate with a man, so fearlessly exposed to a man.

When his head slowly lifted, the depths of those dark eyes drew her in, pulled her into a hypnotic spell. She was sinking deeper and deeper into the recesses of sensual escape, and she didn't fight it—for once, she was ready to let go.

As if he welcomed that silent declaration, he spoke then, his voice gravelly. "You're beautiful."

His fingers climbed up her thighs, his calloused prints rasping at her skin with erotic results, teasing her with where he was going, what would come next. She gasped as his thumb found her clit, biting her lip as pleasure charged through her body, moaning as he used the other hand in combination, expertly caressing the slick folds of her sensitive flesh. He leaned forward, kissed her neck, nipped her ear. Whispered, "Forgive me, Laura, but I have to see you come before I turn out that light." With that declaration he kissed her, his tongue delving into her mouth at the same moment his fingers slid intimately inside her core. With long, sensual strokes he caressed her to the edge. Caressed her to the point where she clung to his neck, her hips arching into his hands, her mouth begging for more of his taste. The buildup was fast, intense, overwhelmingly hot. She shattered with such intensity, her mouth tore from his; her head fell back against the headboard, and her breath lodged in her chest. She shook with the impact of pleasure each spasm delivered. And he expertly stroked the spasms, stroked faster and then slower, into waves of gentle completion, easing her into blissful satisfaction.

Her body eased into the mattress, and she blinked up at him. A rush of newfound heat flushed her cheeks, this time borne of how easily he'd taken her completely over the edge, how easily he'd made her forget everything but pleasure. And she'd done nothing for him, leaving him on the brutal edge of arousal without release. She could feel the impact of that neglect, the hunger eating away at him, the need.

Suddenly, she burned to pleasure him. In one quick

act, Laura adjusted onto her knees, leaned forward, and tugged on his shirt. The buttons snapped and flew, scattering here and there, from the bed to the floor. Her gaze raked his broad chest, her fingers touching the taut skin that covered sinewy muscle. Perfect amounts of light brown hair sprinkled across the expanse and teased the sensitive flesh of her palm. She lifted off her heels, and her gaze collided with his. Holding his stare, she peeled his shirt off his shoulders, the act pushing her body close to his, her chest into his. Heat radiated off him and enfolded her.

He shrugged away the shirt and brought his hands to her hips. Face-to-face, on their knees, their lips lingering a breath away from a kiss. A moment, two. His mouth touched hers, sensual, slow, a caress that lingered, erotic, compelling. He leaned back just enough for his eyes to search hers, his hands inching again beneath her hemline, up the back of her thighs. His palms cupped her backside, a finger sliding intimately along the crevice.

Her lips parted in a gasp. "Rinehart." She spoke his name, not even sure why, only that she wanted this man more than she remembered ever wanting anyone before.

Satisfaction flared in his eyes for a moment before they darkened with challenge. "What happened to me being the enemy?"

What did happen? A question easier answered if his fingers weren't exploring with such delicious precision. She swallowed hard against the pleasure, somehow finding a desire-laden whisper. "You said to keep my friends close and my enemies closer." Laura traced the flexing muscle of his bare shoulders. "But I'm not sure you're close enough yet."

His eyes narrowed in response, his hands stilled where they had been caressing, teasing. Something in the air shifted—no, something in him shifted. She felt it the way someone might a storm blowing in over the open sea, swift and intense. Wildly evident. "What if I don't want to be the enemy, Laura?"

Emotion welled in her chest. She wasn't sure if it was his or hers, maybe both. *I don't want you to be.* But she couldn't say that. Not without exposing herself in a way she wasn't prepared to do, a way she had vowed to never do, ever, with anyone.

He stared at her, willing her to answer, willing her to say what he wanted to hear, eyes probing with such intensity she thought they might set her on fire. But she couldn't give him what he wanted. Take her body, her passion, but she couldn't give beyond that.

A barely perceptible growl slid from his lips a second before he moved, the heat of his body gone from hers, leaving her exposed in an entirely different way. Not sensual, but cold. Alone. It was over. He'd wanted something she couldn't give, and now he was leaving.

She sat up, swallowing hard against a new wave of emotion. But she was proven wrong. Her eyes went wide as Rinehart's boots disappeared, followed by his pants and boxers. And all that was left was one gorgeous hunk of naked man.

Rinehart had felt how much she wanted to open up emotionally, felt how she'd fought to keep up her walls.

How he had felt these things, he could not say, but he had. If she could not pull down the walls herself, he would do it for her. If not forever, then for at least this one night. Rinehart stood before Laura naked and aroused, ready to give himself to his mate, a silent message in his actions. There were no barriers between them tonight, nothing to separate them.

Her gaze traveled his body, exploring, making him hotter with every touch of her eyes. Making him burn for the touch of her hands, the taste of those lips against his. Her eyes lifted to his, desire burned from her to him. And she responded to his silent invitation. She raised up on her knees and reached for the hem of her dress.

With one agile move, Rinehart's knees pressed down onto the mattress, his hands stilling hers. "No," he warned. Uncertainty flared in her eyes that he quickly answered with explanation. "No one sees you naked but me." It was one thing for him to be naked on camera, another thing altogether for her to be.

Understanding settled in her features, and he leaned over and flipped off the light. Darkness surrounded them, a seductive blanket growing warmer with each passing second. His hands found the bottom of her hem; his lips, the gentle curve of her neck just below her ear. He nibbled and she sighed with pleasure. He smiled against her soft skin, pleased at how easily she responded to him.

Together their hands slid the hem of her dress upward, and he helped her maneuver it over her head. His erection settled between her legs, the wet heat of her core invitingly hot. He helped her remove her bra, covering her full breasts with his hands. Her nipples pebbled against his palms, and he yearned to see them, to know the color—pink? red? a rosy color, perhaps? Without the ability to see, he used his hands and mouth to drive a sensory exploration—one where her moans were erotic bliss; her sighs, erotic taunts that drove him to elicit another. He kissed her, touched her nipples with his fingers and then with his tongue.

Laura answered his seduction with one of her own. Her teeth found his shoulder, scraping it lightly; her lips found his arm, his stomach. She pressed him backward, urged him to lay down. The wet heat of her breath brushed his cock; her tongue lapped at the tip. He bit back a groan, feeling as if a leash had snapped, and the Beast inside him suddenly flared to life. He reached for her, pulling her up his body, tight against his side, and willed himself back under control.

"I wanted to do that to you," she said, her breath warm on his neck, her lips delivering a soft caress.

Primal burn set him into action again. Rinehart rolled her to her back, spread her legs and settled between her shapely thighs. "I need to be inside you, Laura. I need…" He slid his cock along the slick center of her body, aroused, hot. "I need to be inside." He sank deep into her body.

"Yes," she whispered, arching upward, breasts pressed into his chest as she tried to pull him in deeper. He rotated his hips, easing to that deeper spot he longed for, that pocket of wet heat that would consume him fully. And when he found it, she moaned, "Yes."

Several seconds ticked by as they lay there, bodies

joined, his head buried in her shoulder. How long, he didn't know. But slowly, they shifted into motion, mouths melding in a scorching kiss, a kiss that devoured, a kiss that provoked. They were hungrier now, their bodies pumping, swaying, clinging. Hands all over each other.

Suddenly, he wanted to claim her, wanted her to know that in every possible way, she belonged to him. A primal burn evolved, a demand to ensure that she knew what he already did—she was his. He arched his back, thrusting harder, faster. Possessiveness flowed through his veins like molten heat through his body. He had to have her. Had to take her. She was saying his name, calling out to him. She wanted him to claim her. She was telling him to with each pump of her hips, the muscles in her core taking him deeper.

He had to have more. He had to…the Beast in him suddenly latched on to his control. Desperate to rein in his urges, thankful for the dark that shielded him from her gaze, he thrust hard against the demand of his body. Over and over he thrust, lunged, delved deep into her body— using the fire in his loins to control the burn of the Beast.

Laura answered him with pleasure, crying out a moment before the spasms of her orgasm pulled him deeper, stroking his hard length with her release. Again, the urge to sink his teeth into her shoulder, to claim her, washed over him again. One last, desperate thrust, and he exploded inside her with such intensity his body shook until they eased into one another, still pressed close together. He didn't want to move, afraid of losing the short time he had with her. Instead, he rolled onto his back and pulled her with him. She sighed and snuggled to his side. Her hand reached up and brushed his jaw before settling in the center of his chest. The tenderness of the act stole his breath. He'd experienced nothing like that in fifty years, perhaps in a lifetime.

He stared into the darkness, his heart thudding so hard against his chest he was certain she could hear it. He could never give her the life she wanted, but holding her now, he wished that weren't true. In the dark, hidden from the rest of the world, they had come together— they were one. But he could not escape the cold, hard reality that the light of a new day would soon bring upon them. That light would shine on the differences, on the walls of separation between them. She could never know the key she held to his salvation. That knowledge would take away her freedom, obligate her to be with him by destiny, not choice. And she *would* feel obligated. He'd seen how she embraced her patient's needs and sacrificed for their happiness.

Laura would escape this island; she would be safe. He'd make sure of it. He had to give her a happiness beyond a life with him; he had to be willing to walk away. And he couldn't find the strength to do that by staying in her bed. But his need for her was too strong. Tomorrow he'd clear his head, he decided, and he'd face reality. Tomorrow he'd be a Knight, a soldier, a warrior with his mission. He stroked her shoulder and pulled her closer. Tomorrow.

Chapter 13

Laura blinked, fighting the haze of heavy slumber; an irritating stream of light was cascading from the nearby window straight into her face. She inched farther back on her pillow, moving away from the offending sunbeam. Snuggling farther beneath the blankets, she started to fall back to sleep.

Her eyes snapped open, and she surveyed the bed. Realization slammed into her mind. She was in bed, his bed, alone—naked, but thankfully covered by blankets. The sound of a running shower caught her attention. She lifted her head, noting the bathroom door, slightly ajar, a few feet away. Rinehart was in the shower. A visual of him whipped through her mind, water streaming over his lithe male perfection. She dropped her head back onto the pillow, cursing the distraction created by that man and his muscle, willing it away. But more distraction followed. Memories washed over her, sensual, wonderful memories. But it was morning now, and her night of escape had passed. The new day forced her to face the complications of those memories, choices she would have to live with.

A thought occurred to her, and she chastised herself. She'd never considered a condom. Not for a minute. And her a doctor! Thank God she'd taken the pill for years, although not because she was having sex.

She glanced at the clock and focused on the urgency of the here and now. It was seven-thirty. She had an hour and a half until the kids were scheduled to be in the lab. That gave her time to shower, check on Kresley and not much more. But she had to make time. Because what she hadn't prioritized with Rinehart, and what should have been at the top of her list, were her questions—even though she dreaded the answers. Her stomach fluttered thinking about it. Perhaps subconsciously she'd allowed herself to put off the inevitable discussion to come, no matter how necessary. The prior evening she'd been able to read Rinehart's emotions. He didn't want to tell her what was in store for her, not because he was trying to be deceitful, but because he didn't think she was going to like what he had to say. Regardless, she wasn't leaving here without those answers.

The shower stopped running. Laura tugged the covers to her chest and sat up, her gaze searching. Her dress might as well have been miles away. Pooled on the floor, it would take some doing to get to it without her blanket. She contemplated going for it, but hesitated.

Damn Walch and his cameras. She wondered if Kresley and Carol were being subjected to his perverted monitoring. They probably were. An unfamiliar emotion surfaced: a red-hot desire to make Walch pay for all he had done.

"It'll be over soon."

Laura's gaze rocketed to the bathroom door as the sound of Rinehart's voice tore her away from her dark thoughts but brought with it a new turbulence. How had he known what she was thinking? Could he read her mind? Could he mask some of his emotions? New fears surfaced about him manipulating her desire.

Her attention riveted to his face, she was ready to demand the truth—but the words died in her throat as she took in the sight of him.

Rinehart loomed in the doorway with nothing but a small white towel roped around his lean hips. Rippling abdominals glistened with droplets of water, and her imagination didn't need any help to conjure what was beneath that towel.

Slowly, her gaze traveled over his waist and his chest, then lifted to his face. "I guess I still need convincing," she said, cynical not by choice but by necessity. But she wanted him to give her a reason to let go of doubt, wanted him to say something to make her believe in his words.

He offered a blank stare in response. Her fears mounted. Had she read him wrong in the heat of passion? Silence fell between them, thick and unnerving. Desperately she searched for a connection. Her ability to read his emotions was useless. He'd become distant, untouchable on all levels. He'd become the enemy again or…something. She didn't know what.

A man who regretted his actions? A man who blamed her for one of his men being injured and now he wanted to get the hell away from her? She narrowed her gaze on him and decided that was it. Opening her mouth to ask about Lucan, she had second thoughts, not wanting to make matters worse. She wasn't sure what to do. Rinehart's coldness had blocked her ability to read him. It seemed he confused her senses easily. She struggled to get a grip on what was happening.

It was Rinehart who broke the silence, and the conversation detoured to new and just as unsettling territory. "I took the liberty of going to your room early this morning and picking up clothes and a few items on your bathroom sink."

Her eyes went wide. "You did what?" she demanded. "You went into my room?" Her hand went to her throat, where her breath seemed to hang. Every bit of privacy and control she'd believed she'd owned had been stripped away. She didn't even want to know how he'd managed to get into her room. No doubt Walch had given him a key.

"I assumed you wouldn't want to leave my room looking as if you'd spent the night," he said coolly, apparently unaffected by her reaction.

Her hand covered her face a moment, the other still clinging to the blanket. "I shouldn't even be here," she murmured. But now that she was, leaving in a wrinkled, day-old dress with no shoes would be an attention grabber to anyone who saw her exit. She hugged the sheet a bit closer and cast him a direct look, firming her voice to a facade of calm. "I appreciate the clothes. Wherever they are."

"In the bathroom," he said flatly. And that was it. He said nothing more. He wasn't giving her anything to go on here. No help getting past this naked moment waking up in his bed.

Could this be any more awkward? "Ah. Yes. Thanks. Don't know how I am going to take a shower with the cameras, but thanks." Her chin indicated the dress where it lay on the floor. "Don't suppose you could hand that to me?" His eyes narrowed a bit, darkened; finally, she saw a hint of fire in them. Fire he quickly banked.

He tore his gaze from hers before he made a frustrated sound, took several steps and scooped up her dress. He stood beside the bed, his towel precariously low and right in her line of sight.

She snatched the dress from his hand and turned her head away. The dress balled in her hands as she awaited his departure. She wasn't going to struggle to pull it on and hold the sheet with him watching.

"Once you're dressed," he said, with that same flat tone she found she didn't like one bit, "we'll talk."

"You won't get an argument from me on that," she said, glancing up at him just in time to note a spark of twisted emotion in those deep blue eyes. He wanted her, but wished he didn't.

"I feel the same," she whispered before she could stop herself.

His brows dipped. "What?" he asked, lowering his gaze.

"Nothing," she replied, and decided it was time to get out of his bed. Cutting her gaze from his, she maneuvered the dress over her head, struggling to keep the blanket in place.

When she finally completed her task, she straightened and found Rinehart was gone. She scrambled to the side of the bed and stood up, tugging the dress down her legs. She hesitated, not sure what to do now.

He reappeared in the doorway partially dressed in similar attire to what he and his team had worn the previous day. Well-pressed Dockers. Boots. A white dress shirt he was buttoning. "The bathroom has no windows. Crack the door and turn off the light. The camera won't pick up anything but shadows, and you should see well enough to be okay."

She thought of all the times she'd dressed and undressed, all the long baths to ease the day's stresses. "I hate that he's watching."

"He'll pay for what he's done before this is over." The words were low, lethal, the emotions he'd suppressed spiking with a quick jab, overflowing into her. "I'll be waiting for you in the other room."

He walked away then, and she squeezed her eyes shut. Confused, overwrought by a combination of her own emotions and Rinehart's, Laura walked toward the bathroom and flipped off the light. She stared into the darkness, and anger burned in her gut. She *wanted* Walch to pay. She hated that she felt such a thing, but nevertheless, she did. Her father had often preached about the danger of driving one's actions out of anger. Soldiers didn't operate on emotion, he would say. But he hadn't understood what she did now. Everyone acted on emotions. Emotions controlled and manipulated.

Walch had crossed a line. He'd invaded more than her privacy. He'd stolen the hopes and dreams that she'd promised her kids. She was angry. But she couldn't allow those things to eat her alive or she'd end up no better than him. She had to use that anger to refocus on her goals.

Somehow she had to keep her promises to her kids. If Rinehart could help her with that, fine. If not, then he was, indeed, the enemy.

Rinehart sat at the kitchen table, nursing a cup of coffee, replaying the list of reasons he should keep his distance from Laura. But more than all of them, being around her seemed to drive the Beast in him closer to the surface. The more he put temptation in his path, the more he feared he would become dangerous. All these things made sense. Except for one issue: How was he going to keep his distance from Laura and maintain the necessary facade in front of the cameras for Walch? He wasn't. The more under his control Walch believed Laura to be, the easier it would be to keep Walch at bay until their escape. Which meant Rinehart was in trouble. Because already this morning, seeing her in a bed, naked—a mere reach from being beneath him again— had him fighting the Beast within. The desire he bore for her was damn near uncontrollable.

Abruptly, the bedroom door opened and he set his cup down, preparing for the impact he knew she would have on him. The instant she appeared, his heart hammered in his chest.

She hesitated at the door, casting him a look full of trepidation before walking toward him. The sleek lines of the navy dress he'd chosen for her outlined her slender curves; a determined look was etched on her beautiful face. The rose-color lipstick she wore was alluring and impossible to miss against the pale perfection of her ivory skin.

Her hands curled around the back of the chair directly across from him. "How is Lucan?"

Regret twisted him in knots. "Lucan will be fine, Laura."

She didn't look convinced. "You're sure? Can I check out his wounds? See if I can help?"

"That's not necessary," he said. "He's amazingly resilient." His lips thinned. "I regret the way I told you what happened."

She studied him a moment, as if searching for something. Then she said, "You were upset about your man just as I am worried about my patients." She inched the chair away from the table to sit down.

"Beside me," he said, standing up and offering her the chair to his right. Again she hesitated, uncertainty in her expression. No doubt because of his behavior in the bedroom. He'd been withdrawn, cold. She'd been alluringly naked, and he'd been desperate to restrain himself, struggling with the best way to handle their attraction. Staying close to her outside the bedroom was the only answer he could come up with.

"The camera's still rolling," he warned. "The more Walch believes you are under my control, the more time he will give us to escape."

Laura cast him an unblinking stare; the displeasure at his answer was evident in her green eyes. "You're sure the audio is scrambled?"

"Absolutely," he said, confident after talking with Max on the beach the night before. The other Knight had created some sort of dual computer virus that attacked Walch's communications and electronics systems as a cover. A text message that morning from Max had confirmed the virus was still functioning. No doubt their tech guys were climbing the walls trying to fix it.

She studied him a moment, as if she might ask questions. Instead, she nodded, seemingly satisfied with whatever she found in his face—or maybe in his emotional mojo or whatever it was she read—because she sat next to him. He then walked to the kitchen and filled a coffee cup for her, setting it and vanilla creamer in front of her before claiming his seat again. She frowned at the creamer. "How did you—?"

"It's yours. So is the coffee. I figured the empty pot that came with my apartment wouldn't do us much good." He shrugged. "And you might as well use it before we go."

"I see," she said primly. That proper little scientist from the lab shone through once again as she poured creamer into her coffee. "When exactly would that be?"

"Monday, at sunrise."

She hesitated, her cup halfway to her lips. "How?"

"Helicopter."

She shook her head, setting her cup down and pushing it out of the way. "You can't sneak a helicopter into a military facility unnoticed."

"You can if you have a tech whiz like Max. He's arranging it to look like training missions are being run nearby. By the time they realize we've deviated from the flight plan, we'll be gone."

She leaned back in her chair, her attention fixed on his face, her stare unwavering. "I'd ask how Max manages all this stuff, but that isn't the real question. It goes back to what I asked last night." A pause, deep scrutiny. "Who are you, Rinehart? And what do you want from me?"

Rinehart had anticipated this question and given great consideration to how to handle it, concluding there was no way around some hard truths. "We're Hunters, Laura. A group of covert soldiers who hunt this group Walch is involved with. It's what we do and why we exist. When you found yourself on their radar, our radar followed."

Her reply came slow, her words measured. "What are they, exactly? Some sort of cult?"

"That's a relatively accurate description. A cult that has inhuman abilities. We call them the Darkland Beasts because they originate from a certain territory in Mexico and because of their violent nature."

"Stop saying inhuman," she said, her spine straight as a steel rod. "No matter how evil they are, having special abilities does not make you inhuman."

Damn it, she wasn't listening. He moved his chair around, faced her directly; then he reached for her chair and turned her to face him. She gasped with surprise but he didn't care. He pinned her in a hard stare. "Beasts are damn near invincible. Shoot them and they don't die. Cut them and they heal almost instantly. And they're strong, Laura. And they're fast." He had no intention of outright telling her they were Demons—not yet. This was close enough. There were other hard truths she had to face first. "They are not like you, Laura, and if you continue to try and make all people with special abilities like you, you'll end up dead or under their control." He sucked in air through his teeth and let it out. "And I can't let that happen."

"I knew there were others like us," she whispered. "Others who would abuse their abilities."

He ground his teeth. "They are *not* like you. They were not born this way. They were created."

"What?" she asked, her eyes going wide, her expression registering shock. But as he expected, she wasn't as shocked as someone who hadn't seen the things she'd seen inside her lab and in her own life. "What do you mean, 'created'?"

"They were all once—" he hesitated, struggling to keep the word *normal* out of his description "—without abilities." He scrubbed his jaw, looked at her. Considered. Decided they had to get some of this out in the open. "Look. Here is the cold, hard truth. You're dangerous in their hands. The others, your patients, they aren't the real targets. The twins are strong—that means nothing. The Beasts are strong. Kresley and Blake have skills they want, but they are only two people. They only matter in the big picture of things if cloned. Once they clone the skills, they can take those humans and turn them into Beasts. Then they will have a new army with all the skills of the past and new ones to boot."

"And Carol?" she asked. "You said nothing of Carol."

"I know you sense the change in her. They've gotten to her, Laura."

Denial flashed in her eyes as she shook her head. "No. No." She grabbed the front of his shirt as she had the night before. "She was such a sweet girl. She's mixed up. I won't let you write her off. I know how soldiers operate—they weigh the risks. She's not an acceptable loss. None of my patients are acceptable losses."

He wasn't going to argue the hard choices in a mission. Decisions were made to save the most lives. It had to be that way. "We'll sedate her and take her back with us, but I make no promises that she can be saved." He reached out and tried to stroke her cheek. She leaned away from the touch, and his heart twisted with the rejection. "We'll try, Laura." His hands covered hers as she tried to retreat, her eyes flashing to his in anger. "The place we are taking you to is our headquarters. You will have every resource you need to help Carol and to complete your work. No strings attached."

"So your people can use us like these Beasts want to do?"

It was a reasonable assumption, but no less hard to swallow. For someone who could read his emotions, she judged him harshly time and time again. Perhaps the darkness in him was more than he could contain. He shoved away that unsettling thought. "We don't need your research. We have our own abilities or we wouldn't be able to fight the Beasts."

"What kind of abilities?" There was accusation in her tone, and he jerked back from her, releasing his hold.

"I cannot control your actions, Laura, if that is what you are implying. Only you do. Regret what you might about last night, but that choice was yours, not mine."

Her lashes fluttered, lifted. "I'm sorry. I... This is all so confusing."

He didn't want apologies and ignored it, answering her previous question instead. He was tired of being in knots. Ready to get this over. "We can do everything our enemies can, minus their evil intentions."

"Yet they didn't create you?"

Rinehart hesitated, treading on dangerous water, not about to tell her the full story. Not yet. Letting her think he was a lab invention would make this easier for her to process. "Our abilities are born of the efforts made to stop the Beasts. We have no agenda but stopping the Beasts, Laura. None."

She wet her lips, the act driving his attention to her mouth and tightening his groin. Damn, he needed to get out of here. He needed air and time to clear his head.

"And saving us fits that agenda," she said.

"You, specifically," he said, hating that admission. "You're dangerous in their hands, Laura. And I am not talking about any ability you might possess. I am talking about your skill in a lab. Your capability to clone people like your patients and turn them into dangerous soldiers."

"I don't have that ability," she argued, her hand going to her forehead for a second before motioning to him. "That's why Walch brought you here."

"Because Lucan convinced him that using your work and his together could make it happen. Lucan based those assumptions on the same science Walch has already gathered himself. He just wanted someone who would do what you wouldn't. They know you're capable of making it happen."

She didn't deny his claim. "I don't believe it," she said, her voice emotional, tight, her gaze drifting to his chest. "All my life I've tried to find a way to set people free, and I've done nothing but put us all on the radar screen."

"Not everyone, Laura," he said softly, reiterating the hardest blow. "You."

She raised her gaze. "So there it is," she said, her eyes glistening with anger. "You didn't come to take my patients out of captivity. You came to take me."

What could he say? He'd come to her by destiny a lover and by order, if needed, a possible executioner.

Twelve hours he'd been in that snake pit. Long enough to know he didn't want to go back.

Walch flung the telephone against the wall. He didn't want to hear about technical difficulties. He sat down on the edge of the mattress and ran his hands over his head, fury barely contained. Rinehart was behind this; he had to be.

Somehow he had to salvage the situation. But he couldn't do it with everything going wrong at once!

"It's not as bad as it seems." He glanced to the doorway to find Carol leaning against the wood frame. She looked like the Carol of the past, with a schoolgirl skirt and flat shoes that looked sexy instead of prim. "Tezi doesn't want your glory. He wants his army. Give him that and he'll go away."

"You get friendly with a couple of Demons, and suddenly you know everything, I guess."

She sauntered toward him and stopped when her knees touched his. "I don't have to know everything," she said, staring down at him. "I have Lithe and Litha for that. You showed your cards too soon. You told them about the cloning before it happened. They were greedy. Greed made them impatient." She slid one leg over his lap and straddled him, arms lacing around his neck. "Greed feeds impatience." He didn't touch her. It infuriated him to want her when she'd betrayed him. "The guardians want to help you make this go away. *I* want to help."

"Help," he said, his hands reaching behind him on the bed. "Why would they help me?"

"They like making new friends." She smiled. "Friends who owe them favors."

As long as it served Tezi. He wasn't a fool. He was being manipulated. The fact that Carol, his creation, was the messenger only made that bitter pill harder to swallow. "And what favor do they want from me?"

"Nothing now," she purred, her hands traveling across his chest. "I'll help you now. You'll help them later."

"You can't do anything at this point," he said, his tone disgusted. "You can't even go back to the lab. Your blood is black. It cannot be tested."

"You really should have thought of that before you bit me the last time," she said. "But that's okay. I have a plan. We'll have everyone marked by the guardians by morning. Then, Tezi will get his army, and you will be rewarded with all that power you so desire."

"And what will you get, Carol?"

"You," she said. "I get you." She smiled. "You won't mind sharing a little power with me, now, will you?"

Chapter 14

Hours had passed since Laura's conversation with Rinehart. Hours since he'd been man enough to admit the truth—that he couldn't let her fall into enemy hands, no matter what the cost. She'd felt the pain in his admission and knew he was battling to reconcile his feelings for her with his obligation to his duty. She'd sworn she would never do anything to aid wrongdoing. But he'd grimly promised that the Beasts would convince her to cooperate in any painful way they could. She didn't want it to be true, but she was a realistic person, if nothing else. Everyone had weaknesses. They'd torture her, torture people she cared about. Reality drew a clear picture. And it was clear to her now that the Beasts *were* evil. No matter what the intentions of Rinehart's superiors, she shared at least one agenda with them: She didn't want herself to end up with the Beasts.

Laura stuck a vial in the rack in front of her and glanced at the desk a few feet away, where Rinehart had lingered most of the day, always close, always watchful. She studied the man now as if he held the answers to every question in the universe. There was a measured reserve about him, a precision to everything he did that spoke of the military, of the inbred soldier. Except when they were alone, making love. Then there had been wildness, uncontrolled, primal. And Lord help her, it excited her to know she was the one capable of doing that. Her head said caution, but her passion had a mind of its own, and, it seemed, so did her heart. Those parts of her preferred to listen to instinct; they preferred to get close to Rinehart rather than to push him away.

He looked up from the paper he studied, perhaps feeling her attention, and raised his brow in silent inquiry. She shook her head, turning away from him as she did. There was tension between them, sexual and otherwise. How could there not be, considering everything that had happened between them in the past twenty-four hours?

A few feet away, Lucan studied the samples of the twins' blood under a microscope. The sight of him that morning up and about had been a relief. She hated knowing he'd been hurt because of her. She didn't want *anyone* hurt because of her. Whatever that might mean for her, she had to live with it.

"Unbelievable," Lucan said, leaning back in his chair and running his hands over his tan dress pants. "No wonder they aren't sick. All signs of the viral infection are gone."

Laura frowned. "That can't be. Did you rerun the test?"

"Three times," Lucan confirmed. "Could the original test have been off? Maybe they were never infected."

"They were infected," she said. "All of them." Blake had woken up with a fever and chills. Kresley still felt horrible. And Carol, well, Carol was nowhere to be found. They'd tried her door, no answer. What if Carol was sick? What if she was injured? Laura fingered the master key in her pocket, considering whether she should use it. She hated to intrude on her patients' privacy.

Rinehart rolled his chair closer to the conversation. "I take it this is unusual."

Laura shook off her thoughts of Carol momentarily and tapped her fingers on the lab table. "It's not entirely impossible to never develop symptoms, but unlikely. Especially both of them."

"Or maybe it's another ability," Lucan suggested. "Something to do with their immune systems. Have they ever been sick since you started working with them?"

This was a perfect opening to explain how she'd created this flu bug, but she hesitated to do so. She didn't want to take any chances of being overheard, although the computers and phones were down, so Max's cyber virus was still wrecking havoc in all kinds of ways, cutting off communication and surveillance.

"The twins haven't been sick, but before this, none of them had more than a sniffle. They've led a pretty sterile life, so that didn't raise any red flags. Whatever the reason, it's good they aren't sick." They all knew escaping would be easier without everyone ill. "I wish I could say the same for Blake and Kresley." She glanced at the clock. "It's time to give them their injections."

Lucan pushed to his feet. "I can do it."

Protectiveness flared and Laura opened her mouth to reject the offer and then reconsidered. Lucan had been working by her side for hours now, and she'd gotten nothing but help from him. The man had been tortured and still worked as if nothing had happened. These men shared an immediate goal, getting everyone she cared about off this island. And she had to take care of other matters, like copying her work, which would have a long-term impact on everyone.

"Yes," she said. "Okay. Can you stop by Carol's room again, too, while you're at it?" She scooped the key out of her pocket and hesitated before offering it to him. "I have access to all the patients' rooms for medical emergencies."

Lucan took the key. "I won't use it unless I have to," he promised. He cut Rinehart a look, which seemed to include some silent message she didn't understand, before he headed to the back room to collect the supplies he needed.

Rinehart pushed to his feet and then stepped to her side, his hands running down her arms, sending darts of warmth over her skin. "We'll find her," he promised, and she had no doubt he meant the words. But he also believed Carol couldn't be saved, and that wasn't acceptable to her.

"We have to find her," Laura said, and dropped her voice to a whisper. "Because I won't leave without her."

"And I won't leave without you," he said.

"You mean *can't*," she countered.

"*Won't*, Laura. I'm not going anywhere without you."

She clung to those words in a way that scared her, so she turned away from him. "I should get back to work," she said, sitting down in front of the microscope, trying to ignore the way he was silently willing her to look at him again. But she wouldn't. He had a mission and she was it. This could only end badly for them.

About forty-five minutes after leaving the lab, Lucan knocked on Kresley's door. He'd stopped by Blake's apartment first, which proved a hostile experience and a dangerous one, too. The kid not only didn't trust him, he'd made accusations about kidnapping the patients and taking them off the island. It was all he could do to keep from grabbing a sock and stuffing it into the boy's mouth. He could only hope Max's technology overhaul of the building was still causing havoc with the surveillance equipment. Lucan had done his best to calm Blake, but he hadn't been nearly as effective as Blake's fever, which had spiked and forced him to rest.

The door opened and Kresley appeared—and for Lucan, that moment would be forever engraved in his memory. She affected him deeply, her very existence like a warm blanket sliding around him. On some dim level, he had known she would. After all, when he was being tortured, she'd been the hope he'd clung to. He studied her now, trying to understand why that was.

Red hair, light eyes, light freckles brushing her delicate nose. Her lips were dry, her skin too pale from illness. She wore old gray sweats and a pink T-shirt. And she was the most beautiful woman he'd ever seen.

There was an innocence about her that reached beyond her youth. A rightness he couldn't explain. Perhaps that was why he had thought of his sister and Kresley in the same moment. Two innocents who didn't deserve to be victims in a deadly war. Beyond that, there was no comparison between the two, and certainly what stirred in him now spoke of her female allure, not a family resemblance.

Kresley delicately cleared her throat, and he realized awkwardly that he'd been staring. Lucan blinked and shook himself inwardly.

"Hi. Kresley, right?" She nodded, and he smiled. "I'm Lucan. Laura asked me to give you an injection."

She frowned. "There's no way Laura asked you to give me an injection. Not unless I went to sleep and woke up in some alternate universe."

"That's pretty much what Blake said," Lucan acknowledged. "It took me about an hour to convince him the shot wasn't laced with arsenic."

She laughed and then pressed her palm to her forehead. "Oh. Don't make me laugh. It hurts." She motioned him forward. "This bug is kicking my backside."

"Hopefully, it's almost over," he said, entering the apartment. "But the flu can hang on awhile."

"I guess Blake is sick, too?" she asked, shoving the door closed behind him and then motioning him to the living room.

"He's feeling pretty rough," Lucan confirmed. He followed her to the couch, noting the pillow and blanket there. The television was on mute; she turned it off with the remote.

Kresley curled up on the corner of the couch opposite him and pulled the blanket to her neck. "And the others?"

"So far they are fine," he said, hoping to avoid the topic of Carol, as he deposited the hard-bottomed bag he carried on the coffee table. He pulled the zipper back. "Any trouble controlling your powers since you've been sick?"

"Why?" she asked, a teasing quality to her voice. "Afraid I will set you on fire when you stick that needle in my arm?"

"Will you?" he asked, and withdrew the injection from the bag.

"It's doubtful," she said in mock seriousness. "But I keep a fire extinguisher handy for emergencies."

Lucan smiled. A genuine, heartfelt kind of smile that he hadn't experienced in at least a century.

He pushed the coffee table out of the way and knelt down on the floor beside her. She smelled clean and female, without the scent of perfume or unnecessary fluff. Just woman. But then, she was more girl than woman. A virgin, he was almost certain—someone who should be running from someone as dark as he.

He uncapped the needle. "You ready?"

She cast him an incredulous look. "After a million needles in my lifetime, I am always ready."

He quickly completed the injection, his mind wrapping around her announcement. Her life had been complex, full of challenge, yet she seemed untouched by it all, completely without bitterness.

On his knees beside her, he found himself full of questions. "Where are your parents?"

"I scared them," she said simply. "They left me with Laura." Again, without any hint of reproach. But it was there, it had to be—the pain, the hurt. His gut said that the biggest fire she had waiting to explode was the emotional one that she had buried. She tilted her head and studied him more closely. "I don't scare *you*, though, do I?"

"Not much scares me," he said, but the truth was, she did scare him. She scared him because he didn't understand his reaction to her. She seemed to soothe him in some unexplainable way. Perhaps some of her innocence slid into the darkness in him and gave him hope. He disposed of the needle, but found himself unable to move. He leaned back on his heels, still close to her, by her side. "You're very brave," he said.

She let a tiny laugh escape her lips. "Obviously you haven't talked to Rinehart. I had a minibreakdown last night." She explained to him what had happened. "So, see? I am not brave. I am terrified. Terrified I'll die before I do whatever I'm supposed to do."

That statement puzzled him. "Which is what?"

"I don't know," she said. "I just know there is something. Don't you ever feel as if you have a purpose?"

She has just said the same words he'd spoken to Rinehart, as if she knew he needed to hear them from someone other than himself. "It's what keeps me going," he admitted softly.

"Then you understand." With that she reached out

and touched his jaw. Desire jackknifed through his groin, and he bolted to his feet.

She jerked back into her couch corner and pulled the blanket over her. "I'm sorry. I don't know why I did that."

He wanted to tell her it was okay, to comfort her, but he couldn't. Because it wasn't okay; he wasn't okay. The primal part of him was on the rise, too long without a battle or sex to sate its demands.

"Laura will stop by later," he said, grabbing his bag, zipping it and heading for the door. He couldn't look back. Because if he did, he feared she would see the darkness in him, of him, all around him.

Lucan exited the elevator on Carol's floor, which was two stories above Kresley's, having barely pulled himself under any semblance of control. But Kresley was right. He had a purpose. That purpose included completing this assignment and getting her, and the others, off this god-forsaken island. He rounded the corner and was about to turn down the corridor leading to Carol's door when he heard male voices; he pulled back and hesitated. Standing in front of Carol's door were two familiar, dark-haired males—the twins, Jacob and Jared. She stood in a robe that hung open in the front, the bare skin a telltale sign she was naked beneath. "See you tonight, guys," she said a second before the door shut.

Lucan stayed in his position and waited as the twins approached. They rounded the corner, each a good six feet tall, but Lucan still towered over them as he stepped in front of them.

"Hello, boys," he said, inventorying who was who

based on their attire from the morning's blood drawing.
To his right, in a red, short-sleeved T-shirt and light blue
jeans, stood Jacob. To his left, in a black T-shirt and
black jeans, stood Jared. "Guess we were all worried
about Carol."

Jared lowered his eyebrows. "Worried? Worried why?"

Lucan patted the medical bag on his shoulder. "The
flu bug. Came to give her some antiviral drugs."

Jacob laughed. "Carol?" he asked. "She's not any
more sick than we are."

"Really?" Lucan said. "I must have misunderstood.
I guess it was just Blake and Kresley who got unlucky."

Jacob cast Jared a sideways look that Lucan didn't
miss—a look that indicated they had a secret they didn't
want to share. "Maybe she just recovered fast," Jacob
finally said.

Lucan studied them a moment, determining that he
saw no beastly influence. They seemed more like two
young men planning mischief without a lot of practice
at pulling it off well. "I'll check in on Carol just to be safe.
You boys take it easy." They murmured a reply as Lucan
sidestepped the two of them and started down the hall.

Lucan stopped at the door and knocked. No reply. He
knocked again. Reaching in his pocket, he retrieved the
key Laura had given him and then paused, flipping the
key between his fingers over and over, thinking, considering. He put it back in his pocket. He didn't want
Carol to know they were onto her.

Watching her would be a good distraction from his
own hell. Let Carol make her next move. And then
he'd make his.

Chapter 15

The desire Rinehart felt for his mate was automatic, the respect she had earned from him this day was not.

Telling Laura the true nature of his duty—to protect her, but also to protect humanity from her ending up in the wrong hands—had been one of the hardest things he'd ever done. She'd taken the news with amazing resilience, determined to save her patients, working tirelessly to prepare the supplies needed to ensure their safe escape. But he'd watched her work twelve hours straight with no break, leaving her lunch untouched. Enough was enough.

Rinehart headed for the mess-hall door with his bag of food, planning to insist that Laura take a few minutes to eat. He wanted her to accompany him to the picnic area behind the building where they could discuss her progress while they ate. It would take some prodding to get her out of the lab, but he planned to play on her logical side to convince her. If she collapsed, she wouldn't be helping the people she cared about.

He quickened his steps as he approached the dining room exit, finding himself driven by a sense of urgency, a need to get back to Laura's side. He reassured himself everything was fine, reminding himself that he'd left Rock to watch over her. But he came to an abrupt halt as two soldiers stepped in front of him. "Walch wants to see you."

"Don't suppose he'd wait until I've finished my dinner?" He received blank looks in return. "No. Didn't think so."

As expected, Rinehart found himself being led to Walch's office. Walch sat behind his desk, the facade of the dutiful officer, a disgrace to the military uniform he hid beneath. Rinehart claimed the visitor's seat before Walch could have the pleasure of ordering him to sit.

"I see I interrupted your dinner," Walch commented drily, indicating the bag of food.

Rinehart regarded him with boredom and set the bag on his desk—an intentional sign of disrespect. "I assumed you would have a good reason." He laced the words with sarcasm.

Walch clenched and unclenched his jaw, then, without warning, leaned forward, and shoved the bag off his desk. Rinehart could barely contain his laughter as he watched Walch's lack of control, but he schooled his features into that of the obedient soldier.

Walch fixed Rinehart in a glare meant to intimidate before settling back in his chair and adjusting his army-issue tie, exceedingly pleased with himself. "Now then," he drawled. "Where were we? Ah, yes. I'm quite sure you've noticed our technical difficulties since your arrival." Walch reached for a remote on his desk and hit a button. A television to his left clicked on; a view of Laura filled the screen. She was leaning over a microscope at her lab table. Rinehart pretended indifference despite the punch of fear in his gut for her safety. Walch continued, "We've managed to restore video and all of the other functions. But oddly enough, we can't keep the audio online." A pause obviously meant for effect. "You wouldn't happen to know anything about that, now, would you?"

Of course, Rinehart knew the audio was still screwed up, and it would stay that way. Max had random scrambling going on throughout the building to detract from the few safe zones they'd established.

"I know I've spent the day on the backup generators in that lab trying to create miracles." Rinehart smirked. "So if your army techs can't get the job done, perhaps one of my men should take a look."

Walch leaned back in his chair, his expression mocking. "I think you and your men have done quite enough in that venue for now." With his elbows resting on his chair, he steepled his fingers together in front of him. "And after tomorrow, I doubt the audio will be much of a concern." He leaned forward slightly. "See, Mr. Rinehart, I've managed to recover enough video to be quite impressed with your expedient actions to bed our little doctor, and I've decided to maximize your potential."

Rinehart steeled himself for what was to come, certain he wasn't going to like it. He didn't hide his irritation, which felt more than appropriate in this game of cat and mouse that Walch continued to play. "My dinner is getting cold," he said sharply. "Get to the point, Walch."

Walch's expression turned to a satisfied twitch of his lips. "Rather than take a wait-and-see approach on this project, I've decided I require insurance. Since the doctor isn't motivated by the simple greed that seems to serve you so effectively, Mr. Rinehart, I'll be meeting with her in the morning and providing her with a different kind of motivation." His eyes lit with malice. "I imagine she will be quite rattled when I'm done with her, so please, feel free to tend to her wounds." He leaned forward, fingers laced on the desk before him. "A 'good cop, bad cop' type scenario. I'm sure you get the picture. After we've both done our part, I expect our cloning program to be kicked into high-octane production."

Somehow, Rinehart kept from leaning across that desk and yanking Walch over it. Somehow, he came off mildly amused. "As enjoyable as licking Laura's wounds might be," he drawled, "I would be far more effective if you actually gave me a clue about what you have planned."

"I'm simply offering her ways to protect the patients she adores so much."

"Threatening them," Rinehart said flatly.

"Threats are for people who are afraid to act," Walch said. "I'm not afraid."

Instant anger rushed at Rinehart, his protectiveness for Laura affecting more than the man in him. His dark side flared, already far too close to the surface. It clawed at him, raged with insistence that he act against Walch. With every ounce of will he possessed, he reined in his Beast, finding his control. Somehow he pressed onward, coolly composed on the outside. "Your inability to stick to one plan for more than twenty-four hours makes me nervous. Not to mention this new plan of yours requires more effort on my part. I'm going to require some insurance of my own, as well. Half my bonus, up front."

Walch sat up, his back stiff. "Did you forget so quickly, Mr. Rinehart, the pain I can cause your men?"

Rinehart quirked a brow. "Did you forget how easily I've managed to influence Laura?"

"She'll cooperate regardless," he countered. "To save her patients."

"Or she'll make you think she is, while that brilliant mind of hers plots against you."

Walch's eyes flashed red—his control over his primal side seemed limited at best. Seconds passed as Knight and Beast sat in silent standoff. "You'll get your money by morning," Walch growled between his teeth. "But if you cross me this time, I'll kill you."

Rinehart smiled and pushed to his feet, looming over Walch as he stared down at him. "You're welcome to try." With those words, he turned and left, a slow saunter that said he felt no fear, his mind already on Laura.

He had promised Laura dinner, and she was going to get it—and not let it sit on her desk and get cold.

They would eat together on the beach. Only now, that shared meal wouldn't be about taking a break. It would be about him warning her about the hell to come the next morning. He would make sure Walch found his version of hell, too, before this was over.

Oh, yeah, Walch. Please. Try and kill me.

When they were alone in the lab, the evening hours crept forward far too quickly, with so little time left until their departure. Even so, Laura took the time to look through the microscope at the same specimen for a fifth time, amazed at what she saw. She blinked. Blinked again, and smiled despite the hellish threats surrounding her every move, because she'd found a very good reason to be positive.

Rinehart's voice sounded outside the door as he exchanged words with Rock, her resident watchdog per his directions. Rinehart acted as if someone might come in and steal her away. Unfortunately, her nerves said they just might.

Laura pushed to her feet a moment before the door opened, anxious to share her discovery with Rinehart, excited in a way that completely defied their circumstances.

"You won't believe what I found," she said as he crossed the room. The scent of food floated from the bag he held, awakening a rumble in her stomach that she quickly dismissed for more important matters.

"You're smiling," he said, surprised. He stopped in front of the lab table and scrutinized her. "And beautiful."

Despite herself, the warmth and sincerity in his expression had her blushing, her lashes fluttering and lifting. The look he gave her was tender, adoring, but without an ounce of lusty male intrusion. It was dumbfounding, considering her lipstick had long ago worn off and she was completely exhausted.

"Thank you," she said, feeling out-of-character shyness.

He didn't instantly respond, but stood there in all his male perfection, regarding her as if she were some sort of hidden jewel he'd found. What woman wouldn't be flattered? He was gorgeous. Sexy. Protective. She had needed none of those things, but yet, here and now, she wanted them all, and more.

"Tell me what has you so excited over dinner," he said, closing the distance between them. The heat of his body lanced through the numbing tiredness in her limbs. "We'll sit on the beach and eat."

"I can't leave, but I—"

The bag settled on the lab table a second before his fingers slid into her hair, his mouth slanting over hers in a passionate kiss. When it was over, he stared down at her. "I want to hear what you have to say, but I really need you to go outside with me."

Her hands went to his, her need to share her news too great to contain. "Okay, but I have to tell you this. The twins. I had Lucan run some tests. We combined their blood with a variety of viruses. Rinehart, it killed the virus every time."

He leaned back a bit to look more fully into her face. "Are you saying they hold the cure to these viruses?"

"Yes! Isn't it wonderful?" Her mind was racing.

"Hypothetically, each twin's strength must be connected to his immune system."

His thumbs stroked her cheeks. "You really love this stuff, don't you? The science. The lab. The discovery."

She considered that for a moment. "The discovery, yes. I like finding answers for people. I like changing lives for the better. I had no choice but to embrace science to make that happen. Life made that choice for me."

He seemed to digest that with something that felt oddly like tenderness, though she couldn't say why the subject matter would provoke such a feeling. Amazement, excitement, yes. But tenderness? Regardless of how misplaced that tenderness seemed, Laura found herself responding, found her heart squeeze with emotion. It was truly wonderful to share her excitement and her work with someone, but also terrifying and unfamiliar. Had the circumstances created such openness or had he?

"Let's continue this conversation outside while we eat," Rinehart urged.

Suddenly, the idea of escaping the continual surveillance seemed more than appealing, it felt necessary. There was a concern, however, that she couldn't quite discount. And that was the menace she'd sensed the night before. She opened her mouth to say as much, but didn't have to. Rinehart seemed to have picked up on her concerns. "We'll stay close to the building, but not so close—" he said, sliding a wayward lock of her dark hair behind her ear "—that I don't have you to myself."

The fire in his eyes left no doubt he, indeed, wanted her to himself, but there was another message there, too.

One that spoke of a need for privacy that they wouldn't find anywhere in the building.

Privacy would never truly be theirs while they were on this island, and she couldn't help but wonder if there would be a time or a place where they might find it in the future. A place without Walch and the Beasts.

In sweats, a T-shirt, and tennis shoes, Kresley wobbled toward the front door of the building, her body weak from her illness, her stomach queasy. But dang it, Blake had insisted he had an emergency and had to see her outside, so what could she do? She climbed out of bed and hiked outside, praying she didn't run into Lucan again when she was looking like death warmed over. Or maybe hoping she would run into him. She couldn't get him off her mind.

Distancing her thoughts from the steamy new addition to the island, Kresley reminded herself of her real reason for dragging herself out of bed. Blake tended toward the extreme, but he'd mentioned Laura, and that was enough to get her attention. She opened the front door of the building and paused on the top steps leading down to the beach. "It took you long enough." Kresley jumped and let out a little yelp at the sound of Blake's voice as he materialized beside her.

"I told you to stop doing that to me!"

"You knew I'd be here."

She shoved her hands to her hips. "So *be* here. Don't be invisible." Dizziness made her head spin, "Ugh. I feel...not so good." She sat down on the step and glanced up at Blake. "And you don't look so good yourself. Why are we out here?"

"I—" He hesitated and claimed the spot beside her. "Sorry, Kres. I'm just worried. Everything is going wrong." He studied her. "Are you okay?"

Kresley pressed her hand to her throbbing head and rested her elbow on her thigh. "I'd be better if you told me what was going on. Then maybe I can go sleep in peace."

Blake grimaced. "Laura is out on the beach with Rinehart." He grumbled something else under his breath, and then added more clearly, "I don't trust him or any of his people."

"I like Rinehart," Kresley countered. And Lucan, too, but that was an entirely different matter, better left untouched. "I like that Laura likes him even more. She hasn't had a man in her life in forever, since she began taking care of us. Don't blow this for her, Blake, or I swear I'll singe your brows and make you look like a freak so you'll never find a woman."

He rotated around to face her and blurted, "I heard two of Rinehart's men say they are planning to take us off the island."

"What?" Kresley was a bit surprised by that news, but since she and Laura had talked about taking a trip off the island, it didn't seem so odd. "You told Laura this?" He nodded. "And she said what?"

"She said…" He narrowed his gaze over her shoulder, looking into the distance.

Kresley turned to see what had caught his attention. She frowned as she noted two male figures walking toward the woods. "Is that Jacob and Jared out there? And Carol?"

Blake stood up. "Yeah, it is." He gave her a pointed

stare. "I'm telling you, Kresley," he said. "Something is going on and we're the only ones who don't know what it is. You go to bed. I'm going to find out what's happening." He faded to invisible.

She grabbed where she thought his arm was and latched on. "Not without me."

Blake grimaced. "Fine." He grabbed her hand. "But hurry up."

Keeping step with each other, they ran down the stairs. Kresley's stomach protested with each jolting move, but she kept pushing herself. What Blake had said about something being wrong—deep down she knew it was true. That was why she'd melted down with Laura and Rinehart the night before. She'd felt the trouble but couldn't identify the cause. She'd blamed it on being sick, but there was more to it.

They started across the sand in a rush and entered the edge of the woods. With light steps they followed the path they'd seen the others take, and a clearing came into view. Then they saw Jacob and Jared, who were standing in front of two gorgeous twin females. Blake grabbed Kresley's arm and pulled her behind several large rocks.

"Oh, God," Kresley whispered, cringing as she took in the sight before her. Jacob and Jared were kissing the two voluptuous blond beauties. "We don't belong here!" she hissed at Blake, irritated she'd been reduced to a Peeping Tom.

Blake blinked at the scene and leaned closer. "Something isn't right. Who are those women?" he asked. "And where's Carol? I know I saw her."

Kresley's eyes caught on the scene beyond the rock with a jolt of fear, terror racing through her body. Jared and Jacob were now on the ground, unmoving. She blinked as the two women seemed to shift and change.

Blake grabbed her arm. "What is this? What's happening?"

She didn't know, but whatever it was, it wasn't good. She cast Blake an urgent look and said, "Disappear and get help."

He gasped and pointed at the scene before them, and Kresley whipped her head around. The women were gone, and two silver snakes were in their place. And thanks to Blake's big mouth, the snakes had turned and were staring at the rock where they were hiding. "Go, damn it," she yelled at Blake.

"I can't leave you."

She grabbed his arms and stared at him. "I can fight, you can't. Not those things. Go now, and get help." He didn't move. "Do it!"

Blake disappeared, and Kresley stood to face the snakes as they slithered toward her.

"Kresley, run!" It was Lucan's voice—she knew it anywhere. Out of her peripheral vision, she saw him to her right, darting toward her. Running wasn't an option, not with one of the snakes fast approaching the rock. Besides, she wouldn't leave Lucan or the twins to these creatures. She had a gift, and today, at this moment, it had a purpose.

Kresley steeled herself for what would follow, ready to use her firestarting for the first time ever to save the lives of people she cared about.

Chapter 16

The water crashed against the nearby shore; the stars twinkled in the sky. Laura sat at the picnic table beside Rinehart and finished off the last bite of her barbecue sandwich.

"That was good," she said, dusting off her hands. They'd spent the entire meal talking about the discovery she'd made with the twins, and she knew Rinehart was trying to give her an escape, if only for a few minutes. Not the act of an enemy. The act of a friend. Her gaze drifted over the dark water. If not for the tingling, warning sensation inching along her nerve endings, she might have actually relaxed a few minutes.

"You've been living on mess-hall food too long if you think that was good," Rinehart quipped, tossing their bags in a metal trash can beside the table.

His mood turned serious. "You'll have a taste of the real world again soon, Laura."

"The real world," she repeated. "For me that means hiding. Secrets. Lies."

"And making a difference," he pointed out. "Making discoveries like the one you made with the twins' blood. That makes you special. Someone to protect and keep safe."

Her lips thinned, a growing sense of discomfort setting her nerves on edge, a discomfort that had nothing to do with the conversation, though. Her uncertain future was enough to twist her in knots. "Someone to lock away."

He took her hand. His thumb stroked the sensitive flesh of her wrist, and heat darted up her arm. Pleasurable as it might be, it did nothing to defuse the thrum of unease building inside her. "Protecting you isn't locking you away," he promised.

A rush of warning crashed over Laura. She traced the surf with her eyes and tugged at her hand, suddenly needing her freedom. Rinehart misread her intentions as rejection and tried to pull it back.

"Something is wrong." She pushed to her feet, with Rinehart following, adrenaline lighting a charge in her body. "You can't feel it, can you? That horrible sense of evil intent filling the air."

His gaze lifted, scanned. "I sense only one kind of evil. Whatever you are sensing now isn't that kind."

Laura's eyes caught on the horizon, and she sucked in a breath. Blake was running toward them. "Laura! Laura!"

Her heart pounded like a drum in her chest. "Oh, God."

Blake was under the parking lot lights now, his face filled with absolute terror, his voice blasting her name over and over.

Laura's gaze briefly touched Rinehart's a second before as they both started off running.

Even so, it felt as if a lifetime passed before they came face-to-face with Blake, though it must have been mere seconds. "Jacob and Jared," Blake said, heaving out the words in heavy breaths. "The women." He sucked in air, struggling for words, hyperventilating.

Laura ran her hands down his arms, desperate to calm him down and find out what was wrong. She was trying to be collected when fear was eating her up inside. "It's okay. It's okay." But she wasn't sure it really was; the warning in her stomach told a different tale. She forced Blake to take several slow breaths. Rinehart's presence by her side comforted her for reasons she couldn't explain.

When Blake seemed semicomposed, she pressed him again. He choked on the words, and she felt the rise of desperation. She needed to know what was happening. "Calm down and tell us," she encouraged Blake. "What women? Has something happened to Jacob and Jared?"

He sucked in air and let it out. "Can't…can't calm down. The snakes, the snakes are killing Jacob and Jared."

Killing. That was the word she latched on to. "Where? Where!"

"Kresley," Blake said, his voice shaking. "Kresley is there, too."

Kresley. Her knees wobbled and Rinehart was suddenly behind her, steadying her. She cursed her weakness, but her recovery was fast—her adrenaline was over the top, blasting her with yet another rush. She was desperate for answers, and she found herself lightly shaking Blake—she'd never done *that* before. "Where Blake? Where!"

"The woods," he gasped out. "The woods at the other side of the building."

Rinehart grabbed Blake and turned him toward the woods. "Take us to the exact spot, Blake," he ordered. Blake obeyed instantly, launching into a run.

Suddenly Laura's hand was in Rinehart's, and they were in fast pursuit, the wind whipping against her face, fear beating at her mind.

She turned her face to the stars and did the only thing she knew to do. She prayed. *Please let them be okay.* A prayer she continued over and over across the parking lot, until finally Blake turned to them again. "Here!" he said, as they reached the edge of the woods. "We went in here."

And now, they had to go in, too.

Lucan called for backup, but couldn't wait for help. He'd let Carol and the twins out of his sight for all of three minutes, and trouble had spiraled out of control. Jacob and Jared were spread out on their backs in the middle of the clearing, unmoving, with moonlight streaming down on them as if they were some sort of sacrifices. Two long, silver snakes circled them. Suddenly, Kresley was there, too. The snakes whipped around, their focus now on her.

Lucan sprang into action, heart thundering in his

chest. He had to get to Kresley before the snake—no, two snakes, now—reached her. He tore through the clearing, jumped over one of the twins, desperate to get to Kresley before it was too late, more desperate than he'd ever felt in his life. And he was going to fail. One of the snakes was close, too damn close.

Kresley wasn't moving, either. "Run!" he screamed. But she didn't run.

As the snake approached, she stood her ground, and abruptly fire shot from her hands, lancing the skin of the snake. Lucan froze in his steps at the same moment that the snake screeched. A moment later, it disappeared into thin air. The second snake retreated, disappearing into the brush—out of sight, but not gone, Lucan was certain. Regardless, relief and wonder washed over Lucan. Kresley was safe and by her own brave doing. He'd known she could start fires; he had no idea she could call it up at will, or direct them like that.

"Jacob! Jared!" she yelled, stumbling toward them. "Are they okay? Are they okay?"

Uneasy about the remaining snake, Lucan pivoted around to check the area. Scanned. Pivoted again. Kresley screamed, a second before he brought her back into view. One of the snakes was flying through the air, in a way no ordinary snake could do; it struck her wrist before she could react. Lucan felt as if someone had ripped a knife through his gut, but that did nothing to delay his reaction. He tore through the space separating him from Kresley, lunging forward. His hands closed down on the slimy width of the snake, and, thankfully, it released Kresley and fell to the ground.

Kresley shot fire at it, sizzling Lucan's pant leg in the process. He quickly patted out the flames. The snake screeched and disappeared.

Barely able to breathe, he raced toward Kresley, who was pushing herself to a sitting position. "Are you okay?" he asked, kneeling by her side. His hands went to her face, to her wrist.

"Yes. I…your leg." She was patting his leg. "How bad is it?"

With his peripheral vision, Lucan saw Max and Des rush into the clearing, toward the twins. But he didn't care about them right now; he didn't care about his leg. He grabbed Kresley's wrist and stared down at it, blinked. Stared some more. She stopped patting his leg and gasped at the sight of her wrist. There was no blood, no bite marks. Just two small, connected circles that looked like a tattoo. She looked up at him. "That wasn't there before."

"Does it hurt?" he asked, a sick feeling in his stomach. If it were a simple wound, then their healer, Marisol, could have dealt with it, but this—this was the act of a Demon and something far more complicated. Something that reached between worlds.

She shook her head. "No, Lucan. I know this sounds insane, but there were two women here who turned into those snakes." She offered him a pleading look. "Please. I have to know you believe me. Blake saw, too. I'm not delirious."

He considered denial and quickly dismissed it. She was too smart for that and Blake too outspoken. "I saw them, too," he said. Relief washed over her features.

Before she could begin to ask the questions he saw floating in the depths of her green eyes, he forced himself to think calmly, though he felt wildly unbalanced. They had a lot of people to consider and a lot of potential panic to control. "I know this is scary, and you have been very brave today, Kresley. Amazingly so. I need you to keep doing that. Just keep the mark on your wrist quiet for now. I'd rather tell everyone when we know what it is and how to fix it."

"You're afraid I'm going to die," she said, searching his face. Her bottom lip quivered, but her chin was steady, strong.

"No," he said, and that was the truth. There were things worse than death, but he didn't say that. He touched her cheek. "You aren't going to die. I won't let you. Which means there is no reason to scare yourself or anyone else into thinking so."

He glanced up as Max approached. "Give me a minute," he said, pushing to his feet. He was praying the other Knight could reach someone, anyone, who could get him answers.

Because protecting Kresley had suddenly become everything to him.

Standing on the edge of the woods, Rinehart had a choice to make. Leave Laura alone and exposed, or take her into the woods with him where danger obviously lurked. Neither was a good option, but taking her with him seemed the worst of the two.

Decision made, he faced her, his hands going to her shoulders. The ominous darkness of the woods was only a few feet away; the well-lit parking lot allowed her to see the determination in his expression. "Stay with Blake." He released her, already on the move.

"Not a chance," she said between her teeth, and started for the woods. He shackled her wrist, not as shocked at her actions as he was frustrated.

"Stay here!" he blasted back at her. "I'm trying to keep you safe, Laura. Help me."

"I can't," she yelled. "I can't stand here and pray they're okay when I could be helping."

The sounds of movement in the woods drew their attention, and Rinehart instinctively moved to shield Laura. But before he could, Lucan called out. "Everyone is fine!"

Laura heaved out a sigh of relief. "Oh, thank you." She looked skyward. "Thank you, Lord."

Slowly, the light illuminated Lucan and Kresley. The twins followed, with Max and Des framing their positions. Rinehart released Laura as she darted toward her patients, Blake on her heels. His Knights converged with him and the exchange of information began.

The next few minutes passed quickly, filled with action from all directions. The relief Rinehart had felt as he'd seen Lucan lead Kresley and the others out of the woods faded as Lucan explained what had happened.

As soon as Rinehart had processed the details, he tracked down Rock and sent him and Des to scout the woods for signs of Carol and the snake Demons. Max had immediately gone to contact Jag, and try to find out something about the snakes.

Rinehart hovered protectively near Laura as she

listened to everyone relay their stories. Lucan was by his side, both of them impatiently waiting for Max's return with some answers. Kresley, Blake and the twins were all sitting down beneath a tree not far from the parking lot; Laura was in the middle of them all, working to calm everyone down. With Carol missing and the snake attacks, there was a lot of fear over her fate and a lot of effort to make logical events that seemed illogical.

"All I remember is hooking up with Carol to go to some club she'd convinced us to go to," Jacob said, having the sense to look guilty over the choice. "She said she'd been sneaking out for months now, and we wouldn't get caught. She convinced us to go, too."

"Convinced *me*," Jared confessed. "I convinced Jacob. I should never have talked him into going out." He cast Laura an apologetic look. "I know your rules."

"We can't go back in time," Laura said. "Focus on remembering what happened to Carol."

"She's still out there," Blake said. "She has to be."

"The last thing I remember is being in the parking lot when Carol showed up," Jacob said.

"With her two hot friends," Jared added.

"She went to the woods, too," Blake volunteered, shivering from his fever despite the muggy night.

"I saw her, too," Kresley said, leaning against the tree for support.

Max approached from their right. Rinehart and Lucan met him several feet from the group so they could talk freely. "Anything?" Rinehart asked, hoping for some news.

"Jag and the rest of the team back at the ranch are researching snake Demons," he reported. "But no one knew anything off the top of his head."

"We need to know before extraction," Lucan insisted.

"I'm sure answers will be forthcoming," Max assured him. "But we have to move forward. We can't wait."

"I recognize that," Lucan snapped. "But we need to look at the potential backlash from what happened back there. What if this is some sort of ticking bomb meant to ensure they can't leave the island?"

Max snorted. "You think her head is going to turn in circles and explode if she gets too far from the island. I don't think so."

Lucan lunged at Max, who sidestepped him. "Whoa," Max said, hands up protectively. "It was a joke."

Before things could get out of control, Rinehart stepped in front of Lucan, his hands going to Lucan's chest. He kept his voice low. "Easy, man. Easy." Lucan inhaled slowly, and Rinehart's gaze went to Laura, whose concern was etched on her face. He inclined his chin to tell her everything was okay, and then immediately spoke to Lucan. "I don't know what is up with you, but it's not helping us or Kresley."

Lucan eased back a step and focused on Max. "What if the mark allows her to be tracked?" he suggested, the easy quality of his voice suggesting their confrontation hadn't happened, the fury still livid in his eyes saying otherwise.

Insurance, Rinehart thought, remembering Walch saying that word. He replayed the conversation. "Walch planned to use the patients against Laura in a meeting tomorrow morning. This has to be part of his plan."

Max held nothing back, unfazed by Lucan's attack, speaking his mind. "Which means we need to face facts here. I don't care if that mark simply tracks her location or eventually turns her into a Demon, she has to be considered a risk to the others. Secluded with precautions taken, before we decide to take her to the ranch. We don't want an army of those snake Demons led right to us."

"I agree she has to be kept separated," Lucan agreed. "But we can't be sure the others weren't marked in some way, too. Just because it's not obvious, doesn't mean it's not the case. Any one of them could be a danger to everyone at the ranch. They all had some form of contact with the snakes."

Rinehart listened to the grim exchange as it whittled away at their options. "Okay. Here's the deal. We can't risk whatever happened to Kresley happening to anyone else, but we can't assume it hasn't already. So orbing them out without knowing where the hell we are taking them isn't an option. Furthermore, we have to assume that if they haven't already been marked in some way, the Demons will be back for them. So they can't be here when the Demons come for them."

"Stay the line until extraction and keep everyone inside, well guarded," Lucan argued. "Have Laura go to that meeting tomorrow morning and find out what he did to Kresley."

Was he nuts? "You evidently have forgotten how dangerous Laura could be in enemy hands. Obviously, whatever was planned tonight didn't go as expected. We have no idea how they will respond to that. None."

"He's right," Max said. "We have to move and we have to move tonight. Get these people into hiding."

"You're forgetting something critical here," Lucan reminded them. "These kids can't travel without medication in hand."

Rinehart digested that piece of reality as comfortably as a blade in his gut. "Okay." He scrubbed his jaw. Scrubbed it again. Thinking. "Let's detail the obstacles, because it's a hell of a list. First off, the patients have to be told what is going on and accept our help. If anyone resists leaving, we've got that to deal with on top of everything else."

"Blake doesn't trust us," Lucan said. "He could be an issue."

"He's scared shitless over what happened in the woods," Max countered. "He'll go if Laura says to go."

"Agreed," Rinehart said. Blake was darn near shaking in his shoes just talking about those snakes. "Next hurdle. We can't allow Laura's research to fall into the wrong hands. The records have to be destroyed. Something Laura and I will deal with, while I get the medication needed for the patients." He glanced at Lucan. "They had their injections today?"

"All but Carol," Lucan confirmed. They all knew Carol was a lost cause. Convincing Laura to leave without her was going to be another nightmare—something Rinehart would contemplate later.

Rinehart continued, "We'll retain our original extraction time and split up into the separate shelters that we set up, then converge at the extraction point." He was damn thankful they'd prepared, scouting out possible escape locations. "That way if some of us are captured, everyone won't be lost." Again he spoke directly to Lucan, knowing he'd studied Laura's work intently. "How long can they go without the shots?"

"They've never gone more than twenty-four hours." He glanced at his watch. "Extraction time is six hours beyond that." He got out the next words with effort. "Kresley is the only one who is a true risk to others without the medication. Another reason to keep her separated. I'll take responsibility for her."

"I'll get your back," Max offered, and grinned. "That way if you wanna fight again, I'll be handy. Besides, I have the most direct line to communication. The faster we get answers, the faster we can undo whatever they did to her."

Anger slid from Lucan's eyes, but Rinehart continued before he could respond. "I'll take Laura to collect the medication. The twins can go with Des and Rock."

"Check," Max said. "And I'll contact Jag and update the other Knights."

Which meant the ball was in Rinehart's court. His gaze shifted to Laura. "I'll have her talk to her patients."

She seemed to sense what was coming; her gaze lifted to his, their eyes colliding in a turbulent connection of pain and dread. He'd never felt anything like what he felt with her, the preciseness of shared emotions, the depth of instant understanding between them.

Laura spoke to Kresley and then pushed to her feet,

her eyes holding his as she walked toward him. Lucan and Max faded away, leaving him to tell Laura that a journey was beginning. But to get to the end, they might just have to climb through hell.

Laura thought she had digested the information about the mark on Kresley's wrist with remarkable calm. The scientist in her, the person of reason and hard facts, said Demon snakes didn't exist. That whatever had attacked Kresley and left that mark had been a military creation, perhaps a device to insert tracking chips. But the darkness she felt on this island, the danger, spoke of more than a military operation gone south. It spoke of evil beyond that of man's making.

With Rinehart by her side, his silent strength flowing into her, Laura had delivered the speech about their situation to her kids, after having practiced the words a million times in her mind. They were in danger. Someone wanted to misuse their abilities. Rinehart and his men had come to take them to safety. It was a reality they lived with every day of their lives, a reality she'd prepared them for and had hoped would never come. But it had. That day was today.

Laura hugged the twins goodbye. Then Blake. "I want to stay with you," he argued, struggling with being sent away.

"You can't," she said, noting the flush of his cheeks. She hugged Blake again and said a few more words to him before turning away in search of Kresley.

The minute they looked at each other, Laura's promise to herself about not crying faded. She pulled Kresley into her arms. "Be safe."

Lucan stood over her shoulder, and Laura pinned him in a stare. "Take care of her, damn it."

"She's safe with me, Laura," he said, the intensity of his vow a surprisingly welcome comfort.

Emotion lodged in her chest, and Laura couldn't find her voice. Rinehart's hand touched her back. "We should go." He spoke with gentle urgency, and she nodded. With one last long hug, she turned away from Kresley.

Not looking back was the hard part.

Chapter 17

How she had acted calmly as she hugged Kresley goodbye, Laura didn't know. Perhaps it had been the absoluteness she'd felt in Lucan's promise to protect Kresley. Or perhaps it was the man now walking by her side across the parking lot toward the lab—Rinehart. The quiet strength he offered had done more for her than a million words. He'd been there by her side as she talked the kids through their fears, helping her stay strong for them.

They paused at the bottom of the stairs. "You're sure Walch doesn't know anything is wrong yet?" Rinehart asked. She looked at the building and reached out to it, feeling the life within it, the emotions.

"I'm sure," she said bringing Rinehart back into focus.

"All right then," he said. "We'll get in and get out, and leave this place behind forever."

"Just walk in like nothing is wrong," she said, reminding herself of his instructions.

"That's right," he said, his hand brushing her lower back as he urged her to start making their way inside. "Simple as baking a cake."

She laughed. "Since I've never baked a cake in my life, that's not the best comparison."

"Really?" he asked. "Never?"

"What?" she challenged. "I'm a woman, so you think I have to bake?"

"Never known a woman that baked," he said. "I was hoping you might be the first."

Unbelievably, she was laughing as he held the door open for her. A good thing considering that two soldiers exited at the same time. She punched the elevator button. "Sorry to disappoint you."

"You are many things," he said softly. "But a disappointment is not one of them."

Warmth climbed through her body as she allowed herself to fall into the depths of his eyes, melting into a place where the danger of their present circumstances didn't seem to exist. Why that was, how he delivered her there, she didn't know. Nor was it relevant. It simply helped—he helped.

The elevator dinged, the sound of reality calling her back into action. Together they faced forward and stepped inside. Together they hoped and prayed it wouldn't be the last ride of their lives.

Thirty minutes later, Laura pulled the flash drive from her computer and slipped the drive's lanyard around her neck, tucking it beneath her dress. And then, heart racing, she punched the key to destroy all remaining data on the computer.

It was done. The only documented record of her work was hanging around her neck. Legs more than a little wobbly, she pushed to her feet and grabbed the bag on her desk. Rinehart sat a few feet away at the lab table, pretending to look at samples under a microscope. He looked up from what he was doing and smiled. "Do I finally get you to myself now?" he asked, referring to the facade of a dinner date they'd started talking about in the elevator for anyone who might be watching on the monitors.

"I feel guilty for leaving," she said, playing along. "You're sure Lucan can look in on the patients?"

"Absolutely," he promised, stretching languidly as he rose—the facade of being in no rush whatsoever. But he *was* in a rush. Laura could feel the urgency beating at him, pressing him to grab her and run. They both knew that at any moment, Walch could discover her patients weren't even in the building. He studied her a moment, his hot inspection sliding down her body with such precision, she was almost certain he wasn't in a hurry after all. His attention lingered on her feet and lifted to her face. "Let's stop by your room and get you into something a little more comfortable."

Translation—shoes she could run in without injury. Check. She was eager to get out of here, but equally as eager to survive. A thought that had her anxiety spiking, as she remembered the menace she'd sensed in those woods. She'd just sent her patients, the closest thing she had to family, out into those very same woods. The woods that she and Rinehart were about to travel, as well. The only safe place seemed to be no place at all.

Walch walked into his apartment to find Carol sitting at the head of his dining table, a wineglass in her hand. With supreme effort he shut the door with an easy, unaffected nudge, restraining the anger that the audacity of her actions created. He'd *made* her; her soul had been claimed by him.

"So glad you're home, darling," she purred, as if she were his woman, as if she belonged anywhere but beneath him in bed.

He took a step toward her, his gaze brushing her throat, his hand touching the knot of his tie. He loosened it, and contemplated wrapping it around her neck and torturing her. But then, she was the pet to Lithe and Litha, and facing them again gave him pause.

"I take it by your presence that you've completed your duty?" Another step and he hesitated, sniffed. The air was filled with the scent of fear instead of the arrogance she'd acquired from the guardians. She was without their protection. This realization would have pleased him if not for the formidable message that scent disclosed. Something had gone wrong and he would pay the price, not her.

Her response came slowly, her actions proof she was in avoidance mode. She sipped her wine and painted on a smile. Her lips quivered. "I can't wait to see Laura panic over her darling Kresley's meltdown."

Skeptical in light of her nervousness, he pressed her. "So then, Kresley has been marked?"

"Oh, yes," she confirmed, perking up with pleasure lighting the evil in her soulless eyes.

"And the others?" he asked, closing the distance between them, one slow step at a time. "What of them?"

Her chin lifted with uneasy defiance. "Why are they necessary?" she challenged. "Kresley is the only one Laura truly cares about. If you have her, you have Laura. If you have Laura, they will all follow."

"You fool!" Walch blasted. "They will run."

He charged across the room to the kitchen and turned on the monitors while already dialing his phone. "Lock down the building," he said, flipping through the channels. In a matter of seconds he quickly verified that the patients were absent from their rooms. He dialed the phone again, gave orders to hunt down Laura and Rinehart and everyone associated with the two of them, and bring them to him.

"You're upset over nothing," Carol said from behind him.

Rage shifted him from man to Beast as he whirled around to find her in the doorway. "Do not think Tezi will not hear of this. And do not think I will not ensure he knows it is the guardians that failed."

Her eyes suddenly flashed with anger; whatever fear she had been harboring slipped away. "You do not want the guardians as enemies any more than you want Tezi as one." She hissed the threat, standing taller now, confident again. "As for the patients, in case you forget, this is an island. If they were stupid enough to run, they cannot go far. We will find them through Kresley's mark."

Walch knew the empty rooms confirmed they had,

indeed, run. "Then do it," he challenged, thinking of the human survival instinct. He'd once seen a man cut off his own leg to save his life. Leaving behind medication was nothing in comparison. "Call Lithe and Litha to you. Have them find Kresley."

Her bravado melted instantly, and he realized that the source of her fear came back to this moment. "Lithe and Litha were forced to go underground to replenish. Lithe was injured while marking Kresley."

Interesting. So fire was the weapon to use against the guardians. Stupid woman was full of useful information. He schooled his face into a blank expression. "What of Litha?"

"They function as two parts of one existence."

"So they can do nothing to aid our efforts," he said flatly, his mind processing.

"They can," she insisted.

"When?"

She swallowed hard. "Soon."

He turned away from her, processing, planning. The guardians were manipulative. They offered him aid, but he knew it was all part of the game they played. They'd help him if they received a favor in return, but only if it cost them nothing with Tezi. And soon, they would all face Tezi, and someone would fall. That someone would not be him.

He turned back to Carol. "If you want to live," he said, "come with me."

Rinehart wasn't sure which one of them reacted first, but as he and Laura stepped out of the building, warnings rushed though his head, and his nerves tingled with the threat of Beasts ready to attack. One quick look at Laura confirmed she felt it, too. In silent agreement, they launched into a run, down the stairs, only a second before shouts came from behind them.

Soldiers charged at them from the left and right, at least five or six from each direction. "Damn!" he yelled, with no option but to keep running. He had no weapons, and hand-to-hand with Laura to protect wasn't going to work.

"Over here!"

Rinehart looked up at the same moment that Des tossed him a sheathed sword and Max stepped from the woods, already matching blades with another Beast. With a fast cut of his blade, Max beheaded a Beast. The head fell to the ground. A second later, the Beast burst into flames.

Laura gasped, but Rinehart didn't have time to respond, rotating to catch the weapon Des had thrown his way—and not a second too soon, as a Beast charged at him, a sword in hand.

Rinehart shoved Laura behind him as Rock and Des fell into a line with him, creating a wall protecting Laura from the ongoing attacks. He could only pray no one came from behind. "You aren't supposed to be here," he yelled at Des, who stood to his left.

Des sliced his blade through the air in an attempt to disarm one of his attackers, casting Rinehart a sideways grin as his efforts paid off. "You thought you could have a party and not invite me?" He ripped his blade through the air and took the Beast's head.

"He had another vision," Rock said, from the right.

As even more Beasts charged their way, Rinehart wasn't complaining about the help.

"Want to tell me what happens next?" he asked Des.

"Nothing you're gonna like," Des said. "So just keep on fighting."

Stunned by what she had just seen, Laura found herself shoved behind Rinehart and two of his men. She was living a nightmare in some sort of alternate universe. There was no other explanation for saber-toothed monsters and chopped-off heads that turned to fire and ash.

But the evil was all around her, oozing from all directions, seeping into her pores, through her mind, into her senses—screaming with how very real this was. Fight. She had to fight the monsters. No one was coming at them from behind, so she whirled around to face forward, then sidestepped to get a good view. Her heart raced like a pounding drum, chased a rhythm straight to her throat. She was out of practice, afraid she would fail. She watched as one of the creatures cut Rinehart's arm, and she gasped; fear for his safety driving her to act. Her hand lifted and sliced through the air. The attacker's weapon flew to the ground.

Relief over Rinehart's safety filled her with the will to continue.

Five more Beasts were charging in their direction. Laura raised her hand again. Their weapons ripped from their hands. Confidence filled her.

"Laura!" Rinehart yelled in warning, as an attacker charged at her, obviously trying to take her captive rather than killing her. She whipped her hand in his direction, and imagined a great force. He flew through the air and hit a tree. The Beasts began to retreat.

Rinehart grabbed her arm. "Let's go."

She glanced up at him for only a moment, but still saw the shock in his expression at all she had done, felt it in the others—Des, Rock and Max.

Laura prepared to run, stilled by the familiar voice that lashed through the air.

"Laura!"

"Carol," Laura whispered, turning to see her approaching. Walch was by her side and he looked human, but the two soldiers with them were beastly and horrid, like the soldiers Rinehart and his men had killed. One side of their face was human, the other, animal, each with a huge eye and ragged features. Fangs snarled over their lips. Laura couldn't look at them, didn't want to. Instead, she focused on Carol—her patient, her friend, part of her family—trying to find something human beneath the taint. Her eyes were darker, her skin whiter. Clothes tighter, more revealing. Hair, wild.

"This isn't the Carol you once knew," Rinehart warned her, eyeing the speed at which Carol and the others approached. "We have to go while we can."

"I know," Laura said, not taking her eyes off of Carol, noting the two long blades in her hands. "But I have to try and find her again." Somewhere inside of this Carol was the gentle woman Laura had once known.

"You can't. Think of the others. Think of the research in our possession that is at risk."

Carol stopped abruptly, and, to Laura's horror, the

blades the other woman held flew through the air, not thrown by her hands but launched with her mental abilities. The steel rocketed toward Des and Max.

Laura raised her hands, and the blades fell to the ground. There was a moment of shocked silence, all eyes on Laura. The hatred in Carol's eyes sent chills down Laura's spine. Walch shoved Carol behind him, as if he feared Laura would connect with her.

"If you think your grand abilities surprise or frighten me," he drawled, "they don't. I've always known you were more capable than any of your subjects." He eyed Rinehart. "I know who you are now. I've heard stories of the Knights with their grand swords. But hear this, Knight. Know this." Anger lashed through his words. "You picked the wrong enemy. Your deceit has done nothing but seal my will to see every one of your kind destroyed."

"You opened the door and invited me in, Walch," Rinehart said. "Made my job easy." He smiled. "Face it. You screwed up and the consequences are coming." He pointed his blade at the ground. "Why don't you drop to your knees and give me your head. Spare yourself the torture headed your way."

Laura watched in horror as Walch's face shifted, as he became a Beast, his big, red eye fixed on her. "You will bring everyone back to me."

"No," she said, shaking her head. "Never."

"We've marked them," he said. "We own them now."

"Only Kresley bears a mark," Rinehart countered.

Walch arched a brow. "Are you sure? Are you one hundred percent sure it's only Kresley?"

"He's lying," Laura said, sensing the lies within him. "I can tell you are lying. Only Kresley is marked."

He narrowed his eyes on Laura for a mere moment and then he waved a dismissive hand. "More important, here is the power those marks bestow upon me. They allow me to order her a fate far worse than death. Hallucinations that will make her go insane. Think of this, my dear *doctor*. Your patient, little Kresley, in the corner, screaming because she thinks snakes are crawling all over her. That is what awaits your little darling. And only I can stop it. Only I can remove the marks."

Laura felt the sting of tears; the fear for those she cared about, almost more than she could bear. "Take me instead," she said, taking a step forward. "I can be everything you need."

Rinehart's hand was instantly on her arm, pulling her back. "No," he spit out. "No."

She looked up at him, the darkness of his expression something she'd never seen in him. There was anger, pain, fierce determination. He would fight her, but she would fight hard. "I have to. I cannot let the others suffer for me."

"You will not do this," he said, his grip tightening on her arm as he faced Walch. "She doesn't have the ability to clone these people anyway, Walch. None of us do. We never did."

"Since she has used herself to create control in the others, she can figure it out," Walch snarled, and fixed his attention on Laura. "You probably already know how."

Instant denial came to Laura. "I don't! It could take

years to discover, but I'll try. Free everyone but me. I'll stay and I will find a way to do it. You can clone my abilities."

"Oh, you *are* staying," he said, and motioned to Rinehart. "And he can bring back the others. You will both work faster with incentives."

"They won't come back without Laura's influence," Rinehart said. "She has to come with us. Send Carol to watch over us."

Walch laughed. "You'd like that, wouldn't you? A chance to save her, too? Not possible, and that's a no anyway. Laura stays."

"Take me in her place," Rock said, stepping forward; he dropped his weapons at his feet.

"No," Laura said. "No." She looked at Rinehart. "No one else sacrifices for me."

"I've told you, Laura," he said, his voice low, pain lancing his words. "You are dangerous in their hands. You cannot go with them."

"I would never do anything to hurt anyone," she rasped back. "This is my responsibility. I have to stay. I have to make this all right."

Walch smiled. "A Knight of White in my possession. I quite like that. Yes. It serves me well." He motioned to his soldiers. "Take him."

Two Beasts charged forward and shackled Rock. Dampness clung to Laura's cheeks as she watched them take him away. He'd given himself up for people he didn't even know. Sacrificed himself. It wasn't right.

"You have twelve hours," Walch said.

"Can't do it," Rinehart said. "We cut off communications with the rest of the group until our ride gets here. That's seventy-two hours from now."

Walch growled, anger raging off of him. "I will not wait three days. You have one."

"Three days," Rinehart said, leading Walch astray from the true plan. "And then we trade. The patients for Rock."

Walch seethed. "It behooves you to get her sooner than later. Every second he is here will be painful. A moment over three days and he is dead." With that, he turned on his heels and stormed away.

Carol reappeared as the line of Beasts disappeared. She stayed her position long enough to glare at Laura, hatred shining in her eyes for several moments before she followed Walch and the soldiers in their departure.

Laura wanted to scream, to run after Rock, to demand Rinehart make this right. "It should have been me," she said. "Walch needs me. He wouldn't have hurt me. Get him back." She grabbed his arm. "Please."

Rinehart's expression was grim. "I'll come back for him when everyone else is off this island."

"No," she said. Then stronger, "No. I *have* to bring Kresley back and make them undo whatever they did to her."

He strapped the sword onto his belt with some sort of leather strap Des tossed him, his tone cool, calm. Expression almost cold. "You're not thinking straight right now. You're emotional and upset. Walch will not help Kresley. He'll turn her into one of them. Just like he will you."

"What of the torture he promised Kresley?" she demanded. "What of that?"

His eyes flashed with anger. "Kresley has all of us to help her and we will find a way to free her. Rock is on his own in there, and he, too, has been promised torture."

She regretted the words once spoken, more so after hearing his response. Rock was his friend, his family. "I'm sorry." And he was right, she was emotional. Out-of-character emotional. Her common logic gone, eaten alive by panic and fear. "I'm sorry," she repeated.

He didn't respond, abruptly cutting his gaze away from her and speaking to Des. "This was your vision. Rock knew he was going to do that when he came here."

He nodded. "Yes. We knew it was one of us or Laura. He is without a mate. He insisted it be him."

Laura listened to the exchange without under-standing the talk of vision any more than she understood how man could become Beast. Nor did she dare ask. She'd hurt him. She didn't want to hurt him. She didn't want to hurt anyone. So why did it keep happening?

Chapter 18

Standing outside a flaming fire ring, Tezi watched the two Beasts inside it battle to the death. Both were seasoned soldiers who'd survived centuries of immortality. Both wanted their place in the Dark Knights. The one who lived could have that spot, and their first duty would be killing Walch.

Tezi had received the news of Walch's failures only hours before. The guardians had faced the Knights of White, men known to Carol as Walch's hired researchers, in battle. The idiot had invited *Knights* into his operation, offered himself and their plans up as prizes.

The guardians had fled when Tezi's anger had erupted; they were hiding in the Underworld until he regained a semblance of tolerance. Since then, Tezi had killed dozens of Beasts, enraged by the decision he had to make: to cut his losses, take what he could from the island and move on. Build his army one by one. Seek out those with gifts and convert them. Use the best of the Beasts until they could be replaced.

But in the end, one simple truth prevailed. Tezi would not be stopped.

A warming sensation on his wrists disengaged his interest in the battle; his bracelets were returning to arms, with a plea from the guardians to be heard whispered in the air.

"Show yourselves," he demanded of the guardians.

They appeared at his feet, bowing down to him. He was their master, their leader; Adrian had given them to him, and they were indebted to Adrian for some unknown reason that mattered not to him. All he cared about was how they served his purpose. And their purpose had reached beyond simply marking the patients. They had been there to test Walch's loyalty, to report his actions, which they had done well.

"What say you?" he asked, allowing them to rise with a motion of his hands.

"All is not lost, Tezi," Litha said, rising to her feet.

Lithe took a position next to Litha. "The firestarter was marked. We can track her, and she can be yours. And where she goes, so does the doctor. The doctor is said to be brilliant. She could be useful, as well. We can still make them yours."

"Would this please you, master?" Litha said.

One Dark Knight at a time. "Yes. It pleases me."

He turned to the scene behind him, snuffed the fire with the rush of his hand, instantly stilling the battle underway. "Both of you, come here." The two Beasts snarled at each other before obeying.

"There is one more thing," Lithe warned. "The twin boys. They are Healers, undiscovered. They must be slain."

Tezi arched a brow. "You are certain of this?"

"Certain," the guardians confirmed together. "We tasted their blood."

The blood of a Healer was deadly to a Demon. "Yet you survived?"

"They have not come into their full powers yet. Still, they weakened us," Lithe explained.

Litha was quick to add, "We barely had the magic to mark the firestarter."

"We were almost destroyed by her fire," Lithe said. "We must return to the Underworld to recover."

"How much time do you need?" Tezi demanded, impatient to get on with this.

"Not long," they said together.

"Already we feel the threads of Carol's mind again, but she is more tightly bound to us," Lithe reassured him. "Soon we will be able to reach for the firestarter, as well."

He turned to the two warrior Beasts and gave his orders. They were to go back in that ring and fight, but for more now than merely a place in his army. Whoever survived would lead his mission: hand Walch over to the guardians; kill the twins; convert the firestarter and the boy; and bring the doctor to him.

The guardians owned Walch now.

He waved his hands and willed them back to the Underworld. Satisfaction began to expand in his chest. All was definitely not lost.

They'd been walking a good hour.

Rinehart treaded a light path through the woods with Laura by his side; he cautiously avoided leaving a trail. But there was nothing light about his mood. She'd begged to go to Kresley's side, and he'd shut her down. He had nothing to say to her until they were in the shelter. Then, he'd have plenty to say. It was time she understood who and what he was. Time she understood there was more at stake than a facade of normalcy.

With his sharp denial of her requests, she had gone from apologetic over what had happened with Walch and Rock to angry, and it had happened in a snap of fingers. Well, welcome to his world. He was angry, too. Damn angry. He said the words in his head and let the roughness of them rasp through his chest, fill him up, drive him onward. Let it remind him why he couldn't comfort Laura, why now was the time to be tough. Comfort wouldn't keep her alive. A strong dose of reality just might, though.

He glanced at the sky, the natural light fading as clouds encroached on the stars. Darkness made him nervous and he didn't get nervous. But then, in all his long life, he had never had an assignment quite like this one—an assignment that could require him to destroy Laura before she could become a destroyer herself. Nor had he forgotten the malice they'd felt in these woods, thankful now that it had not surfaced again. The sound of a river indicated they were nearing their destination. He angled to the right, cut through the trees and found the waterside. Clouds scattered across the sky, brushing the stars, and then wiped out the moon. Instantly, the ground went pitch-black, a pit that seemed to swallow them.

Rinehart grabbed Laura's hand, steeling himself for the impact of her touch. With her soft palm against his, awareness jolted his body, but he shoved it aside, frustrated at his lack of control. He paced out the steps his men had mapped out until he found what he sought— an obscure rocky formation, its foliage overlay making it damn near impossible to find in the dark. Hopefully the daylight would leave it hidden, as well.

Stepping cautiously, he led Laura to the far right of the foliage and lifted. Sure enough, there was a hole, an opening to what should be shelter, with supplies waiting for them inside.

"Stay here while I make sure it's safe," he said to Laura, confident enough in her ability to protect herself to leave her for a few moments.

She clung to his hand. "Be careful." He couldn't see her face, but he felt her concern. Felt her like he shouldn't. Felt her damn emotions when he didn't want to. She was still angry, but also worried for his safety. His heart squeezed and he couldn't say why. He shoved aside the softness. Of course she was worried, he reasoned. This wasn't about him. Laura worried about everyone. She probably worried about that Demon bastard Walch. That bit him in the backside, and he yanked his hand from hers.

"Stay alert," he warned.

He inched behind the wall of vines and squatted down, unable to stand to full height in the small space. Taking a moment to ensure he sensed no danger, he crawled to the back of the space and felt around for another rock formation, finding it and reaching behind it. Sure enough, a stash of supplies, compliments of his men. First things first: the lantern. He turned it on low, to offer them just enough light to function, fearful more would be visible to someone passing. A quick survey showed rock and dirt and not much more. No hidden dangers.

Crawling back to the entrance, he motioned Laura forward. "I don't believe you have a lantern," she said, sliding past the entrance.

He didn't speak. He was fuming, madder now than before. He unrolled a sleeping bag, the only one they had. She could have it. He'd sleep on the ground. Wouldn't be the first time, wouldn't be the last. That is, unless he died. The way things were going, that seemed to be an upcoming event. Laura would resent him if they mated, if he stole her opportunity to fit in with the rest of the world. He couldn't spend eternity seeing that in her eyes. Couldn't believe that was what was in his destiny. Death would be a better choice. Dying in battle, dying fighting, just as he'd lived fighting.

He patted the bag and she sat down. He took a spot directly across from her and reached into the supply bag, retrieving a bottle of water, offering it to her.

"Thank you," she said, accepting it. But she didn't

open it. She sat there, staring at him, as if she knew he wanted to say something.

"Say what you want to say to me so we can put it behind us."

Right to the point. Good. He wanted to get right to it himself. "You have to stop hiding. Stand up and fight like you did back there with Walch."

The water was disposed of instantly, her response whipping back at him. "Hiding? I have never hidden from anything."

"You've spent your entire life hiding your abilities, and that's what you are teaching your patients to do, too."

Even in the dim light, he could see the flush of her cheeks. "I am teaching them to protect themselves."

"There are better ways."

"So easy for you to say," she said. "You don't have to fear being a lab rat. Or to have your own family act as if you are a freak to be hidden away."

"Yet you teach them to hide."

She threw her hands up in the air. "What are they to do? What? Maybe they should be circus acts." A frustrated sound slipped from her lips. "What's wrong with wanting a normal life?"

"Normal is relative, Laura. What is normal for a professional ballplayer is not normal for a stockbroker on Wall Street. The only normal we get is our own normal. Our destiny, our place in this world. What we choose to do with that is up to us."

"I don't know what you want from me here," she said, confusion and frustration in her voice. "What would you have me do?"

For all the turmoil he'd been through, he knew who he was and what he was supposed to do. He was supposed to fight for those who couldn't. He'd questioned that once in his life over a woman. He didn't question it now. In fact, it drove him onward. "You tell your kids that their abilities are gifts, but you see your own as a curse. They feel that, Laura." She glared at him and then abruptly cut her gaze away, pulling her legs to her chest and hugging them. He pressed onward—he had to. "Giving them control was something I believe you were meant to do. Just as I believe all of you are meant to use your gifts for a greater purpose."

She turned back around. "To fight. To become soldiers. That's what you want from us, isn't it? That's why you came here."

Damn it. He ground his teeth. She wasn't listening, and he had to make her. There was no time for words, or secrets. "I came here because I was ordered to save you or destroy you. I choose to save you and I am begging you, Laura—*Let me save you.*"

She rotated to her knees, facing him, with her attack lashing through in her words. "Save me to be some sort of soldier? No! I can't be that. I won't."

"War isn't always about death. It's about life."

"I'm a doctor. I heal people. Yet you tell me what you want from me is necessary and right. Bloodshed is not right. War is never about life."

"You're wrong."

"Of course. What else would my would-be executioner say? Kill me now. Get it over with. I will not join anyone's army."

"Damn it, Laura. I am not suggesting you throw on some armor and go to war. This isn't about staying off the radar anymore. You're on it and that won't change. The Beasts will keep coming. They will never stop. Either fight or run. You have to choose."

"Only a military man would call avoiding a war running away."

He drew a calming breath that didn't work. "It's time for a wake-up call, Laura. No one can see what you saw out there today and not know the truth. You're in denial and I don't know why. You are hunted. Your patients are hunted. Not by men. Not by a cult. By Demons. Those snakes—Demons. Walch—human turned Demon, which is what they plan to do to you. You will become one of them, and you won't even care. They'll rip your soul out and leave you with nothing but evil. You don't hide from the Underworld. They will find you."

Driven by emotion, he acted, not willing to hear her argue, not willing to hear her blasted illogical logic. He drew her into his arms and stared down at her. "I won't let them have you." He laced his fingers through her hair. "I won't." Rinehart kissed her then, a wild, passionate kiss. A kiss that freed his Beast. She could choose to run, she could choose to hide. But when he was done, they would never turn her into a Beast.

Primal instinct poured through his veins as Rinehart drank of Laura with long strokes of his tongue, kissing her with insatiable passion, his hands possessively branding her body. He'd unleashed the Beast within him, told himself it was okay, told himself that she was his to claim this night. That taking her wasn't selfish, that claiming her was her salvation rather than his own. And she gave herself to him, her anger not forgotten, not at all—simply redirected into passion.

They were naked, intimately entwined. He hardly remembered undressing, though he would never forget the way her hand stroked the hard edge of his erection through his jeans, or the soft way she had said his name—a plea for more, a promise of pleasure.

They faced one another, his thick erection pressed between her shapely legs, nuzzled inside the core of her body. He wanted to melt into her, become one with her. He'd never needed like this, never wanted anything as much, and he wondered at how the simple touch of her hands on his face, his neck, his chest, could affect him in such an intensely provocative way. Wondered how a kiss was not simply a kiss: passionate kisses, hungry kisses that drove his hunger. Her sweet moans filling his mouth as his fingers lingered on the sweet ripe peaks of her breasts.

Somehow, Rinehart held back, waited until they burned with need. Then and only then, with their lips a breath apart, did he press past the silky folds of her body, easing her on top of him, the hard ground his to bear. Her hips widened over his, taking him fully, impaling herself on his length. He shoved aside the silky mass of her hair and pulled her lips to his, kissing her. His woman. His mate.

"Rinehart," she whispered, her body hungrily clinging to his, her stomach aligned with his, her breasts flush with his chest. Her hips swaying, stroking him with erotic friction.

His hand slid down her back, pressing her closer, molding them into one, the depth of his need beginning to shift, darken. Demand formed deep in his groin, expanding through his body, to his chest. Unfamiliar need that reached into his soul. He thrust into her, thrust again. He pressed her hips into his, lunged upward. Harder. Faster. He had. To. Have. More.

They were panting now, their movements, their touches, taking on a desperate quality, two people trying to become one. A frenzy of wanting until her body clamped down on his cock with wild demand. Instantly, his gums tingled, ached. The moment of truth had arrived. A moment that came only one time for a Knight—the one time his teeth elongated, and that was to claim his mate.

Guilt flashed in his mind as he pumped into her body, driving toward her satisfaction. Regret over how this had to happen, over claiming Laura without consent. Feelings he swiftly shoved aside. He'd made his decision, chosen his path. Lost himself in the warm, wet heat of her as he replayed Jag's words in his head. Keep her out of the Beasts' hands *at all costs.* Jag had never meant death; Rinehart knew that now. He had meant this, claiming her. Taking away her susceptibility to the enemy.

Laura might hate him for stealing her will, her choice, would most likely resent him, but she would never become a Beast.

Yes! This was what they both needed. He pumped

into her, kissing her, touching her, driving them both over the edge. Burying himself inside her body as his soul reached out to hers.

Laura arched into him with a gasp of pleasure, her body tensing for a moment before the spasm clamped down on him, pulling him deep into her release. Rinehart was shaking with need when he rolled her onto her back without fully giving her his weight. Pumping into her one last time as he exploded, shuddering with release. His cuspids extended and he didn't hesitate, didn't give himself time for second guesses. He buried his face in her neck and sunk his teeth into her shoulder.

Her fingers dug into his arms, and she cried out, not in pain, but in pleasure, her body clenching around his as she once again found release. Wildly, their bodies quivering together, and he could feel the connection of souls. Slowly, they eased into each other, their bodies calming, sated.

He heaved a breath as he released her shoulder from his bite. But he couldn't let go, couldn't move away. Not yet. *Please, Lord, not yet.*

Chapter 19

Overwhelmed, Laura lay beneath Rinehart. His emotion, her emotion, it all pounded into her, fogging her brain. Something had happened between them. Something she didn't understand. Was she losing her mind? Had he bitten her? She swallowed hard. And she had liked it?

It was all so confusing. The male perfection of muscle pressed close, only serving to make matters worse, reminding her of the pleasure he'd given her. The connection she had felt in those incredible moments with him; the connection she felt now, and in truth had felt since the moment she had met him. "Rinehart?" she whispered, a question in her voice, a plea to understand what had just happened.

Slowly, he eased up onto his elbows and stared down

at her, his eyes telling the story she couldn't read in his emotions. Whatever had just happened held some sort of consequence she wasn't going to like. A consequence he had knowingly bestowed upon her. "What did you do?" she demanded, urgency growing inside her. She knew he wouldn't hurt her, but she could also sense his feeling that he knew better than her. That he could make choices on her behalf. Her hands tightened on his arms. "What did you do?"

Torment filtered into his face. "I had to protect you," he declared, his voice lowering into a hissed whisper. "I had to."

The raspy declaration rattled her, and suddenly Laura needed to be up. Already, passion had driven away her good sense, made her forget the argument they were having. She couldn't think molded to him, as if they were about to make love again.

Laura pushed at Rinehart and worked to scoot herself out from underneath him. Receiving no resistance, she found herself illogically disappointed.

Nevertheless, space had been the right choice; her mind was clearing with disturbing results. She grabbed his shirt, an easy solution to cover up, as he reached for his pants. Demons. They had been talking about Demons. Then they had made love and—her hand went to her shoulder, searching for a wound that wasn't there—erotic images of him biting her flooded her mind. Inwardly, she shook herself.

Her arms slid into the sleeves of his shirt, the tear on the right arm catching her attention. Her gaze riveted to his arm as he buttoned his jeans, to the injury she'd forgotten. Her mouth dropped open at what she saw. She closed the distance between them and grabbed his elbow, holding him steady to survey the gash on his bicep, and saw that it was nearly healed.

Laura touched it, her lashes slowly lifting. "I saw that cut. It needed stitches only hours ago."

He stared at her, his eyes half-veiled, his emotions a hard wall she struggled to bypass. "I heal quickly," he said. "And now, so will you."

"Explain," she said, acutely aware she had not buttoned his shirt, that her breasts were exposed. Somehow, he was sitting against the wall, and she was between his legs. Heat darted to her core, and she yanked her hand from his arm. Leaning back on her heels, Laura tugged the shirt together, crossing her arms protectively in front of her body. "Stop talking in circles. Stop telling me half of everything. We've had the 'Demon' talk. I get we are not dealing with normal here." She cringed at the choice of word and then defiantly added, "Not what I consider normal." She swallowed, not sure how to frame her question. Was he a Demon? Did she even want to know? "You're… What… You said you were like them—like the Beasts. Like them how?"

Laura didn't give him time to answer; her shoulder seemed to tingle as she thought of him biting her. Her hand shoved under the shirt to probe the wound that didn't exist. She shoved the garment off her shoulder, desperate to prove she wasn't insane, that he had bitten her. And there she found her proof. She gasped as she saw a marking, a star of some sort. Instantly, she thought of the snakes, of Walch, of the threats he'd made against Kresley. God, Kresley. Momentary fear for her twisted her stomach.

Her head was spinning as she fixed Rinehart in an accusing stare. "What did you do to me? What...what are you?"

He didn't react to her obvious emotional state, his demeanor cautious, his words seemingly chosen with care. "I am as I said, Laura," he replied. "A Hunter. A member of an elite group that fights for humanity, who were once victims of the Beasts ourselves, recruited by the leader of our group." Without warning, he moved, his knees to hers, their thighs aligned. The heat of his body flowed into hers, his hand branding her shoulder as the mark had. "It is my offer of protection. Something I can give to only one human in my life, and that human is you. No Demon will ever steal your soul now, Laura. They will not make you one of them."

He'd marked her and only her. An intimacy lingered in that confession that she didn't fully understand. On some level, though, she knew they were somehow linked. She had felt that from the moment they met.

Again that overwhelming rush of emotions washed over Laura. His. Hers. Desperately she searched his eyes, trying to confirm information that seemed unreal, seemed impossible, trying to understand. She searched his face, his emotions, and found his resolve to protect her, his unshakable commitment to her safety.

But she knew there was something he wasn't telling her. "There's a consequence that comes with the mark, isn't there? A reason you did it without asking me first."

His gaze shifted, his touch easing from her shoulder. They were close but not touching. "I am immortal, and thus you, too, are now immortal. You will not age, but neither can you suppress your abilities with science. Normal will never be what you wanted it to be."

Normal. A word that had defined so many of her actions in the past. She shoved away any reaction. He had more to say. She wanted to know everything, and she wanted to know *now.* "What else?"

His hands lifted as if he would touch her, then fell back to his sides. "We are bound together as mates now, our souls connected. If we were to separate, I have no way of knowing how it might affect us. There are only a few mated Knights, and each of them made the choice to come together."

"The other mates had a choice," she said flatly, realizing how much this bothered her. She was falling in love with Rinehart, she had no doubt of this. But now, no matter what happened, she feared she would never truly trust their bond. A bond that she realized was becoming exceedingly important to her. He was that missing thing in her life, the person she could confide in, the person who she didn't have to hide from. She needed that to be real. Could it ever feel real with this mark on her shoulder?

Fear, pain, hurt, all rallied inside her. She was saved from the Demons, but faced a life unknown. "Why didn't you talk to me? Why didn't you explain?"

"I tried, Laura, I—"

"Not hard enough. I've been bombarded with Demons and monsters and hell, right here on earth. I can barely stand the thought of what might be happening to Kresley right now. Rock is in danger because of me. How could I not feel confused? How could I not fight for the few things in my life that felt normal?"

He raised his hands as if to reach for her, and she shrank away from him. His expression tensed. "I was told to ensure you stayed out of the enemy's hands *at all costs*. I had to make a choice for us both. I had to choose your death or your immortality. I chose your immortality. I chose to claim my mate. I did this to save you, Laura. I need you to know that." His chest rose and he cut his gaze before turning back to her. "But you deserve to know you saved me, as well. When I was given my soul back, I retained the stain of the Beast. It was eating me alive. I was turning back into a Demon. It would have consumed me again, and not far down the road. My salvation was you, Laura. Only a mate can bind the Beast within the Knight. But I didn't mark you for me. You may decide that *is* the case, but it's simply not true. You still have a chance to build a decent life, to live among humans. That has never been my life, and it never will be." Conviction formed in his voice. "I would have walked away. You would never have known what was happening to me."

His voice rasped the words one last time. "I would have walked away."

If ever she was glad for the ability to sense emotion, it was in that moment. He meant those words. He really had been prepared to walk away. "I would have done it for you," she whispered. "I would have saved you without a moment of hesitation."

He shook his head forcefully. "No, you wouldn't have," he said. "I wouldn't have let you. Don't you see, Laura? I don't want you out of obligation. I want you because you want to be with me. I still do. We'll get through all of this, Laura, I promise you that. And we'll figure this out. We'll find out how to make it work. If you want happily-ever-after, I'll do my damndest to find it for you."

Her heart swelled. That sounded so unimportant right now. In fact, it sounded frivolous. People were dying. People were in danger. How could she turn her back and not do something about it? Pretend that Demons didn't exist? She slid into Rinehart's arms, thankful when he welcomed her, holding her close, his heart beneath her ear, his lips on her hair. "I don't even know what that is anymore," she whispered.

"I'll help you find it," he said. "I promise."

And she believed him.

Kresley was his mate.

Deep inside a large cavern well-hidden by a hollowed-out tree trunk, Lucan held her as she sobbed; he was terrified for her safety, praying an answer would be found to end the hours of hallucination that had tormented her. She was relatively calm at the moment, but it wouldn't last. It came in waves that seemed never-ending. Some were mild—but some were intense, powerful crashes.

Gazing down on her tear-streaked face, his chest tight, his need to comfort her immense, he knew in his heart of hearts she belonged to him and he to her. They had barely found each other, and already she was slipping away from him.

"I don't know what to do for her," Lucan said, eyeing Max, who sat on the floor a few feet away, edginess surrounding him. A sheathed saber sword lay across his lap. "I wish like hell I had a way to sedate her."

"I wish like hell we could, too," Max agreed, eyeing the eight-foot cavern door as he rotated the saber handle over and over. "For her and for us."

Max had made his concerns over being discovered more than vocal and Des had agreed. Which was exactly why Des had opted to take the twins on to a separate shelter. Rock's situation reeked of a chilling reality none of them wanted to think about. The chances that a Knight survived captivity with Beasts was unlikely.

Two silver-clad females shimmered into appearance just inside the entrance. Lucan's gut wrenched. "The snakes," he warned, forcefully setting a clinging Kresley aside as he snatched his sword and came to his feet.

"We've come for the girl," they said in unison.

"You've come for my sword," Lucan countered.

"And mine," Max added.

"Your swords will not stop her pain."

Kresley screamed behind him, and somehow he managed to remain as he was.

"We will find a way to remove your mark."

They smiled. "We are sure you will," one said.

"But will it be before she goes insane?" the other questioned.

Kresley screamed again and Lucan cringed visibly. The Demons smiled.

* * *

Kresley huddled against Lucan, screaming about the snakes on her face again. She needed help and Max had said "screw it" to the helicopter. If there was any chance their Healer could help Kresley they had to try and reach her and do so now. But an hour had passed and no Max. One more hour toward Kresley's unraveling.

And she was screaming in a way he knew meant those Demons were returning.

They shimmered into view, directly in front of where he sat against the wall, holding Kresley. With all his will, Lucan wanted to fight, but could not. He was afraid to let go of Kresley, afraid she would lose the last bit of sanity his touch seemed to offer her.

"Are you ready to give her to us?" the Demons asked, staring down at him with silvery eyes.

"I will not," Lucan said, and reached for his sword. "I will kill you both before you take her."

They laughed. "Your sword will not kill us."

"But releasing her might," one of them said.

Desperation formed inside him, a deep need to protect Kresley. She'd spoken of a purpose that day he'd given her the injection. Spoke without fear, with resolve. He believed deep in his soul that purpose was real. That something important awaited her. "Tell me what I can do to save her."

"You wish to negotiate for your mate?" they asked.

Kresley jerked in his arms, smacking at her arm as if to beat off another snake. "Yes," he hissed. "I wish to negotiate."

"Will you trade yourself for her?"

And there it was. Would he trade himself for Kresley?

Would he turn his back on the duty, the honor, he had clung to for three centuries? Lucan stared down at Kresley, searched his soul as he did. Without her, he would surely fall to the darkness. He was a lost cause without her. They would both end horribly or she could be saved. What option was there? He had to save her.

He brushed hair from her face before nodding to the twins. "Make her pain go away and we will talk conditions."

The two woman-Demons joined hands, lacing their fingers together. Instantly, Kresley went slack in his arms. Lucan panicked, his heart racing as he touched her face, her cheeks. Her breath brushed his palm. "Oh, thank God."

The Demons giggled. "God didn't do that. *We* did."

For a moment, Lucan stilled with that taunt, every muscle in his body tense. He was turning away from the light, giving himself to the darkness, and they were enjoying every minute of it.

Composure somewhat regained, Lucan settled Kresley on the blanket and stared down at her for a moment. He touched her lips, then tore his gaze away and pushed to his feet, sword in hand. A rush of malice filled the air. The twins stepped aside and a man appeared. *Tezi*. Lucan could not believe his eyes. Before him stood the Knight who had once been their leader, a Knight he respected and followed. A Knight who once had been symbolic of all that was good and now reeked of evil. Now he knew what Max and the others had sensed in the woods. It had been Tezi.

"How could you turn to them?" Lucan hissed, his

grip on his sword tightening. "How? You told us to hang on. You told us we had a purpose."

"How could I?" Tezi bellowed angrily. "How could *they?* How could they recruit us to fight evil and then allow us to die a slow, painful death? You know it is true."

"They never meant for us to rot, Tezi," he said. "Some of us were simply proven stronger than others."

Suddenly, Max charged into the cave and drew to a halt. "Tezi," he gasped, stunned. He, too, had once served under the former leader.

Tezi did not look at Max; his eyes flashed red at Lucan. "Come with me now or this ends here and now for your little firestarter."

"Lucan!" Max yelled.

Lucan sought out Max's gaze, looking for hope that help was on the way and found the answer he did not want. He had not reached Marisol. Help was hours away. Too long to wait for Kresley.

He dropped his head, defeated, lifted it and looked again at Max.

"Don't do it," Max pleaded. "Don't do it."

"I don't have a choice," he said. "She has a purpose. Saving her is mine."

The twin Demons were suddenly by his side, latching on to his arms. His skin crawled with their touch, but he did not fight. Nor did he turn to look at Kresley. He couldn't. Leaving her was too hard.

"Take care of her," Lucan pleaded to Max.

Lucan steeled himself for his departure. Tezi's gaze sharply cut to Max. "Adrian has a message for your divine leaders." Tezi's words were laced with a taunt.

"He has chosen to make my presence known now, because with the claiming of your Knight we declare a new war. We need not defeat you with swords. We will defeat you from within, and we announce this because you are too weak to stop us. Mark my words—many will soon see our way as the true light. Today a new world begins."

The bitter promise lanced through the air a moment before he was gone—with him, his Demons…and Lucan, now a fallen Knight of White.

Chapter 20

Hidden within the cavern that she and Rinehart had called home for nearly a day, Laura nibbled on a piece of beef jerky as Rinehart did the same. His clean-shaven military persona had roughened to a thin layer of stubble, which rasped across her skin in a way she had found decidedly erotic.

In the twenty-four hours they'd been hiding, Laura had worried often for her kids, and Rinehart had become her willing distraction. A distraction she had needed desperately to set aside the obstacles they faced outside these walls.

"What's wrong?" Rinehart asked, drawing her out of her reverie. She noted he was studying her intently.

She shook her head. "Nothing," she said, trying to mean it, but failing.

Looking unconvinced, Rinehart pressed. "Talk to me, Laura."

She hesitated. They'd talked about so much locked inside these walls. About her work, about his past in the army and then in the FBI. She'd even opened up about how being different had affected her growing up. About feeling like an outcast. But Rinehart had held back, avoided certain subjects that seemed important for reasons she couldn't pinpoint. About his transition into the Knights. All she knew, thus far, was that he was born in 1912 and had become a Knight when he was thirty-two.

With their escape planned for only a few hours later, Laura decided that now was the time to ask about this. "Will you tell me about becoming a Knight? About how it happened?" A shell-shocked expression flashed across his face, telling her how off guard she'd taken him, a second before he squeezed his eyes shut. Several seconds of silence followed before he slowly leaned back against the wall. Laura had the mental impression of him steeling himself for what was coming, and she found herself doing the same thing.

"I'd been thinking about leaving the FBI," he said, finally, his voice low, monotone. "Frustrated over things I was asked to do that felt unnecessary. They weren't about protecting Americans, but servicing certain interests that, frankly, I thought were corrupt." He hesitated. "I was engaged to be married. A woman of society who wanted me to move into politics. Looking back, I know I never really wanted that. I simply wanted to make a difference in the world. My thoughts on the agency turned around when I was made agent-in-charge over a

case that seemed important—taking down a radical
group who planned attacks on our country. Of course,
my fiancée wasn't happy. We fought the night I was
leaving for a sting operation in Mexico." He hesitated,
regret and guilt lacing his features. "I had eight good
men with me, many with families, all looking to me for
sound decisions. I was distracted, not myself at all." He
gritted his teeth, shook his head. "I never saw the attack
coming. Never had an indication we were being hunted.
But I saw my men attacked. I saw every one of them
fall." His eyes were bloodshot, his voice hoarse. "I let
them fall to the Beasts, yet I was the one saved. I am
the one here, now. That's always been hard to swallow."

Laura's heart exploded with grief for him. She
crawled across the floor, and slipped between his legs,
trying to get close, to offer comfort. "You are not to
blame," she declared huskily. "Distraction be damned,
Rinehart. You were attacked by *Demons*. You were
human. Your men were human. They would have fallen
no matter what you did."

"You don't know that." His eyes were heavy with
blame, his hands settling possessively on her waist,
pulling her closer. "I couldn't let you fall, too, Laura. I
couldn't. You're right about me stealing your ability to
make that choice. I justified my actions, but deep down
I knew what I was doing and why. I simply wasn't
willing to let them have you, too."

She pressed her lips to his. "I know," she whispered. "I know."

"Forgive me," he said, a plea in his voice that reached
straight through to her soul.

"There's nothing to forgive," she promised, and she meant it after hearing that story. She understood why he would fear letting her choose. That didn't mean she liked it, didn't mean she agreed with his actions. But she understood. In fact, listening to him speak, she'd begun to realize that all war was not about death. That her abilities were meant to save lives in ways she'd never thought she'd consider.

He inched back enough to probe her expression a moment before pulling the shoulder of her T-shirt down to expose the star. One long finger slid over the mark there as he studied it with heavy thoughts. His gaze lifted, seeking hers. "I have always been some kind of soldier, Laura. It's who I am. It's what I am."

"Then be that," she said softly, her voice catching in her throat. "Be who you are. I've never been able to do that."

"There's nothing normal about the life of a soldier."

Her hand caught his and she kissed it, her lips lifting in a fleeting smile. "Normal is relative, remember?" Then, more seriously: "I just have to figure out what that means for me. Everything has happened so fast."

His lips brushed hers, his hand sliding up her back as he pulled her down on the sleeping bag with him. "I'll try not to rush you," he said, his mouth slanting over hers, his tongue flicking against hers for a brief, sensual moment that defied his words. "But don't take too long. I really don't know how long I can keep from falling in love with you."

He kissed her then, and there was nothing brief about it. A kiss that was filled with tenderness, a kiss that branded her in ways that the mark on her shoulder could not.

And Laura decided then, that if she could escape this island, she might just find a purpose that reached beyond "normal." Perhaps it was time she did more than talk to her patients about looking at their abilities as gifts, and embrace her own.

Extraction time arrived at 4:00 a.m. The rendezvous for Laura and Rinehart with the rest of their group was at the edge of the woods overlooking a vacant beach area. Though there were no signs of Beasts, Rinehart was edgy, ready to get this done. Ready to take Laura to safety and get Rock the hell out of Walch's hands. But despite all this, he watched with satisfaction as Laura greeted the twins, Blake and even Kresley, in good health.

Any peace he took from that sight faded as he watched Kresley start to cry and heard her speak of Lucan. Max appeared by Rinehart's side, leaving Des to guard the others. "Lucan," he said, his voice low, barely above a whisper, but still rasped with roughness. "He made a deal with the Demons who marked Kresley, traded himself for her."

Rinehart damn near doubled over with the news. *Not Lucan.* "There was another way. We would have found it." Lucan had made it for three decades. "Only days ago he told me to hang on. He spoke of our purpose."

Max's expression was grim. "He said saving her was his purpose."

Rinehart knew then. "She was his mate."

"Yes." Max scanned the beach, his jaw clenched.

"The Demons weren't working on their own." He hesitated. "Tezi came for him."

Rinehart shook himself, certain he had heard wrong. "The former leader of the Knights?" he asked, disbelieving.

Max gave a jerky nod. "The one and only."

A chill raced down Rinehart's back. Every Knight vowed to see death before allowing themselves to turn.

"I always assumed there were some of the early Knights remaining, ones like me who hung on to hope," Max said. "I guess we know now what happens when they hang on too long."

"You think that's it?" Rinehart asked. "That Tezi hung on too long?"

"Yeah," Max agreed. "I think he hung on until the darkness became such that he couldn't see what he was becoming anymore. I think there are others like that out there, too." He cut Rinehart a sharp look. "And so does Adrian. He sent us a message. A new war has begun."

Rinehart would have asked more, but Laura was suddenly by his side.

"Oh, my God," she whispered, her hand on his arm a silent comfort he'd never thought possible. "I heard about Lucan. Kresley's a mess. I'm sure you are, too. I… *We'll* go after him. I have powers and—"

Max eased away, leaving them alone.

Rinehart wrapped his hand around her neck, under her hair and kissed her forehead. "You're powerful, baby, but not powerful enough to take on the Underworld." She was changing, joining their place in this world, whether she knew it or not. And it pleased him in a way he would never be able to put into words.

"We can try," she pleaded. "We ca—"

"We can't," he said, cutting her off. "Lucan might as well have made a deal with the devil, and he did so willingly. There is no turning back from that." The sound of a chopper in the distance put him on alert. It was time to leave—and not a minute too soon, in Rinehart's book.

The Knights exchanged a "go ahead" look and launched into action. They'd opted out of arming the others in the planning stages of the escape. None of them had handled guns before, and bullets slowed the Beasts, but did not kill them. The best bet was a focus on fast action.

Des and the twins headed for the helicopter first. Max followed with Kresley and Blake, then Rinehart and Laura broke out of the woods to follow. At that same moment, a group of at least twenty Beasts charged from the woods. The enemy's position was not more than half a mile down the beach, and they were headed straight for the chopper.

Everything happened quickly from there, but it played out for Rinehart in slow, torturous motion. He and the other Knights drew their swords, and Rinehart looked protectively to Laura.

"I can handle myself," she said, already running to attack, her intention to fight clear.

"Damn it," Rinehart growled, charging forward to keep her close, a tactic that proved impossible as he found himself attacked on all sides. His sword swiped viciously at an attacker, taking the Beast's head. Then another. But two more came at him.

He could see Des and Max in the distance, both heavily engaged, as well. Desperate to get to Laura, he fought with a fierceness beyond what he'd possessed before. He had come too far to lose her now. He would not fail. One Beast at a time, he turned his attackers to ash and flames.

His heart pounding, keeping a tight grip on his sword, he scanned for Laura, running toward her the moment he had a visual. She had her patients all together, but a group of Beasts were stalking them. His heart lurched at the sight, a roar escaping his lips as he charged toward them.

A second later, relief washed over him as Laura used her abilities to disarm the Beasts, sending their weapons flying across the beach. Kresley shot fire at one of them, a successful hit that sent the Beast running for the water but also seemed to weaken her. Rinehart was close now, his strides eating away the distance, crashing into the sand as his heart slammed into his chest.

Kresley stumbled and fell, and to Rinehart's distress Laura wavered in her stance, seeking a visual of Kresley. The Beasts took the moment as an opportunity. They snatched up Blake and started running. Blake became invisible instantly, only he was still in the Beast's arms. Or was he? The Beast stopped, let his arms fall.

Blake had a chance to escape, and Rinehart could only hope he took it, because Rinehart couldn't go to him, not yet. He was finally at Laura's side, and only a second before Jag orbed to his.

Des and Max engaged the remaining Beasts at their

frontal positions. "I can take two at a time," Jag said, intending to orb everyone to the chopper. Rinehart knew Marisol wouldn't leave that chopper to help; she was forbidden to enter a war zone, her healing ability too valuable to endanger.

Rinehart turned to Laura; Kresley was by her side, their arms linked. "Go with Jag, Laura," he ordered, directing them toward their leader.

Her refusal was instant. "No," she said. "Take the twins. You have to take the twins."

Jacob and Jared instantly objected. "We will stay. We can fight."

Laura ignored them. "Their blood," she said, her plea directed at Jag. "It has healing ability. They could save lives in the future. Many lives. Take them."

Jag hesitated, and Laura immediately saw this, declaring her case. "Rinehart and I…I have his mark. I'm not at risk. I can't turn. I won't turn." Desperation seeped into her face. "Please. I can fight, Jag. I can survive."

"And so can I," Kresley declared bravely, despite the obvious weak state that the Demons had left her in.

Rinehart shoved away the fear for his mate, pride filling him at both Laura's and Kresley's bravery. Jag didn't need to hear more, either, nor did he give the twins a chance to argue further. He orbed to a position behind them, touched their shoulders. They disappeared to safety.

"Go!" Rinehart yelled to Laura, ordering her and Kresley to run to the chopper. He motioned for Des and Max to follow them. "I'll get Blake."

The problem was, he couldn't see Blake, and another

ten-plus Beasts were breaking over the horizon, heading toward them.

"Damn it!" he yelled, and then muttered as he scanned, "Where the hell are you, kid?" Then, in the distance, Rinehart saw him, saw *Lucan*. He carried Blake in his arms as he charged toward the chopper.

Rinehart's chest expanded with relief and hope. Everyone was getting out of here safely. And maybe, just maybe, Lucan had found a way out of his deal, as well.

Now, Rinehart just had to go back and get Rock. New determination formed as he charged toward the woods, ready to make his escape. The heavier churn of the chopper engine had him turning, running backward as he watched the takeoff. His heart stopped at what he saw, his movement stilled. Laura wasn't on the chopper. She was running toward him, as Lucan ran the opposite direction and disappeared into the woods.

Lucan entered the woods and stood there, anger coiling in his gut, fists balled by his sides. The silver snakes that shackled his wrists—the result of his refusal to give up his soul—slithered off, and the two silver Demons appeared by his side.

"Don't be angry," they said, their bodies pressed to his side, hands on his chest. That was a feeling he would never get used to. "We let you save the boy."

He grimaced. They let him because they did not dare stop him, though he did not say so. That was a card better left in the deck. Torturing his mind was their only weapon, and his actions could have gotten him killed. Tezi would not want to lose his prize.

"I was promised my mate's safety," Lucan said. "She could have been killed."

The Demons laughed. "She was saved from us," they purred. "But no one promised her eternal protection. You were the only one who could have given her that."

Lucan's head spun; a wave of remorse washed over him. What had he done?

Rebellion formed in Lucan. There would be an eternity of punishment to endure. He might as well get it started in style. He was going to get Rock out of that warehouse.

Rinehart pulled Laura into the woods and confronted her. "What were you thinking?" he demanded. "You should have been on the chopper!"

"You can't do this alone!" she rebutted. "You need me."

Worry settled in his chest at the same time as acceptance. What could he say? He did need her. "I don't want anything to happen to you."

"I don't want anything to happen to you," she countered. "And you can't go after Rock alone. You'll both die." She pinned him in a stare. "So what's the plan?"

He shook his head and smiled to himself, not about to let her see him do so. She was a little warrior princess in the making. Protecting her was definitely going to be a lifetime endeavor.

Rinehart pointed to the Beasts crossing the beach to their far right. "We follow them to Walch and hopefully, Rock."

"You think he moved Rock to a new location?"

"He's still got military in his makeup," Rinehart said. "He moved him. I'm sure of it. We'll find the place and then wait for the right moment."

Rinehart found that right moment nearly twelve hours later—a long time to wait, considering Rinehart had a good view of Rock hanging from the ceiling of the warehouse they'd tracked him to, his body bloodied and lifeless. The warehouse doors had been rolled open to expose him. It was clear that Rock was bait, and bait they didn't have a choice but to take. His first instinct upon seeing his fellow Knight like that had been to charge in and cut him down, blast through the Beasts and take him. Then logic had taken hold, and he had endured the wait for the cover of night.

They planned to have Laura cave in the front wall to create a distraction. "You're sure you can do it?" Rinehart asked.

"I'm sure," she said. "Just be careful." He kissed her and didn't give himself time to worry about leaving her alone. He crawled through the woods toward the warehouse to make his move. As planned, the minute he arrived near the side of the warehouse, Laura did her thing. The walls began to rumble. Rinehart waited for the collapse that didn't come. Instead, the walls kept shaking, so hard it felt like an earthquake. With a mental shrug, he decided that would have to do.

He drew his sword and rushed the warehouse, ready to be charged by the enemy, but no attack came. The walls stopped moving abruptly, and he hoped like hell that Laura stayed her position and waited for him.

He moved toward Rock's bloodied body, the sight of him far grimmer up close. The wound in his gut was deep; blood oozed from it, pooling on the ground. Rock needed Marisol before he bled to death. And Rinehart was going to get him to her.

Rinehart reached up to cut Rock down, feeling a renewed urgency about Rock's condition.

"I wouldn't do that if I were you." Walch spoke from behind him. "He's wired with some pretty heavy firepower."

Rinehart turned slowly to find Walch alone. Walch held up a remote control. "One wrong move and *boom*."

Rinehart digested that bit of news with a sickening feeling in his stomach. Rock was wired with a bomb. Interesting, though, that Walch hadn't blown them both up the minute Rinehart had entered the building. "What do you want, Walch?" he asked, certain there was an agenda behind his actions.

"Wanted," he corrected. "We both know the patients are gone. But not their doctor. I saw her powers. The shaking walls were a dead giveaway that she is here. My soldiers should retrieve her shortly, so you can be together. Though I have to tell you, I haven't decided on your fate. Push this button or hand you over to Tezi? I really have to weigh the rewards and get back to you."

"They'll never touch her," Rinehart said, certain of his mate's skills.

"Rinehart!" Laura yelled, appearing in the doorway with a Beast holding each arm. "He has a bomb."

"He knows," Walch said drily, and quirked a brow at Rinehart. "She really did take to you quite quickly. One little mention of your destruction and she restrained herself." He motioned to the Beasts. "Tie them both up." He smiled at Rinehart. "Tezi will find two Knights a worthy sacrifice, I believe. I should save *you* for *him*. He has a wicked way with a knife, I hear. All that Aztec history of his. Likes to cut the hearts out, you know?"

A Beast tossed Laura against Rinehart, and he caught her, keeping her from falling, but he didn't look at her. His gaze was riveted to the doorway, and he found Lucan standing there, a lethal menace crackling off him. Laura seemed to sense him, too, her attention reaching for the door. "Lucan," Laura whispered.

Yes, Lucan. But had Lucan come to take them to Tezi or to aid their escape? A question quickly answered as Lucan shouted across the room. "Walch!" Lucan yelled, drawing his sword as he walked toward them. "Time to die." Rinehart could see the anger in Lucan, the resolve to kill Walch.

Walch laughed, appearing unfazed. "Three for one. I love it!" He pointed to several Beasts. "Take him!"

Suddenly two snakes slithered off Lucan's arms. Laura gasped at the sight as they watched the snakes transform into two beautiful females with silver-clad bodies and silver eyes. "Tezi said Walch is ours to take," the Demons said, looking up at Lucan. They stepped away from Lucan and joined their fingers together. Walch collapsed onto the ground and started screaming in a painful fit. The Demons sashayed to his side and squatted next to him, each resting a hand on his shoulders. He disappeared with them, and so did the remote to the bomb.

Rinehart launched into action. With one swift movement he raised his sword and sliced Rock's hands free, then wasted no time turning to meet the sword of a Beast that was charging at him. Lucan was doing the same. The soldier in him remotely assessed the situation, tallying his adversaries and counting four more Beasts.

Out of the corner of his eye he saw a Beast charge Laura. A moment later it flew across the warehouse. She repeated the action one Beast at a time, until those four were in retreat.

Rinehart sliced his blade through the air and took the head of the Beast he was battling. Lucan quickly managed the same. The two Beastly bodies lit up in flames and turned to ash.

Lucan yanked a cell phone from his pocket and tossed it to Rinehart. "In case you don't have one handy. Call for a ticket home."

"What about you?"

His expression was blank. "It's too late for me." He said nothing more, turned and walked away.

"He needs help now, Rinehart!" Laura's yell had Rinehart turning away from Lucan, already dialing the phone. She was leaning over him. "I can't feel any air at all."

Jag answered the line quickly, and by the time Rinehart hit the end button, Jag and Marisol had appeared. Marisol leaned over Rock and sobbed, her hand going to the wound on his stomach and lighting there.

Jag turned as Lucan reached the exit. Lucan seemed to sense his presence. He turned to Jag and saluted. Jag stood there, utterly still, and Rinehart knew he was hurting. Jag cared about his men. He'd die for any one of them. "He retains his soul," Jag said softly.

"Yes," Rinehart said, having thought the same thing. He'd seen Lucan's eyes, and they were not that of a Beast. "I don't know how, but they have him captive."

Jag said nothing more, but he didn't have to. They both knew the war had changed, shifting in a way only time could define, in a way that threatened to reveal a battle of enemies once considered friends.

Marisol looked up at Jag and nodded. "It's time." She didn't wait for an answer. She and Rock shimmered out of the room.

Rinehart grabbed Laura's hand, noting her worried expression. "They went home," he told her.

Jag reached out and touched them. "Where we all need to be right now—home."

They disappeared from the warehouse, finally departing the island.

They appeared on the lawn of a ranch house. Rinehart immediately pulled Laura close, fitting her beneath the shelter of his shoulder as Jag released her hand. But her heart still raced as they waited for Rock and Marisol to appear. "Where are they?" she asked. "We have to go back."

"They are fine," Jag assured her. "Marisol is caring for him someplace more suitable than the front lawn." He smiled. "Rock will recover fully. Marisol's gift of healing will have him well in no time. But you were a big part of getting him here to safety. And we thank you,

Laura." He held out his arms to the surroundings. "Welcome to Jaguar Ranch. It is your home if you wish it to be." The screen door opened and Laura looked to the porch as Kresley, Blake and the twins ran down the stairs to greet her. A moment of sadness over Carol's absence washed over her, but she clung to the hope that the others would now be safe.

She looked up at Rinehart a moment, a feeling of belonging filling her she could hardly comprehend. He kissed her head and she darted away to greet everyone. She could feel a new beginning forming, a new place called *normal*. And she thought she just might want to call it home.

Epilogue

Rinehart stood in the back of the sparring studio and watched Laura match blades with Kresley, both doing remarkably well for having never touched a sword until six weeks before.

When finally they completed their matchup, Laura pulled off her mask. Her cheeks were flushed, and her auburn hair spilled wildly down the white protective gear she wore. *Beautiful,* Rinehart thought. His mate was beautiful.

She smiled at him and set down her helmet. "That's all for me," she told Kresley.

Kresley pulled her helmet off, as well, and frowned. "Fine," she said, sounding as if she were disappointed. "The twins are supposed to be here anyway." She eyed the clock. "But they're late. Again. They spend all their time working with Marisol and all those healing herbs." She placed her sword across the rack on the wall and crossed her arms. "Blake spends all his time in Jag's library. Which is fine and all, but I really think they need to learn to use a sword."

Laura's expression sobered. "Everyone is not as hell-bent on learning to fight the Beasts as you. Besides, you don't even need a sword. You have fire."

Kresley's lips thinned. "Fire might not be enough."

Enough for what, Rinehart wondered. Lucan hadn't been seen or heard from since the island, and with each passing day Kresley grew more focused on fighting. She was going to go after Lucan. He could feel it in his bones. And nothing good would come of it. She would get herself killed if they didn't stop her.

He shook off the grim thoughts and watched Laura discard her gear, his nerves on edge over what he was about to do. The first night at the ranch had been the only one they had spent apart, and it had been a miserable one. She'd come to his room the next night and stayed after that. They'd become closer with each passing moment. And he loved her. He loved her with all his heart. He believed she loved him, too, but he desperately needed to know for sure. He couldn't fall any harder and survive her departure.

"All ready," Laura said, walking toward him. She wore black jeans and boots along with a snug-fitting T-shirt, and somehow looked just as classy as she did in her high heels and skirts. She pushed to her toes and kissed him. "What's this big surprise you have for me?"

"It's not a surprise if I tell you," he chided, stealing

one last kiss, fearful it would be one of his last, trying not to hold her too tight, or press his lips to hers too hard.

She frowned. "What's wrong?"

He laughed. "You're always analyzing my feelings."

She nodded, lips pursed. "Right. So what's wrong?"

He grabbed her hand and pulled her out the door, their destination the Jeep waiting out front. Laura drew to a halt on the porch, staring into the near distance. Marisol and Rock stood beneath a tree in intimate conversation. "They love each other," she said. "It doesn't seem right that a Healer would be forbidden such a thing."

"There is something about Marisol's past we don't know," Rinehart said. "Some wrong she is meant to right. That is all she has ever said about it. But Marisol is aware of why the rules are as they are for her."

"I see," Laura said, studying the couple a moment before looking at him. "Why does she fear the twins? I sense it every time they are near her."

Rinehart's jaw set with tension. "She says there can be only one Healer in this realm at a time."

Laura frowned. "But there are three of them."

"She believes that the twins can exist together, and that soon she will not."

"Oh, no," Laura said, her hand going to her throat.

He tugged her to the Jeep. "Come with me now. Your surprise awaits."

A smile quickly returned to her face as she willingly followed. The ranch was one of the largest in existence, stretching for miles and miles. But they drove only a mile this day, and they pulled to a halt in front of a small white house. A work in progress, but Rinehart and Des would finish it soon. They'd put priority on the pavilion-style building next to it, and completed it that morning. And that pavilion was her surprise. Or part of it, at least.

"What is this place?" she asked, climbing out of the Jeep before he could help her out. She had an independent streak the size of Texas. Not that he minded, but he wanted her to know he was there for her now, and he tried to show her that in any way possible. Like getting her door—when he could manage to beat her to the punch.

"You'll see," he said, taking her hand.

She hesitated a moment before letting him lead her forward, her hand brushing his cheek, telling him she was aware he was nervous, but deciding not to push him. Damn, how easily she read him.

He opened the door to the building and flipped on the light. Fancy white tile sparkled under the masses of special lighting he'd had installed. Laura followed him in and stared in wonder at the large black marble lab tables, rows and rows of glass cabinets filled with supplies and, with Jag's help, every kind of equipment she could ever desire. The temporary lab they'd set up for her upon arrival faded in comparison.

"It's wonderful," she said, rushing forward to examine a microscope on the lab table closest to her. "This must have cost a fortune."

He leaned on the wall and tried to appear nonchalant. "I told you we could provide you with all the resources you need. It's yours, if you want it." He hesitated. "But read the letter on the table first."

She peered at him tentatively, and then picked it up. Frowned at the name on the envelope, and then tore it open as if it excited her. His heart lurched in his chest. She was excited. She would leave him. At least he would know where she was, he told himself. But his heart wanted to explode.

Laura quickly read it, and then looked up at him. "It's a job offer from Scott and White hospital in Temple. They seem to think I want to use my research to help cancer patients. You're the only person I've ever told my thoughts to on that. The only person who knows I believe it can translate to answers in that field. How would they find that out?"

He could barely get the words out. "I wanted you to have choices, Laura."

Instantly, her eyes teared up, and the letter fell to the ground. She launched herself across the room and into his arms, hugging him and then staring up at him. "I want to help people, but I choose to do it by your side. I choose to do it right here in this lab."

He didn't let himself feel relieved or happy. Not yet. "There will always be more than science here, Laura. There is war, and that won't change."

"I'll never get used to you and the others going out to fight every night, or worrying for your safety. But it helps a lot to know you're immortal." She grinned mischievously. "And that you aren't too macho to let me come save you if I have to."

He laughed, pleased with that answer, so happy it took him a moment to choke back the emotion enough to speak. "I love you, Laura." He dropped down on his knee and pulled a box from his pocket and flipped the lid open. A diamond sparkled between the black velvet crevices. "Marry me. Laura. Choose to be with me this time. I want to finish that house next door for *us*. Be my wife."

"Yes," she said. "I do choose you. I love you."

He slipped the ring on her finger, and then stood up, pulling her in his arms and kissing her. And for the first time, he knew this was forever.

* * * * *

In honor of our 60th anniversary,
Harlequin® American Romance® is celebrating
by featuring an all-American male each month,
all year long with
MEN MADE IN AMERICA!
This June, we'll be featuring
American men living in the West.

Here's a sneak preview of
THE CHIEF RANGER by Rebecca Winters.

Chief Ranger Vance Rossiter has to
confront the sister of a man who died while
under Vance's watch...and also confront
his attraction to her.

"Chief Ranger Rossiter?" The sight of the woman who'd stepped inside Vance's office brought him to his feet. "I'm Rachel Darrow. Your secretary said I should come right in."

"Please," he said, walking around his desk to shake her hand. At a glance he estimated she was in her mid-twenties. Her feminine curves did wonders for the pale blue T-shirt and jeans she was wearing. "Ranger Jarvis informed me there's a young boy with you."

The unfriendly expression in her beautiful green eyes caught him off guard. "Yes," was her clipped reply. "When we arrived in Yosemite the ranger told me I couldn't go anywhere in the park until I talked to you first."

"That's right."

"Knowing you wanted this meeting to be private, he offered to show my nephew around Headquarters."

So this woman was the victim's sister.... "What's his name?"

"Nicky."

The boy who haunted Vance's dreams now had a name. "How old is he?"

"He turned six three weeks ago. Were you the man in charge when my brother and sister-in-law were killed?"

"Yes. To tell you I'm sorry for what happened couldn't begin to convey my feelings."

The woman's gaze didn't flicker. "I won't even try to describe mine. Just tell me one thing. Was their accident preventable?"

"Yes," he answered without hesitation.

"In other words, the people working under you fell asleep on your watch and two lives were snuffed out as a result."

Hearing it put like that, he had to set the record straight. "My staff had nothing to do with it. I, myself, could have prevented the loss of life."

Ms. Darrow's expression hardened. "So you admit culpability."

"Yes. I take full blame."

A look of pain crossed over her features. "You can just stand there and admit it?" Her cry echoed that of his own tortured soul.

"Yes." He sucked in his breath.

"I work for a cruise line. Aboard ship, it's the captain's responsibility to maintain rigid safety regulations. If a disaster like that had happened while he was in charge he would have been relieved of his command and never given another ship again."

Rachel Darrow couldn't know she was preaching to the converted. "If you've come to the park with the intention of bringing a lawsuit against me for negligence, maybe you should." It would only be what he deserved.

"Maybe I will."

In the next instant, she wheeled around and hurried out of his office. Vance could have gone after her, but it would cause a scene, something he was loath to do for a variety of reasons. In the first place, he needed to cool down before he approached her again.

The discovery of the Darrows' frozen bodies had affected every ranger in the park. A little boy had been orphaned—a boy whose aunt was all he had left.

* * * * *

Will Rachel allow Vance to explain—and
will she let him into her heart?
Find out in
THE CHIEF RANGER
Available June 2009
from Harlequin® American Romance®.

We'll be spotlighting a different series every month
throughout 2009 to celebrate our 60th anniversary.

Look for Harlequin®
American Romance® in June!

Join us for a year-long celebration of the rugged
American male! From cops to cowboys—
Men Made in America has the hero
you've been dreaming about!

Look for

The Chief Ranger

by Rebecca Winters, on sale in June!

Bachelor CEO by Michele Dunaway	July
The Rodeo Rider by Roxann Delaney	August
Doctor Daddy by Jacqueline Diamond	September

REQUEST YOUR FREE BOOKS!

2 FREE NOVELS PLUS 2 FREE GIFTS!

Silhouette®

nocturne™

Dramatic and Sensual Tales of Paranormal Romance.

YES! Please send me 2 FREE Silhouette® Nocturne™ novels and my 2 FREE gifts (gifts are worth about $10). After receiving them, if I don't wish to receive any more books, I can return the shipping statement marked "cancel." If I don't cancel, I will receive 4 brand-new novels every other month and be billed just $4.47 per book in the U.S. or $4.99 per book in Canada. That's a savings of about 15% off the cover price! It's quite a bargain! Shipping and handling is just 25¢ per book*. I understand that accepting the 2 free books and gifts places me under no obligation to buy anything. I can always return a shipment and cancel at any time. Even if I never buy another book from Silhouette, the two free books and gifts are mine to keep forever.

238 SDN ELS4   338 SDN ELXG

Name _____ (PLEASE PRINT)

Address _____ Apt. #

City _____ State/Prov. _____ Zip/Postal Code

Signature (if under 18, a parent or guardian must sign)

Mail to the **Silhouette Reader Service:**
IN U.S.A.: P.O. Box 1867, Buffalo, NY 14240-1867
IN CANADA: P.O. Box 609, Fort Erie, Ontario L2A 5X3

Not valid to current subscribers of Silhouette Nocturne books.

Want to try two free books from another line?
Call 1-800-873-8635 or visit www.morefreebooks.com.

* Terms and prices subject to change without notice. Prices do not include applicable taxes. Sales tax applicable in N.Y. Canadian residents will be charged applicable provincial taxes and GST. Offer not valid in Quebec. This offer is limited to one order per household. All orders subject to approval. Credit or debit balances in a customer's account(s) may be offset by any other outstanding balance owed by or to the customer. Please allow 4 to 6 weeks for delivery. Offer available while quantities last.

Your Privacy: Silhouette is committed to protecting your privacy. Our Privacy Policy is available online at www.eHarlequin.com or upon request from the Reader Service. From time to time we make our lists of customers available to reputable third parties who may have a product or service of interest to you. If you would prefer we not share your name and address, please check here. ☐

SN09

New York Times Bestselling Author

MAGGIE
SHAYNE

Her last chance to live, her only chance to love...

Lilith awakens cold, naked and alone, knowing nothing—not even who she is—except that she has to run, run for her life…because someone is after her.

When Ethan discovers the terrified woman hiding on his ranch, he knows immediately not only *who* she is but *what*. He's never forgotten her, not in all the time since he escaped their joint prison, a clandestine CIA facility where humans are bred into vampires willing to kill on command. He refused to accept that fate, and since he won his freedom, he's become a legend to those he left behind. With her own escape, Lilith has become a legend, too, and now—together—they have no choice but to fight those who would become legends by killing one.

BLOODLINE

Available April 28, 2009,
wherever books are sold!

nocturne™

COMING NEXT MONTH

Available June 4, 2009

#65 FROM THE MISTS OF WOLF CREEK •
Rebecca Brandewyne
New York Times **Bestselling Author**
After a long absence, Hallie Muldoon is finally returning
to her childhood home. There she comes face-to-face
with a past long hidden and a mysterious yet protective
stranger named Trace…a man who seems more wolf than
human. What secrets have the mists of Wolf Creek kept
all these years?

#66 BACK TO LIFE • **Linda O. Johnston**
Shot by a suspect, Officer Trevor Owens is close to
dying…until Skye Rydell pulls him back. As a descendant
of Valkyries, Skye has power over life and death—and a
definite connection to Trevor. But that connection opens
up a dangerous transference of power between Skye and
the handsome cop. Can they gain control over life, love
and death before it's too late?